ANGEL TROUBLE

A GRIM REAPER COMEDY

D.M. GUAY

For Nerdly.
Thank you for the math. Seriously.
THANK YOU FOR DOING ALL. THE. MATH.

HELLO. MY NAME IS LLOYD,
AND I'M IN WAY OVER MY
HEAD.

As I lay sandwiched between a giant, unconscious, jelly centipede from hell, the ghost of a gill guy, and an incubus pervert in a leopard print thong, I looked to the sky and asked, "Jesus, haven't I been through enough?"

No, Lloyd. No, you have not.

CHAPTER 1

"Wow." DeeDee said. "I knew Steve was mad at us, but I didn't know he was *this* mad."

The three of us stood in the candy aisle, staring at the new cleaning crew. They'd just arrived in a beat-up cardboard box, which Steve had unceremoniously dropped outside by the ice machine without so much as a hello.

There were six of them. They were buck naked, and they weren't zombies. But that's all we could say for certain. They kind of looked like piglets, only not cute. Eight inches tall, with hairless, pudgy wrinkled bodies. They stood on their two hind legs like people, but had hooves instead of feet. They had big ears and lots of sharp, pointy fangs.

"Jesus. They look like the demons on the cover of a shitty Norwegian death metal album. Only the artist didn't get the airbrush right." Kevin leaned against the mop bucket, out of breath just from talking.

Yeah. About that. Kevin wasn't exactly in peak physical condition these days. He hadn't fully recovered from all the cursed combos he'd eaten during the Monster Burger fiasco. The spell had broken, but the fat persisted.

"Really, kid? You got a lot of nerve calling me fat."

Crap. He heard that.

"Yeah. I did. Now focus. What does Steve expect us to do with these things? Look at 'em. They're a pack of dumb asses. And we're already full up on dumbasses." He thumbed a leg back at me.

The creatures chittered to each other as they climbed up on each other's shoulders, forming a chain up to the hanger bags of Starburst. Again. They'd been trying to get that bag of candy for at least an hour, only to toddle and fall, roll to the floor empty-handed, then do it all over again. They didn't seem to be very bright. Or very dextrous. Or very much of anything except hungry. And persistent.

"Do you think they're from hell or from earth? I couldn't find them in the books." DeeDee rubbed her chin. "I mean, how is this going to work? What are we supposed to do if we need a cleanup when there's a customer in the store?"

"Don't you get it, sweets? That's the point. This is Steve shooting us two middle fingers. He sent them here to punish us. It's the only explanation. I hope you like to mop, kid, because you're gonna be doing a lot of it. Starting now." Kevin kicked the mop bucket toward me with his fat back leg. "Double up on the Curse Breaker, will ya? We gotta wash every speck of Katia's bad juju off this place, or we're dead. All dead."

"Come on, Kev. No one has seen her since Monster Burger burned down. We reinforced the gate," DeeDee said. "Don't you think you're being melodramatic?"

"Am I? You ever seen him like this?"

Kevin pointed at Faust, who was hanging yet another workplace safety poster. It said, "BEWARE OF THE BEAST." Yes. In all caps. Screaming—above an old woodcut illustration of a busty brunette tied to a stake, standing in a pile of sticks, on fire. He'd hung so many, they were starting to look like creepy wallpaper. Faust smoothed out the poster. But he forgot to smooth himself. His hair stuck up in all the wrong places. His suit was wrinkled. Black circles ringed his eyes.

"Well," DeeDee said. "He does seem a bit off."

That was an understatement. He hadn't been his usual calm,

suave self since that tentacle monster spit him out of another dimension, we found out his ex-girlfriend cursed our beer cave, and she
turned the burger joint across the intersection into a zombie factory.

"You think? I've worked here since you two were in diapers, and
I've never seen him like this. His ex is nuts. Look what she did to me!
If I get any fatter, I'll pop. Jesus." He rubbed his bulging carapace and
huffed, "Being fat is exhausting. How do you live like this, kid?"

"I'm not—" *fat!* I was gonna say it out loud until I glanced down.

"Yeah. Sure, kid. Sure. You're not fat, and I'm Ozzy Osborne.
Now get mopping."

My cheeks flushed hot, and I wheeled the mop bucket away,
totally humiliated. So wouldn't you know it, Angel eight ball rolled
out from behind the boner pill display, throwing triangles. Great.
Cue more humiliation. My guardian angel was like a kick-me-while-
I'm-down magnet.

I ignored him, but it was no use. He rolled right in front of me.
Well, roll was generous. More like wobbled. Angel still had a strip of
silver duct tape around his middle, to cover the crack Chef left when
he bit him in half.

"Hurrr hurrr hurrrr."

I read his teeny triangle again.

"Hurrr hurrr hurrr."

"Are you crying?"

"Sniff. Shlorrrrrrp." The triangle dipped and turned. Barely. His
water level was pretty low. "Hurrrrr."

"Are you all right?"

"Don't look at me." He swiveled away, and I heard a *pfooooooo*
like he was blowing his nose. Then he swiveled back. "Okay, now
look at me. I've had a rough day, but I can't let my personal life inter-
fere with work. Listen. Head Office is in a tizzy. The entire celestial
order is getting audited. Major scandal."

"Okay."

"This is serious. Pravuil is in charge of accounting now, and he's a
real stick in the mud. You need to make significant progress before he

reviews your file, or we're both screwed. He's counting Old Testament sins again. Do you have any idea how many bacon cheeseburgers you've eaten? So get out your 'Capable Adult' and 'Hero's Journey' checklists, and get to work. Start ticking boxes. I need this job!"

"You're kidding."

"I certainly am not. My rent just doubled, and I'm all aloooooooone. Hurrrr. Hurrrrr. Hurrrrrrrrr." Angel wobbled in slow circles, crying? I didn't know what to say, so I just stood there, watching him roll.

"I said don't look at me! I don't want you to see me like this. Hurrrrrrrrrrrrr. Hurrrr. Hurrrrrr."

"Okay, then." I wheeled the bucket to the back of the store and mopped under Bubby's TV.

Angel rolled up next to me. "What's up with you lately? You're acting weird."

"You told me not to look at you!"

"Not that. You normally put up way more of a fight. You haven't been the same since that zombie stuff. All you do is shrug and sigh and say 'Okay.' You're awfully mopey. Is something bothering you?"

I shrugged. Duh. When you're nearly eaten by zombies, it makes you think. I had all kinds of feelings that I didn't know what to do with, shoved down deep, twisting and churning and festering. I'd felt bad ever since the Monster Burger incident. Not scared, really. Just bad.

"Cheer up. Most people would be happy to know God has a plan for them. Yours is outlined in big letters. You don't even have to think about it. You just have to do it. You should be over the moon."

I wasn't, so I kept mopping.

"Most people never get the chance to save the world once, let alone twice. You should be proud. Well, kind of. I mean, you *helped* save the world, but you weren't like, the Number One Guy," Angel said. "DeeDee and Kevin generally do the heavy lifting. You're more like the sidekick, but that's something."

"Sidekick?" My heart skipped a beat. Huh. "Oh my God. That's it."

Angel's right. I was a sidekick, and I wasn't even a good one! Too fat to climb a shelf, even with a zombie horde chasing me. I had only survived this long due to sheer luck—and because Kevin and DeeDee had skills—because God knows I didn't have any skills of my own. I was about as useful as that Wonder Twin who turns into a bucket of ice water. No wonder Kevin was always on my case. Kevin. Jerk. "If I saved us—just me, just once—Kevin would have to be nice to me."

"Wait. Did you just say you want to be a hero? You did, didn't you? Hallelujah. I might not get fired after all! Bring it in. Give me a hug."

"Uh. I didn't say that. I was just thinking out loud." I mean. Let's get real here. Me? But Angel didn't listen.

"We're finally on the same page. Just in time. We've got a lot to do. You need all the points you can get. Oh. Look. Now's your chance. Go be heroic. Good luck!"

He rolled right into my foot, as if nudging me along. "What are you doing?"

His triangle pointed behind me. I stood up straight. My grip tightened on the mop handle. I swallowed hard and turned around. Super duper slowly, because anything could be behind me. Anything.

Turns out Angel was pointing at a Cookie Scout. She was small and knock-kneed, maybe ten years old. She stood at the very end of the aisle, in a little uniform. She fiddled with a fat pink sash with a big felt cookie badge sewn on it.

"Uh. Hey there, little girl." I moved closer, but not too fast. I didn't want her to think I was a Chester Molester. "Are you lost?"

She looked up at me with a cherubic little face. Hair in pigtails. Tears filling her big brown eyes. She pointed to a cardboard box on the floor next to her. Boxes of cookies. Huh. Poor kid. She must have wandered away from her troop. She must be terrified!

Then she said, "You're fat. I bet you like cookies. You wanna buy some cookies? I need to sell three more boxes to pay for camp. You look like you could eat three boxes in one sitting."

Gee. What a sweet little girl. Not. Still, she wasn't wrong. Universal truth: Fat men do not pass up cookies, not even in an emergency. They just don't. Plus, hello. Everyone knows charity calories don't count.

"They count. Trust me." Angel rolled up next to me. Of course. Always an opinion.

"Yeah. I like cookies." Why lie at this point? Come on. We can all see my fat. I went down on one knee so we were eye to eye. "These look yummy. Tell you what. How about we call your parents, and then I'll buy a box?"

"One box. For real? Wow. Fat and a cheapskate. I know you can eat more than one box. Wait a second." Her eyes darted back and forth. She nervously patted her sash. "Where's my unicorn? Do you have my unicorn? I want my unicorn. I earned it!"

She grabbed my arms. Her brown eyes stared at me, not blinking. Not crying. Nothing. "Where's my unicorn? You stole it. Give it back, now!"

"I don't have any unicorns."

"That big guy said it was in here. He said you had it." She squeezed my arms, tight. Her hands were cold as ice cubes, and her fingers dug in so hard they felt like knives.

Then her eyes rolled back in her head.

Crick. Crick. Crunch.

Uh oh. That sound? It was bones cracking. Her body stretched out, long and longer, like an invisible hand pulling out Play Doh. Her shoulders popped into weird, jagged shapes. She looked up at me with black eyes. All black, even the bits that were supposed to be white. Her mouth split into a gaping maw lined with pointy awful black dripping teeth.

"What the FUUUUUUUUUUUUUUU!"

Yeah. I screamed. Because dude. This kid was a monster. Literally. Cherubic, my butt! I tried to pull away, but her hands turned to claws and clamped down hard on my shoulders. A thing rose behind her head. A fat fwapping tail. The end looked sharp.

Gulp. Not good.

She shrieked, "UNICORN!" and opened wide.

AAAAAAH! SHE'S GOING TO EAT ME!

"Don't you dare die without all your check marks. I'll get written up!" Angel rolled into me. "What are you waiting for? Go on. Get her. Whip out your best moves! Show me what you've got."

I wriggled and kicked, but it was no use. She had a death grip on me. "Why didn't you warn me?"

"How was I supposed to know? What monster brings cookies?" Angel said.

"UNICORN!" That scout smacked me so hard across the face, I flew down the aisle, taking everything in the car section down with me.

She stomped up to me, crunching in tiles with her saddle shoes. Then she was on top of me, pawing at my shirt, my pants, my pockets, tail waving, fangs bared, shrieking, "Give it to me. I earned it!"

I grabbed the closest thing and shoved it right in her mouth. Turns out, it was one lousy pineapple air freshener.

Mmm mmmph mmmmmph.

Ha! Choke on that! Yes!

Wait. Those were yummy noises. Shit.

She swallowed it and licked her fangs. "Give me UNICOR —*Shhhhpppppplllllllllllllllllp.*"

Her black eyes went wide and a hard round white thing emerged from between her fangs, covered in goop. Jesus. It looked like the mini-mouth inside a xenomorph. Her black eyes stared at me, glassy and unflinching.

I shrieked and tried to wriggle free. "Don't eat meeeee!"

Shhhhpppppplllllllllllllllllp.

That white thing shot straight into the linoleum, right between my legs, so hard the tile cracked. The demon scout slumped. She let me go.

Wait. That wasn't a mouth. It was a broomstick, pinning her hell face to the floor. DeeDee held the other end.

Kevin slugged up, out of breath and drenched in sweat, dragging a red canister behind him. He pulled the trigger and a cloud of white foam rained down on me and the ersatz scout. The second it hit her, her body began to bubble and ooze, disintegrating into a black, thick sticky puddle.

I screamed and batted the foam away. "Don't melt meeeeeeeeeeeeee!"

Kevin didn't stop until the canister fizzled out. "Relax, kid. Doesn't work on people."

They looked at me. I looked at them. Then DeeDee said, "You okay?"

"Uh. No!" Hello! Demon Cookie Scout!

Kevin dropped that canister like it was hot, and scurried to that cookie box. He knocked it over and stuck his head in. "The cookies are real! Peanut Butter Patties? Hell yeah! My favorite. Mmm. Pop 'em open for me, will ya? I'm starving." He sat up and rubbed his rather generous belly. "Hold up. Ignore me. I'm not thinking straight. I've had nothing but carrot sticks for three days. My food cravings are out of control. Don't let me eat them. No matter what. Promise me, kid. Kid?"

He looked right at me.

Was Kevin seriously talking about cookies and diets right now? While I sat in the sticky black oozing puddle that used to be a monster trying to eat me? My blood pressure was so high, my lips were numb. All I could say was, "Scout?!?"

"Are you really surprised? Did you honestly think she was out selling cookies this late? It's not even cookie season! Geesh. You shoulda known she wasn't human the minute you saw her. The demon in scout's clothing is the oldest trick in the book," he said. "Plus, if you'd followed standard unidentified entity protocol, we wouldn't have had to step in and save your butt. I don't know what I'm gonna do with you. You've worked here long enough to know that.

Amateur hour is over, kid. It's time to stop being a half ass, and start being a full ass, dumbass."

I won't lie. His words stung. "Wait. Standard what?"

"Standard unidentified entity protocol. It's in your employee manual. See?" He whipped a tiny book out of. Huh. I don't know where. He never seemed to have any pockets when he owed me money.

He cleared his throat and read aloud. "If you encounter a hostile entity of unknown origin, subdue the beast using standard issue slay foam until such time as a proper classification can be made. Slay foam is conveniently located in your gate's weapons safe, as well as in the emergency boxes located throughout your store."

"What boxes?"

He pointed to a bright red "Break In Case of Emergency" box hanging on the wall. Literally right next to me. It had a fire extinguisher inside.

"But. Fire?"

"That's not fire foam, kid. That's a front. Because the whole store is a front. It's what we do here. Now, let's see what kind of demon makes this much mess." He flipped some pages. And he flipped some more. "Huh. She ain't in mine. She in yours?"

"Let me check." DeeDee walked behind the counter and came back a moment later with a book wrapped in purple fun fur. It looked like a goth cheerleader's diary. And it was...purring?

Uh, her employee manual looked a lot different than mine. Like a lot. Cute, friendly and fuzzy. Mine lived in the bottom of my bedroom closet, fighting my cat and chewing up my shoes. Although, Kevin insisted I bring it to work with me, so right now it was loose in the store somewhere. Not exactly a comforting thought.

"That's strange," DeeDee flipped through all the pages. "She's not in mine either."

"What about you, kid?"

Kevin looked at me. I looked at him. He didn't honestly expect me to carry it on me, considering the state it's in. Did he?

"Uh, yes I do." Kevin shook his head at me. "You aren't gonna accomplish anything around here without that book. The point of an employee manual is to read it. So read it, already. Geesh!"

Kevin surveyed the gloppy black mess on the floor. Which was still steaming. And stunk like a horny skunk. "Well, whatever she is, she didn't come out of our gate. We're locked up tight."

"Then how did it get here?" I wasn't proud of my panicked, high-pitched tone.

"How am I supposed to know? There're all kinds of ways these jerks can weasel up to earth. Don't just sit there. Mop her up. You got time to lean, you got time to clean," Kevin said. "Tell you what. We'll make it easy on you. Grab him a bottle of Gut Scraper outta the back, okay Dee?"

DeeDee disappeared into the stockroom. "Don't you dare throw away the cookies, kid. I gotta cheat day coming up soon. I'm gonna go hard on these Peanut Butter Patties."

Kevin scuttled back into the cookie box. Halfway. Because he was too fat to fit all the way in.

"I heard that." He ruffled around inside. "Coconut Stacks. Blech. Ooh. Skinny Mints. Score! I don't know what kind of monster shows up with cookies, but I wish we'd get more of them. Jackpot."

I stared at the pile of disintegrating goop that was once a Lloyd-eating monster disguised as a little kid. My shoulder stung. Her claws had poked a hole in my shirt. And under the hole, blood. Just a little, but man. It really hurt.

"You should probably disinfect that. If I've learned anything since the bubonic plague, it's that human bodies are no match for germs. Tiny, but mighty." Angel shook out from underneath some toppled bottles of motor oil. "Wow. We need to talk. You weren't even a side-kick on that one. You were full on victim. Kevin's right. It's about time you actually got good at this job."

"Tell me something I don't know." I had just managed to peel myself up out of the scout slime, when the front door chimed. A rush of freezing air swept through the store.

Angel rolled behind my foot, like he was hiding. "Why is *he* here? This is a disaster!"

"Who?" I looked and immediately regretted it.

A man stood in the door. He was eight feet tall at least, impossibly thin with sharp bony shoulders. He wore a long, weird black dress with the hood up. He looked at me and holy crap. He didn't have a face. He had a skull. A naked, no skin, white, bone only, full on skull where his face should be.

Is that? I immediately felt like all the blood drained out of me. Cold. Knees shaking. Because yes. It was. The grim reaper just walked into Demon Mart, and he looked exactly like he did in all the movies. Only without the scythe.

I looked at the black pool of dead Cookie Scout. At the trace of blood on my fingers from the scratch on my shoulder.

Oh, no. She'd killed me. It must have been a hell germ or poison or something. I died so fast, I didn't even notice. So that's it then. This was the end. I'm dead.

CHAPTER 2

I MIGHT BE DEAD, but I still tried to hide. Duh. Who jumps up and down, screaming, "Over here! Take me!" when the angel of death comes calling? Nobody, that's who. So I slowly sunk down behind the shelf until only the very top of my head stuck out. I would have gone all the way to the floor, but I had to keep an eye on that reaper. Because I was gonna run the second he floated this way. I wasn't ready to die. Not like this. In mismatched socks and a wrinkled "Shrimpin' Ain't Easy" T-shirt. And still living with my parents?

Fuck. Angel was right. I needed serious check marks.

"Angel. What do I do?" There had to be some way out of this.

No response. His triangle just hung there. Blank. Stupid angel. Now he shuts up? When I need him the most? I shook him. Come on. Wake up! Death is here!

Wait. Maybe he's prepping the pearly gates for an in-person meet and greet. Or...Hold up. I'm not going to hell, am I? Oh shit. He said the Old Testament sins count again. What if I he can't talk to me anymore because I'm doomed? Stupid bacon cheeseburgers! This can't be happening! Aaaaaaaaaaaaaaaah!

I was totally screaming on the inside when DeeDee stepped out of the back room, bottle of Gut Scraper in hand. She stopped dead in her tracks when she saw the reaper. And so did Kevin, who had taken his head out of the cookie box long enough to peek around the end cap. Which means they both saw him. So they must be dead, too. Shit. It wasn't a hell germ. It was a gas leak! How else would we all die at the same time?

"It was the salmon mousse, kid," Kevin said.

"I didn't eat any salmon mousse!" My blood pumped so hard I felt like my head was gonna pop off.

"It was a joke. Geesh. Relax! I can hear you breathing. You're still alive, and so am I."

"Are you sure?"

Shit. The reaper moved at the sound of my voice. He looked at me. I mean, I think he looked at me. It was hard to tell because he didn't have eyeballs, but his empty sockets seemed to be pointing my way.

My heart stopped cold in my chest. I should have kept my mouth shut!

But the reaper floated the other way, to the slushy machines.

Phew.

He wrapped a giant bone hand around a nozzle, lowered his skull down under it, and pulled. Pythias Pomegranate poured straight into his mouth. Well, between his bone jaws. A mouth would imply cheeks and flesh, which he didn't have. Still, the slushy didn't spill on the floor. It disappeared. And he made a gug gug gug sound as he chugged it down into some unseen reaper mouth.

Man. Drinking right out of the machine? Talk about bad manners.

"Funny. You did the same thing the night we hired you," Kevin said.

"What? No, I—" Oh. Never mind. I totally did.

When the reaper finished, he stood up and floated to the freshly stocked Zapp's end cap, ripped open a bag of Evil Eye chips, and started shoving them in his mouth. And I mean shoving. Like a starving walrus. Red bits of chip shrapnel flew in all directions as his teeth chomped those taters down. Once again, despite his lack of cheeks, he seemed to actually be eating them.

When he finished, he moaned like a ghost in a cheap horror movie. "Eeeeeee. Eeeeee. Eeeeee. Hurrrrrp Hurrrrrp Hurrrrrrrp."

His shoulders—well, shoulder bones—jumped up and down. He rubbed his empty eye sockets with his knuckles.

Wait. Was he crying?

"Yep. He's crying," Kevin said. "I gotta be honest, kid. I don't know what the hell is happening here."

"Um. Are you okay?" DeeDee asked him, with an apprehension that was very un-DeeDee like.

The reaper looked at her for a long time. Then he put his arms out. "Can I have a hug? It would really cheer me up right now."

My heart kicked up. Hug the grim reaper? Hell no. *Don't do it, DeeDee! Noooo!*

DeeDee looked at me. Then at the reaper, and asked, "If I hug you, will I die?"

"Uuuuuuuuuuuuuuuuuuuh." He sighed. Then slumped. "No. I've been suspended. I'm not allowed to reap. Eeeeeep. Eeeeeep. Eeeeeeeee."

He stopped hiccup crying just long enough to blow his nose on his sleeve. "Ten thousand years of service and stripped of my scythe. Just like that. I didn't do anything wrong, but no one believes meeeeeeeee. Hurrrrrp Hurrrrrp Hurrrrrrp."

"Geesh. This guy's a mess," Kevin said. "Don't just stand there, kid. Make sure she's okay. We don't know if we can trust him."

"Me?"

"Yeah, you. Now scoot. I'll be right behind you. It's gonna take me a while, though. These muffin tops are really slowing me down."

I didn't want to go, because I was terrified, but I went. Because DeeDee. Plus, Kevin kicked me in the shins until I started walking. By the time I made it to the candy aisle, the reaper had wrapped his bony, shroud-draped arms around her. She held him while he sobbed, shoulders popping, skull wet with tears.

"It's okay," she said. "It will all be okay."

"No. Herp. It's. Hurrrrr. Not. Oooooooh. Kaaaaaaay. Herp herp hurrrrrrrrrrp. My life is over. I can't go on. Eeeeeeeeeeeeeeeeeeeeeee."

"Your life isn't over." DeeDee patted his back. "You can find another job. I. Um. I think?"

"It's not just the uh uh job. Herrrrrrrrrrrr. Everyone hates me. Hurrrr. And my girlfriend dumped meeeeeeeee. Heeerrrrrrrrr urrrrrrrr. Hurrrrrp. I miss her sooooooo mu uh uch heerrrrrr hurrrrrrr hurrrrr."

"Of all the places he could have gone, he's here. HERE! I have the worst luck." Angel's triangle poked out between the packages of Haribo Star Mix on the candy aisle end cap. "He's the reason we're all getting audited, you know. He let us all down. I'm so mad. I can't even look at him."

Angel literally turned away.

"He said he was suspended." I whispered through clenched teeth. "If he can't reap, does that mean we can't die?"

Angel didn't answer. He rolled in between the bags of gummy bears and cried. I assume. I heard the vague sound of sobs.

"Don't get any ideas, kid. He's *a* reaper, not *the* reaper. There's more than one, you know." Kevin leaned against my leg, panting, trying to catch his breath. "There are seven billion people in the world. That's too big a job for one guy."

"How do you know that? Wait. Let me guess. It's in the employee manual."

"No. There's another one right behind you."

"What!?" I turned. Very slowly.

Sure enough. Another tall bony figure in black robes stood on the welcome mat. And this one had a scythe. Reaper two waved his bony hand at the first reaper and said, "Hey man. Heard about your suspension. Shit luck, but you never know. Maybe it'll work out. Probably not, though. Anyhoo, those of us who still *have* a job have to get back to work."

He raised a scroll to his empty eye sockets. "Well, poop. I'm late.

She's already dead. Totally not my fault, though. Celestial 40 is a parking lot. I got here as fast as I could."

We all stared at him. Even reaper one, tears streaking down his bare-bone cheeks.

Reaper two looked at me. "You see a dead scout around here?"

I pointed to aisle six.

"Thanks, man."

Reaper two floated away, and reaper one collapsed in a sobbing heap of ugly cry on top of DeeDee. "Hurrrrr. Hurrrrr. Hurrrrrrrrr. It isn't fair. He never does anything right, and he still has a job!"

Reaper two must have heard him, because he shot him a really mean look. Like, really mean. So bad, that even though he didn't have a face, I could tell. He grumbled. "What goes up, must come down, jerk."

"Aaaaaah!" That was me. Yeah. I Screamed. Top of my lungs, because something bit into my toe, and the way this night was going, it could be anything. It was my employee manual. It held tight to my Puma, growling.

The grim reaper turned around and just stared at me with his empty bone eye sockets. In silence. My legs felt like cooked spaghetti. It's like he was boring into my soul. Waiting.

"I uh." I tugged at my collar. Because no pressure. It's only the grim reaper staring at you. Because you screamed like a terrified gopher. "Uh. I couldn't help but overhear. It'll be okay, man. I got fired, and my girlfriend dumped me, too. I had to move back in with my parents. I felt like my life was over. But it wasn't."

Stupid mouth. Sure. Go ahead. Relay my failures in front of Death and DeeDee. "Don't be sad. It'll be okay. It'll all work out. You'll see."

The reaper rubbed the tears off his cheek. "Really?"

"Really."

The reaper wrapped his bony arms around me and squeezed. "That's the nicest thing anyone has ever said to meeeeeeeeeeee."

Brrrrrrr. He was cold, like hugging an iceberg. I didn't know how DeeDee endured it for so long.

He sniffled, then he said, "You guys are so nice. Thanks for making me feel at home. So uh. Which way is my room? Where should I put my stuff?"

His bone finger pointed to the door, and a beat up duffle bag appeared on the doormat.

"Room?" My voice shook.

I didn't know what to say. DeeDee didn't say anything either. Her eyebrows hit her hairline.

"Woah woah woah. Did I hear you right? No. No way." Kevin stomped right on up to the reaper. "No room for you. This is a gate and a store, not a hotel. You can't stay here. Hit the road."

The reaper recoiled.

"Kevin!" DeeDee shot him a look. *The* look. The "how could you be so mean? Let's talk about this" look. "Thomistic philosophy says angels appear to show us divine reality. We should be open—"

"Stuff it, chica. You can shove that philosophy degree straight up your butt," Kevin said. "We can't have a reaper hanging around here. It's bad for bus—"

Crunch.

Kevin was mid-word when the reaper's big bony foot came down right on top of him. Hard.

DeeDee's hands went over her mouth.

"Wow. Did you guys see the size of that roach? You really need to call an exterminator," the reaper said. "Yuck. I hate roaches. They give me the creeps."

The reaper rubbed his foot on the floor mat to get the Kevin off. Kevin lay on the linoleum. He didn't move.

DeeDee dropped to her knees and put her ear to his chest. Then she looked at me with pink, wet eyes, and said, "he's dead."

CHAPTER 3

DeeDee held the remains of Kevin to her chest and cried. I sat next to her, stunned. This can't be happening. Kevin? Dead? Stomped to death like a common roach? No. No way.

My mind raced. What do I do? I have to do something! Call 911. Yes!

Wait. Would paramedics respond to an emergency call for a cockroach? Probably not. Shit.

"Why are you guys so upset?" The reaper asked. "It's just a roach."

"He wasn't just a roach! He was my manager and my friend." I didn't realize how true it was until I screamed it. Sure, he was a pain in the ass, but I couldn't imagine life without him. Not anymore. An icy cold weighed in my gut. I felt heavy. Sinking. Numb.

The reaper leaned in to get a closer look at Kevin. "Oh. Wow. I'm sorry. I didn't realize. Geesh, guys. I mean, I thought he was just a really big, disgusting roach."

"Well, he is." Angel wobbled out between the bags of Zapp's. "Still, I can't believe he just committed an unauthorized reaping when's he's already under investigation. Maybe the rumors are true. I didn't want to believe it. Hurrrr. Hurrrr. Hurrrrr."

"Help us!"

Angel looked away, but another angel answered the call. A fallen one, but still. Faust stepped out of the stockroom, carrying a fresh batch of posters. He took one look at Kevin, and said, "Again? Oh, my. This will never do."

He snapped his fingers, and the chime on the front door dinged. A rush of cold air swept over me. My fists balled up with rage. Another monster? Now? SERIOUSLY? I swung around, ready to unleash my rage sadness on whatever beast was unlucky enough to step in, but it was Doc. He stood in the doorway, brows furrowed, carrying a small purple bag. "We have no time to waste! Places, everyone. Where is Bug Man?"

He zeroed in on DeeDee, still cradling Kevin. He shooed me and the reaper out of the way. He sprinkled a weird white powder on the floor, into the shape of a circle with lots of scrolly designs at the edges. He arranged small white candles around the outside. When every-thing was just so, he lit the candles, looked at DeeDee and said, "You know what to do."

She does? Then he looked at me, like I knew what to do. Wait, did he mean "you" as in DeeDee or "you" as in all of us?

DeeDee laid Kevin's body in the middle of the weird powdery circle and pulled out her fuzzy purple employee manual. It opened on its own, pages ruffling, as if by magic. Doc reached under Kevin's body and pulled his employee manual out of. Huh. I don't know where. Then *it* opened up on its own, by magic. He looked at me, waiting.

And waiting.

"What?"

His brows wrinkled together. "We need yours, too."

"I'm not touching that thing!" I shrieked.

I'm not proud of the sound. But, hello. Stressed! My boss is dead and my employee manual was alive—mobile, angry, very bitey—and beelining toward the pyramid of 2-Liters by the beer cave. Because the damn thing moves on its own!

I hesitated.

"Do it, or Kevin is lost to us for eternity!" Doc yelled, "Go! Page thirty three, New Man. Quickly. We have no time to waste!"

So I went. I followed that rabid book down the aisle, despite a numb body and fumbling feet. It saw me coming and crawled faster. Spine opening and closing, pulling itself across the linoleum.

Jesus. Was this my life? Really? Chasing an angry magic book across a doomed convenience store so I can resurrect a dead cockroach? When did things go so far off the rails?

Doc and DeeDee's voices rose behind me. Chanting in tandem. "Ortum exsurge a tenebris domain. Kevin veni ad nos in domum suam. Corpus tuum incolunt iterum vivere."

Or something like that. They chanted it over and over, their voices mingling together into one long, low, constant buzz.

"Chant, New Man!" Doc snipped. "Page thirty three! Three must say the words, or they will not work!"

"I'm on it."

For once, I wasn't lying. I had that book cornered, and it knew it. Its cover furrowed like it was looking back at me. My palms were covered in sweat, my mouth ran dry. The book looked at me. Then, it veered right and tried to make a break for the stockroom. I lunged. I missed. I panicked. And I flopped. Literally, a full belly flop. I smacked face first, flat on the floor. Ow. But worth it. My pudge covered a lot of ground laid out flat. Trust me.

The book kicked me in the belly button. I rolled to the side and grabbed it. It bucked and kicked. "We have to save Kevin!"

It stopped for a second, like it was thinking about it, then it opened. That's more like it!

Chomp. "Ow!"

Yep. The spine opened just enough to let me slip a couple knuckles in so it could bite me. "I don't have time for this. Page thirty three. Open up!"

It didn't. At least, not the way DeeDee's magically rippled to the correct page. I had to pry that cover open and pin it to the floor with my knees.

DeeDee and Doc chanted. "Exsurge...something something...Kevin veni something something. Corpus something something vivere."

My page had the same words. Mostly? Hard to tell. There were an awful lot of them. No pictures. I checked the page number: three and the top curve of another three above my hairy knee. All right. "This is it."

I cleared my throat, and... huh. Oof. Everything was in big loopy, old timey fancy people cursive. Aw, man. I won't lie. I'm gonna have some trouble reading that. They barely teach that shit in school anymore.

"Chant, New Man! Now!" Doc snapped.

Well, I'd just have to wing it. Because it was in cursive. And not in English. Guys like me don't exactly ace Latin. But I joined in. Slow, but steady "...tenebris domain. Insert name veni—" Oops. Back up. Try again. "Domain *Kevin* veni ad nos in domum suam."

Huh. Looks like my part is different. Must be why Doc was so insistent. I chanted, but every word I said made the book more angry. It growled and jerked and bucked, and worse, the corners of the pages kept curling down, trying to cover the script so I couldn't see.

"Cut it out! I'm trying to do the right thing here."

But it didn't stop. Its spine tightened and snapped, pages curling, and I had to put all my weight on it to keep it open. I chanted and chanted. But DeeDee and Doc suddenly stopped, and only my voice echoed around the store. "Receperint tui sumus exspiravi!"

I really put some flourish on it. Dude. I just spoke Latin! I'm awesome!

Suddenly, the book snapped shut and scrambled away, taking a mouthful of my leg hairs with it.

"What did you say?" Doc stared at me, his eyes round as silver dollars. "Were you on the correct page, New Man?"

"Yes!"

He looked at me for a moment, like he didn't believe me. "Come here, quickly. We must join hands. We do not have time to waste."

I did. Even the cleaning crew stopped eating Starbursts long enough to join their clammy little hands with me and DeeDee. Doc chanted, and DeeDee rocked back and forth to the beat of his voice. The grim reaper? Well. He just stood by the hot food rollers, sobbing, "I can't do anything right! Hurrrrrrrrr. Hurrrrrrr. Hurrrrrrr."

Yeah. I feel you, dude. I didn't know what to do, either, so I just tried to stay still and not touch anything. I didn't want to mess anything up. We needed Kevin, because DeeDee couldn't count on me to save the day on purpose.

We did this for a long time. Hoping. Praying. Doc chanting and sprinkling oils and rum and powders as candles flickered. I'm not sure for how long, because time seemed to stand still and sprint all at the same time. Eventually, Doc stopped. "We have done all we can. Kevin is in God's hands now."

He covered Kevin's fat roach body with a rectangle of white fabric. We all stared at it for a long time. Hoping? Dealing? I wasn't sure. But the cloth was still. Kevin didn't move. He wasn't magically resurrected. It was over. He was gone.

DeeDee looked at me. Tears had dragged her eyeliner down her cheek in black streaks. "We should bury him. Is there room in the employee plot at Eternal Spector Memory Gardens?"

"Did you say 'employee plot'?"

"For employees killed in the line of duty. It's in the cemetery next to Monster Burger." She did not sound alarmed. She said it more like, duh. "If Kevin's there, we could visit him. He'd be so close."

"It is full, but he is small. We will make room for him," Doc said. "He deserves the honor. I will get my shovel."

My head spun. "There's a cemetery plot for Demon Mart employees killed in the line of duty? And it's FULL?"

Hello! Am I the only one who's alarmed?

Apparently, because Doc and DeeDee were up and moving. DeeDee gathered a handful of Milky Ways from the candy aisle and a couple of mini bottles of Wild Turkey from Kevin's stash behind the counter. She sat down next to him, laid them around the body, and whispered, "For your journey to the afterlife."

Doc disappeared into the back and emerged a few moments later with a tiny coffin and a shovel.

I didn't move. Were we burying Kevin? For real? "And we have coffins in the storeroom?"

"Faust takes his duties seriously. He is always prepared," Doc handed me the coffin. Small. Perfectly Kevin sized. Polished wood. "Place Bug Man inside."

I stared at Kevin's body, lying under his shroud. My hands shook like jelly on a roller coaster. I turned to Faust, who was plastering the beer cooler doors with more of those damned posters. "Do something!"

"Unfortunately, when a soul is between body and judgment, I cannot intervene. It is against the rules. Kevin's soul is out of my reach."

The cleaning crew cried as they emptied Doc's bottle of rum and tore open another bag of Starbursts, ready to eat their feelings. Wow. Kevin called that one. They really were stomachs on legs.

"You know I did. Cleaning crew, my butt. Those things are dumb as a bag of dicks. You just wait. I'm gonna give Steve an earful about this. I'm gonna rip him a new one."

DeeDee froze.

A lump formed in my throat. I turned, very slowly, toward the voice.

An ethereal blue blob floated just above the floor right next to me. It was translucent and shimmery. It was shaped like a roach. A big, fat giant roach. The shape turned to me, then thumbed a leg back at the grim reaper, still sobbing by the hot dog station. "Why is this asshole still here? Get him outta here already. I ain't paying you to stand around scratching your butt. Why are you looking at me like that?"

"Uh..." I pointed at his body, still motionless under the white fabric.

"What the hell is this?"

"It's...you?"

"What? You're full of it, kid." He floated over to his body, and stuck his head right through the fabric, like he was taking a look. A long look. When he reemerged, he stared at his glowing blue body, his legs, every blue bit, for a good long time. Then he said, "You gotta be shittin' me. You didn't read the damn chant right, did you, kid?"

"I did. I swear!"

"Then why am I a fucking ghost?"

"Don't blame me! I chanted every word on that page!" Maybe if my employee manual hadn't run away or rolled down the pages, I could have chanted sooner. "The grim reaper is the one who smooshed you. It's not my fault you're dead!"

Doc stood behind the counter flipping through books, grumbling, "I do not know why you did not properly resurrect, Bug Man. It is possible we have performed the ritual one too many times. New Man. Bring me your manual. I want to see your page thirty-three. Fetch it now."

"That thing?" I pointed. My manual was deep in the chip end cap, ripping open Zapp's bags, growling. "No way!"

"You must tame it if you are to succeed here."

Doc's order didn't override my paralysis. I didn't move. I couldn't. But everyone else did. Doc flipped through more books. DeeDee wiped tears and eyeliner off her cheeks.

Kevin? Well, he floated above the floor, testing his new ghost powers. He hopped up and down a few times to see how high he could fly. Which was barely. Then he jiggled his carapace. "I can't believe I'm still fat. Man. The afterlife really isn't fair. Oh shit. Here we go. HI-YA!" Suddenly, Kevin jumped into his best Chuck Norris stance. "Back off. I'm not dying again!"

The second reaper floated up to Kevin, whose tiny roach legs waved in menacing circles, gearing up to fight. He leaned all the way down and looked Kevin up and down. "Woah. No way. Is that a cockroach with a *soul*? Ten thousand years, you think you've seen everything." He scratched his skull. "Hold on. Did you reap this roach without a scroll? Holy shit. You did, didn't you? I never thought I'd see the day. Mr. Perfect reaping illegally. Wow. Head Office is gonna have a field day with that. They'll never take you back now."

Reaper one offered no defense. In part because he had ten hot dogs, with buns, stuffed into his mouth. The buns were wet with his tears.

Reaper two said, "So, you planning to shack up with these breathers? Talk about slumming it. My, how the mighty have fallen. Sucks to be you."

"Hey. Bonehead." Kevin kicked the second reaper right in the shin. Or tried to. His blue leg was like smoke. It went right through. "Get that dead monster outta my automotive section and move along already. We got a gate to run. I don't need two of your ugly mugs hanging around here. You'll scare away the customers."

Reaper two ignored him. He pointed at the other reaper. "I gotta go, but good luck with your investigation. You're gonna need it. Oh, and if you decide to go rogue and reap the babe illegally, call me. I'll come pick her up. I got a bone she can sit on for the ferry ride, heh heh."

He pointed at DeeDee, then at his. Ahem. "Speaking of hot babes. I'll say hi to your ex next time I'm in the Nobodies Division. See ya around!"

He floated out the front door and vanished the second he hit the end of the handicapped parking spot. Of course, that still left one reaper. One reaper with a guilty look on his bone face, mouth full of hot dogs flopping up and down as he chewed them down to mush. When the last bun disappeared, somehow, into his invisible cheeks, he cleared his throat and floated over to Kevin.

"Ignore that guy. He's a jerk. But, uh. I am sorry, little dude. I had no idea. I've never met a roach with a soul before. My bad." He wiped the crumbs off his mouth with his sleeve. "What do you say we start fresh? Let bygones be bygones."

"Fresh, huh? You just killed me, that's all. But yeah. Sure. Sure, man. It's cool."

Kevin didn't mean it, but the reaper didn't seem to catch on.

"Oh. Great! That'll make living together much easier. Where should I put my things?" He floated over to the door and picked up that weird magic duffle bag, which shimmered as if it was halfway between here and another dimension.

"Hold up. What do you think you're doing?" Kevin dug his fists into his carapace.

"Taking these to my room. Is it somewhere in the back?"

"Oh. Hell. No." He pointed not one but three legs at the reaper. "I told you once, I'll tell you again. You gotta go. You aren't staying. Hello? You killed me!"

"But I said I was sorry."

"I am afraid you must let him stay." Doc looked up from one of the many creepy books behind the counter. "The rules are very clear on this matter."

"What rules?" Kevin snipped.

"These rules." Doc held up a slim leather binder, with the words *Transmundane Gate Management and You, Complete Rules and Regulations* embossed in gold on the cover. He read aloud. "Section seven. Subsection B. All gate locations must provide safe haven for displaced divine creatures who seek it, so long as said creature has not been convicted of crimes in a court of celestial law. Tell us, Reaper Man. Did you break celestial law?"

The reaper shook his head. "No. I'm suspended, pending investigation, so right now I'm just unemployed. And my girlfriend cast meeeeeee uh huuuuh out. I don't have anywhere else to goooooooooo. Hurrrrrrrrrrrrrr."

"Then he is permitted to stay." Doc snapped the binder shut. "Until his case is closed. Or he is formally convicted."

"What? Hell no. Let me see that." Kevin attempted to jump fly to the counter. But even in ghostly form, he was too portly to pull it off.

His wings buzzed, but he didn't achieve even a hint of lift, apart from the inch he was already floating above the floor. That didn't stop him. He grunted and cursed until he finally managed to float crawl up through the counter. He walked directly into the binder Doc held. He stood there, half of his body poking up through the cover. "Wow. That feels weird. Woody. Now back off. Let me read."

While Kevin and Doc had a heated debate, DeeDee grabbed me and locked eyes with me. "If the angel of death moves in here, we need a plan."

We sure the fuck did! Duh! I couldn't wait to hear it.

Then she said, as I hung on her every wise word, "Do you have any ideas?"

"What? Me? I thought you had a plan!" I squeaked it. I'm not proud. Come on. She always had a plan. She was the one with the plan. "I don't have a plan!"

"Yeah, no. I got nothing. I'm sure we'll think of something. Until we do, stay frosty. I mean, he already killed Kevin, and we can't run the store if we're all ghosts. That would suck. So. You know. Don't die."

"That's it? That's the plan?"

She shrugged. "It's a start. Let me know if you come up with anything else."

"Me?" Fuck. We're screwed.

Kevin ran a leg across the paper for a while, reading out loud to himself. Or maybe he wasn't reading, unless that binder was actually a dictionary of creative curse words, because he was absolutely spewing expletives. His shoulders slumped, and he said, "Well, dipshits. Doc's right. Looks like we got a roommate."

CHAPTER 4

MILLIONS of tiny flakes dive-bombed past the streetlights, torpe-doing directly onto my nose, piercing like little ice bullets. Because it's pitch black, freezing outside, and snowing. And no, I was not snuggled up in my jammies, inside, like normal people. Nope. I was outside, riding my busted up Huffy across town in a snowstorm. In January. In Ohio.

Because DeeDee didn't have a plan, but I sure did. It had two parts.

One: Don't die. Duh.

And yeah, okay. That was DeeDee's plan, but I added a part two: Hero up, stat.

It wouldn't be easy, and there were reasons I had avoided it— Namely the lack of readily available radioactive spiders, because that's about what it would take for a guy like me—but it was long overdue. So I pedaled, through the storm, toward Bubba's Yoked & Choked Kick Ass, Take Names Training Center, seeking a miracle.

I had no other choice. My new roomie was the grim reaper, and he'd already killed my boss. Plus, I'd nearly been eaten alive by zombies because I was too out of shape to climb a five-foot-tall shelf.

You may have forgotten about that, but I haven't. It wasn't the high point in my life. Trust me.

Fwump fwump fwump.

"What's that?" I glanced back. It sounded like something flapping against the wind. But there was nothing. Just darkness. Deep. Black. Darkness. No one else was on this street. Just me.

"Meh. It's probably nothing. No one in their right mind would be out in this weather. In this part of town. Talk about a bad neighborhood. Even Gomorrah wasn't this sketchy." Angel eight ball sat on my gym bag, which was in the bike basket attached to my handlebars. "Why didn't you drive? The weather is terrible."

I nearly wrecked the bike. "What? Drive! You didn't tell me I could drive?"

"Why would I? You never bothered to get your tires fixed after God smote you."

"I would have fixed them if you'd told me He'd changed his mind!" I sunk my face deeper into my coat, steeling myself against the cold. The night seemed extra dark. Extra cold. Extra creepy. "I've been biking to work in snow!"

"Hey man. This is your fault, not mine. Chance favors the prepared. Be an adult. Fix your flat tires. You've got money now. Look on the bright side. Shivering burns calories." His triangle turned. "Can you pedal faster? My water's freezing. I can barely turn in here."

"Gee. That would be a loss." I wanted to chuck him out of the bike basket.

"It would. For you. STOP! Hit the brakes! My GGEPS says we're here."

I skidded to a stop. "GGEPS?"

"God's Green Earth Positioning System. Don't even say it. I know, okay? You Know Who prefers a certain flourish."

Angel directed me to park my bike in front of nothing. Seriously. The block was abandoned. Nothing but concrete foundations, worn down to stubble with age, where buildings used to be. We were maybe a mile down the road from where Monster Burger once stood. I could see the faint reflection of white snow accumulating on the arched gate of the Eternal Spector Memory Gardens. You know, that cemetery full of Demon Mart employees? The one that was *full*?

Gulp. Refer to Part One: Don't die. "Uh, wrong address. Let's go!" This block was bad news.

"Praise Jesus. It's cardio time. Finally!" Angel flashed an arrow into the darkness along the fence line at the very back of the block. A small neon sign suddenly buzzed to life. It said, "Now serving 327" in crackling red. The sign appeared to be floating, attached to nothing.

Great. That's not creepy. "Maybe this was a bad idea."

"You aren't backing out now, buttercup. You need check marks before my audit. I need this job."

Angel eight ball plopped out of my cup holder and wobbled through the litter and snow.

I grabbed my gym bag and followed him toward that fizzling neon light. The anemic yellow glow of the streetlight disappeared the second we stepped off the sidewalk, like the abandoned lot had been wrapped up in a big black blanket. Which is great. Just great, because walking outside, alone, at night on an empty block, on a street with "Cemetery" in its name is totally cool. No horror movie in the history of the world ever started like this. What could possibly go wrong?

The lot was deep. We walked and wobbled for what felt like forever, pressing into the ice cold wind, until suddenly the darkness opened up like a curtain. A vintage mobile home sat in the middle of a bright green lawn of plastic grass. The trailer had a fat teal stripe around the middle. A pair of pink plastic flamingos stood in a flowerbed filled with plastic daisies. The scene looked like a souvenir water globe from a tacky roadside attraction. Untouched by snow. Warm, even. Tropical.

This couldn't possibly be Bubba's Yoked & Choked Kick Ass, Take Names Training Center. Gyms had windows lined with tread-mills, so all the piously fit people could show the fatties outside how hard they worked to look flawless. Gyms had juice bars, aerobicizing MILFs in spandex, and abbed-up meatheads with bleach-white smiles sizing up your love handles at check in. They certainly didn't look like this.

There was a sign tacked to the front door. It said, "Closed every full moon."

"We're in the wrong place."

"GGEPS doesn't lie. This is it. Go knock on the door."

"No way. This is someone's house." Plus, this was the Ohio equivalent of a gingerbread house in the forest. "A witch is probably in there preheating the oven. Look at me. I'm the ham!"

"I see ham all right." Angel huffed at me and rolled into the door. *Thunk. Thunk. Thunk.*

"What are you doing? No normal person would answer that door. No one would be out here except robbers. Or worse. Jehovah's Witnesses."

Angel managed to triangle eye-rolled me, despite his low water level.

"I changed my mind. I don't need the free gym membership. You're right. I've got money now. I'll pay. Planet Pump is only a mile from here. It's only ten bucks a month! Roll on over here, let's go."

"Bubba is the best in the business, and you need all the help you can get. Trust me."

I stepped back, and I swear one of the pink flamingos' beady black eyes followed me. Yep. I'm out. Too creepy. Planet Pump, here I come. I turned to go.

Reeeeeee.

Uh oh. Don't tell me. That was the sound of a door opening, wasn't it? Of course. Just my luck. Almost home free, now I'm dinner.

"Number three two seven? Lloyd Lamb Wallace?" The voice was low, gravely, a manly bass. "You out here?"

"Um. Yes?" My heart kicked up. I was in over my head. I wanted to run. Because any gym membership included as a free benefit to Demon Mart employees couldn't be at the mall with normal people. No. It had to be in a trailer full of nightmares on an abandoned lot.

"For real? You? You're Lloyd Lamb Wallace?"

I turned to face my fate. An absolutely hulking man stood in the door, six foot five at least, with wide shoulders and a thick barrel chest. And boy. Let's just say this trailer didn't need a flagpole, because this guy was flying enough stars and stripes for the entire neighborhood. On an absolutely enormous pair of stretchy workout pants, one leg stars, one leg stripes. His pants were so big, they had to be made from one of those giant flags that fly over car dealerships.

Bubba had a bald-eagle print bandana wrapped around a mullet. He had a brown Hulk Hogan mustache, and more chest and shoulder hair than I'd ever seen on one man, so thick it looked like a pelt. It poked out of a tank top with "Bubba" airbrushed in fancy cursive across the chest. Dude. This guy had worse taste in T-shirts than I did.

I looked down. My shirt said, "Fart. Now loading."

Well, maybe equally bad.

He seemed startled by the looks of me, too. "Are you cranking my shank, son? *You're* Lloyd Lamb Wallace?"

"Yep. I'm Lloyd." I should have lied and run home.

"Really? You're the kid who saved the world twice? Well, helped save the world. I heard you weren't Number One or anything."

"Sidekick. Called it." Angel triangled me. "It's gonna take more than abs to turn you into a hero."

Wait. What? "You were the one who kept going on about me needing abs!"

"I said you needed them, sure. But come on. I didn't say they were gonna magically solve all your problems." Angel said. "It's more of a can't hurt, might help thing. Besides, they might make you feel better about yourself. "

Well, my new leaf was not turning over the way I wanted it to. Already!

Bubba sized me up. "I was expecting. Huh. Doesn't matter. In this business, you never can tell by looking, can you? Now get on in here, son. It's time to get pumped."

He clapped his giant meat mitts together and motioned for me to follow him in. I stepped up. As soon as my feet touched the welcome mat, the door morphed into a bright white glowing rectangle. It looked like one of those portals Kevin uses, only without the dickhead demon roommate hand reaching out to steal our stuff. My gut churned. "Uh, Planet Pump's still open. If we leave now, we'll be there in ten minutes."

"Quit stalling." Angel rolled into my feet, and I fell straight into the light.

"Aaaaaaaah! Oh." Yeah. I screamed. Until I realized it felt pretty good. Warm and tingly all over, like I was wrapped head-to-toe in massage chair. Wow. This feels awesome. Why didn't Kevin tell me portals were this great?

Then it stopped. I opened my eyes.

Holy shit. I stood in a huge room filled with exercise machines. The ceiling had to be thirty feet high, with metal trusses and giant can lights. And the gym? It kept going and going, back as far as I could see. This was way nicer than Planet Pump.

"Welcome to Bubba's Yoked & Choked Kick Ass, Take Names Training Center." Bubba put his arms out and whirled around, inviting me to bask in the glory.

Honestly, I did want to clap. I mean, what a great trick. This had to be the best double wide ever.

"Oh, and son, from now on, use the front door." He pointed at a huge stone half circle with symbols carved into it, standing between the locker rooms and the water fountain. The edges moved, and the center lit up bright white. It was a gate, but huge, much bigger than the beer cave.

Something stepped out of the cloud of swirling white mist in the center.

Oh my God, is that? Gulp. No way. I dropped my gym bag in shock. I swear as real as I am standing here, a huge wolf, seven feet tall, standing on its back legs, stepped out, grabbed a towel off a rack, put one paw out in front of him, and leaned forward, stretching his legs like he was warming up.

Bubba didn't seem to think a werewolf stretching his hammies before hopping on the treadmill was strange at all. He waved. "How you doing, Fluffy? Don't forget: Members-only flea dip this Friday!" He turned to me. "Son, your locker isn't ready yet, but you can drop your bag and coat there. The gremlins will take care of 'em."

"Uh, gremlins?"

He pointed to a reception desk. Between stacks of clean white gym towels, a bunch of hairless, naked creatures bounced around the desk, folding towels and doing data entry. One had a pair of granny glasses perched on its nose as it stared at a computer screen, click clacking away.

"Ugly things, aren't they? I thought they were gonna be cute and furry like the ones in the movies, but I'm starting to think Steven Spielberg didn't know what he was talking about." Bubba shook his head. "Anyway, they're great if you get them young and train them right. No one else folds a towel as neat as they do, and their spelling is a lot better than the imps I had in here before. Now where were we? Oh, yes."

Bubba cleared his throat. "Lloyd Lamb Wallace, you are about to embark on a journey. Using the elite fitness and fighting skills I honed during seventeen consecutive world title victories in the Fang Dome, I will transform you from the sad potato I see before me into a majestic beast of a man. Together, we will chisel your body from misshapen hunk of flab into masterpiece. You will become rock hard, like a god. Follow me, and you will go from blimp to pimp, from fat to all that, from hippo to hip, from flub to stud. I only have one question for you: Are you ready, Lloyd? Are you ready to change your bod and your life forever?"

He was fired up like a snake-handling tent preacher. Bubba pointed at me. "Are you with me?"

Angel eight ball hit my foot, rattling with excitement. "I'm with you!"

"I said are you with me?" Bubba raised his arm up in the air like he was hailing a cab. Or Jesus. Either way.

"I'm with you!" A voice boomed behind me.

Bubba looked up, and the color immediately drained out of his face. He tugged at his tank top, and his Adam's apple bobbed up and down as he swallowed hard.

Shit. There's a monster behind me, isn't there? Yes. There totally is. And it must be bad if Bubba's nervous.

"This is a private training session, son," Bubba said.

"It's okay. I'm with him. We're together. We're best friends. And roommates." The grim reaper floated up next to me. "Sorry I'm late. I had a hard time finding you once you stepped off the curb."

I looked at him. He looked at me. I didn't know what to say. Except, now I knew where that fwap fwap noise came from on the ride here. Yep. He followed me, and we were gonna have to have a serious talk about boundaries. I could tell he was shooting me puppy dog eyes, even though he didn't actually have eyes. And his cheekbones had tear streaks on them.

"Yeah. It's fine. He's with me." I didn't have the heart to send him away.

"Next time, give me a heads up, son. We have a firm 'No Reapers' policy, ever since Trog dropped dead during the Thanksgiving Turkey Trot back in '07," Bubba said. "I don't think any of us will ever forget the sight of that reaper chasing him around the track. Of course, Trog probably shouldn't have eaten three whole turkeys before he ran. Poor guy. But you know how trolls are. Very literal. What's your name, son?"

"Zackumzaphielhermesiappotholonian."

"Wow. That's a mouthful. How about I call you Zack? If you're serious—really serious—about your bod, I can bend the rules. Just once." Bubba's eyes narrowed. "But you have to promise me right now no death and absolutely no reaping in here. It's not allowed. Do you understand me?"

"Okay. I promise I won't reeee. Eeee. Eeeeeee. Eeeeeeee."

Here we go again. Tear faucet, full blast.

"Uh, is he all right?" Bubba looked at me.

I shrugged.

Bubba clapped Zack on the shoulder. "Buck up, son. Just stay with Lloyd. You two will be training buddies. No going off on your own, understand? At least 'til the guys warm up to you. The Trog incident is still fresh in their mind. All right, then. First thing's first, boys: Fitness assessment. Drop your gear and meet me by the scale."

I dropped my bag by the front desk. A gremlin hopped down on it to wrap a coat check tag around the handle. That's when I noticed the zipper rippling. Something moved inside. Whatever it was bucked. He unzipped the bag and peered down in.

"Grrrrrrruuuuuu." Something red snapped up and tried to bite him.

"Oh my God!" It was my employee manual. I jumped on the bag and pushed it back down in. "I'm so sorry. I don't know how that got in there!"

I zipped that thing shut, quick, but the book didn't like it one bit. It kicked. "Bad book. Bad! Stay in there. You hear me. STAY!"

It whimpered but stopped fighting. For now.

"Can you keep an eye on him, Angel? Angel?" I looked all around, but Angel had disappeared. Great. Some help he is. I had to improvise. I tied my coat around the bag, securing the zipper. "It's okay, book. Be good. I'll be back soon. If you're a good boy, I'll bring you a treat."

Hey. It worked for dogs, so maybe?

The gremlin looked at me, then at the bag, then at me with a face that said, "WTF, dude."

"It's not my fault! I didn't know it was in there!"

I quick stepped over to Bubba and Zack, who were standing by a row of trophy cases filled with brass cups and framed photos of

Bubba and a really really good looking, impossibly buff blond guy. They both dripped with medals. A framed news story had been clipped from the *Weekly Wolf News*.

Wait. Were these guys all—? You know what? Forget it. I don't want to know.

The headline said, "Five time Mr. Fur-niverse champ (1993-1998) trains record-breaking six-time champ, Mr. Fur-niverse 2016-2021."

World champs. Wow. These guys had clearly cornered the market on radioactive spiders.

Bubba patted me on the shoulder. "Hey, son. I've got some bad news. Normally, I handle all the new guys personally. I like to be there in the beginning, to shape their soft doughy bodies myself, but Spot called in sick so I have to teach obedience school tonight." He glanced at his watch. "I hate to switcheroo on you like this last minute, but don't worry. Hunter will get you started, and I'll check back in on you at the end."

Bubba walked away. "Who's Hunter?"

I was immediately sorry I asked. A man stepped out of the office. I say man, but really I mean an Adonis. Six feet two, sandy blond hair and tan, with shoulders so wide and a stomach so small the top half of his body was the shape of a V. It was the guy from all the photos. Six-time Mr. Fur-niverse himself. Super human.

My intestines just did a somersault. Fat guys avoid the gym because we don't want to stand next to guys like Hunter. He and I looked like the before and after pics in a late night Brazilian diet pill infomercial. See? I told you. Nothing good ever happens at the gym. Ever!

Angel eight ball rolled out from behind a Best Howl 1987 plaque. "Wow. Look at that hunka. Is it hot in here?"

"Well, hello, fellas. Come on in and make yourselves at home. Then, get ready." Hunter stepped right to us and growled. "I'm gonna rip you apart."

CHAPTER 5

I QUAKED in my tube socks.

Hunter's perfect pink mouth split into the biggest, most impossibly large white-teeth smile. "And rebuild you better than before. It'll be great! I'm so excited to meet you guys. Welcome to the Bubba's family. Bring it in."

He roped his muscle arms around us and squeezed. Tight. His rippling muscles were like vice grips. "Let's jump right in. First up. Fitness assessment. Show me what you've got."

I glanced down at my gut. Well, I've got that.

His two giant hands grabbed me by the biceps—definitely don't got that—and lifted me off the floor.

He picked me up like I was nothing, a piece of paper, and sat me on a giant metal square. Numbers blipped up on a digital pad attached to the wall. And blipped. And blipped some more, higher than I'd like them to go. Because this was a scale.

Hunter stepped between me and that horrible number and smiled. But it was a distraction. He produced a pair of large metal calipers out of nowhere and jabbed the points into the front and back of one of my love handles. "Let's get a BMI."

Yep. This was my worst nightmare. But, hello. My new roommate was the grim reaper. If that wasn't an incentive to get fit, what was?

Hunter eased up on the calipers. "Don't worry. We'll get that bod ready for swimsuit season. You're up, Bones."

I stepped off the scale, and Zack stepped on. Hunter slipped the calipers under Zack's robes to check his BMI, too.

Dude. Why? He had no body fat. Like, literally zero.

Hunter said, "Wow. Four percent. Body builder territory. Looks like you're in pretty good shape. I can't wait to see how you do on your muscle endurance tests."

Yep. Pinch me. I'm having a nightmare. I finally join a gym, and I'm stuck with a six-time Mr. Fur-niverse and the world's buffest skeleton.

"Give me twenty, boys. Go!"

Twenty what? I didn't even know what that meant. But Zack had his arms out, knees bent, pumping up and down, doing an absolutely perfect squat.

"Excellent form! Get in on the fun, Champ. What are you waiting for?"

Champ? Did he mean me?

I put my arms out and bent my knees. Oof. It burned. I hadn't even squatted all the way down yet, and I was feeling it. Wow. Was my butt supposed to hurt like that?

And down. *Grrr.* Up.

And...down. Oof. Holy shit. I'm dying.

And up. *Hurrrrrrrr. Hurrrr.* Who was crying now? Me.

And down.

And up. *Eeeeer.* And down. Well, almost. I wasn't gonna make it. My butt cheeks burned hot as a spicy wing under a Popeye's heat lamp. That had to be twenty already. Or four. Yeah. It was four.

Meanwhile, Hunter counted away as Zack pumped up and down without effort. "Ninety eight. Ninety nine. One hundred. Wow. How old did you say you are? You're in excellent shape."

"He sure is." Angel watched Zack pump, with tears on his triangle. Literally. It said, "Hurrrrrrr. Hurrrrrrr. Hurrrrrr."

Wow. I'm being shown up by a guy with literally no muscles. This is the best day ever.

I gave it one last try, but my thighs turned to jelly right under me, and ploop. My butt hit the mat.

Hunter stood me up with one hand, like I was a Ken doll. "Good start, Champ. You can only go up from here!"

This man was so cheerful and encouraging, I wanted to punch him in the face.

"Next up. Mile run!"

He's kidding.

"Now this I gotta see. I need a good laugh. To keep from crying. Hurrrrrrrrr," Angel said. Suddenly, his triangle began to spin. And spin. "Lloyd. Are you still there? I can't see you. It's awfully smoky in there."

Whatever. Stupid angel.

Hunter led us to the track, and I filled with absolute dread. Still, I had to admit this really was the best double-wide trailer on the planet. On the way, we passed a big glass wall looking over an indoor pool. Heated. Olympic sized. Blue flecks of gently rippling water reflected on the wall. So calm, so relaxing. Until something green bobbed up out of the water and rose over the pool deck. It was a green fish man with ruffly gills on both sides of his face.

Nope. I'm out.

"Oh, hi, Glug." Hunter waved.

But Glug the fish guy didn't pay any attention to Hunter. He took one look at Zack, and his scales went white. Seriously. The green drained right out of him. He went belly up and floated, not moving.

"Huh. He's usually more chatty." Hunter shrugged, then pointed to a giant wood door cut in the wall. "This is the sauna. State of the art. Goes up to three thousand degrees, for members from the lower circles, but you can set it to earth temperature. Be sure to double check, though, or you'll burn down to ash. We don't get many humans in here. Gotta keep 'em alive!"

He had to be kidding. I peeked in. Steam hung thick in a room filled with giant hulking dudes, some covered in fur, some with blue skin, others green. All big, all scary, none human.

"Let me see." Zack pushed me aside and looked in.

"Aaaaaaaaaaah!"

That wasn't me screaming. The door kicked open, toppling me and Zack like dominoes. A wave of molten hot air washed over me, and all those dudes streamed out. Totally naked. A rainbow of inhuman bare butts hightailed it down the track.

"Do any of you guys want towels?" Hunter called after them. Then, he poked his head in the sauna and looked around. "Maybe it's too cold in here. I'll get maintenance on that."

He had to be kidding. No one could be that clueless.

Hunter walked us to the starting line. A big muscly dude with dark red skin and a head of twisty black horns took one look at Zack, and dropped his hundred-pound free weight right on his cloven hoof. He hopped around, holding his aching hoof in his hand.

"You all right there, Gunther? Watch those hooves!" Hunter fiddled with his stopwatch.

"And go!" Hunter clicked his stopwatch.

Zack ran—well, floated—around the track, so fast a strange *clink clack thunk tink* noise followed in his wake. Probably literally a wake, given his speed. I swear that reaper was gonna float a one-minute mile.

"Aaaah! Reaper! Run!"

Hold up. Nope. Never mind. Those noises? It was the sound of weights dropping to the floor as demons and werewolves and gill guys ran, tripping over each other to get away from the grim reaper—robes flowing, skeleton arms pumping, floating at them at sixty miles an hour.

Dude. Zack had them running for the doors. Zack didn't seem to notice. Maybe he was used to people running away and screaming? I kinda felt bad for him.

"Uh, change of plans, Champ. No more laps. Zack's really shaking everybody up," Hunter said. "The Trog incident must be too fresh in everyone's minds. Meet me at that machine."

He pointed at a hulking metal thing that looked like a medieval torture device. Unfortunately, it was right next to Fluffy. He was the only one who wasn't ruffled. His huge brown eyes were like glue, stuck on me and on Zack.

Hunter—propelled by thick powerful legs—bounded off to intercept Zack. He pulled him off the track before he could scare the remaining customers away.

I went to the machine and sat down on the pleather bench. The second my cheeks hit, something ice cold seeped into my shorts. And wriggled? "Watch it! Do any of you dipshits look before you sit down? I'm working here!"

I popped up. Kevin reformed in the indentation my butt cheek had made in the vinyl. He was bright blue and had a tiny sweatband around his head.

"What are you doing here?"

"What does it look like I'm doing? I'm working out! Duh. Look at me." Kevin ran his legs up and down his carapace. He had ectoplasmic muffin tops rolling over each of his body segments. "That Monster Burger spell trashed my figure. I gotta get back in shape before I cross over. I don't want to be fat for all eternity."

"Will that even work? You're a ghost."

Kevin ignored me. He thumbed a leg back at Zack. "What the hell is he doing? Reapers aren't allowed in here! He shouldn't even leave the store. Why did you bring him out?"

"I didn't bring him. He followed me," I whispered. "It's not my fault!"

"Hot tip: You aren't gonna make any friends around here with that guy trailing you. Did you hear about Trog? Dumb fat bastard shouldn't have eaten three turkeys."

"I didn't invite him. He just showed up!" I whispered. "What do you want me to do?"

"Well, since you two are besties now, take him back to his room, lock him in, and throw away the key. He can't be out wandering around. Everyone's terrified! You can't tell he's unemployed by looking at him. Know what? You can have the machine. I'm moving over to the squat press anyway. It's leg day." Kevin floated off the bench and away, across the floor mat. "Do your job and get him out of here."

"Help me!" I called after him, but he just flipped me two roach middle fingers. He didn't even look back.

Hunter jogged up. "Hey. Fluffy. Can you set this machine to human level?"

As soon as Hunter said, "human," two very pale, thin dudes by the bench press zeroed in on me. They looked me up and down as they sipped on their water bottles. Wait. No. Not water. The liquid was red. The bottles rose and fell, appearing to magically float in mid-air in the mirror behind them. I looked at the dudes. Then at the mirror. Then at the dudes. No reflections. Holy shit. Vampires. This can't be happening. "Angel, if you let me transfer to Planet Pump. I'll go every night. I swear. Angel?"

But Angel was nowhere to be found. Where the hell did he go? Oh. Never mind. I see him, wobbling in a slow sad circle around the rowing machine, like he's lost.

"Who are you talking to?" Zack said. "Oof. Vampires. Talk about creepy. Dead. No souls, but still walking around. What's up with that?"

I looked at him. He looked at me. "The *vampires* are creepy?"

"Fluffy will get you started, Champ. Bones, follow me." Hunter walked Zack to a clearing of mats, where he did what had to be a perfect burpee. Of course. Because that was a torture straight from hell if there ever was one.

Fluffy stopped fiddling with the weights and rose up on his huge, furry back paws. He leaned his graying brown muzzle close to me and growled, "Are you nuts? Death is not your friend. Death comes for all of us in the end, no matter what. Don't be fooled. You're playing with forces you don't understa—ooh. Ooh. Ow. You tiny bastards!"

He suddenly plopped down on his butt, lifted his back leg, and dug into his ear. Hard. "Flea Dip Friday can't get here fast enough. Can you give me a scratch there, buddy? I'd really appreciate it."

"Uh." I put my hand behind his ear and scratched. Because I was too scared to be rude. He whined and his foot thumped the floor like a happy golden retriever.

"Oooh yeah. Thanks, man. I owe you one." He stood up, stretching to his full seven feet. "I meant what I said, though. You're in over your head. Death plays cruel games, blah blah blah."

He said something else, but I didn't know what. Because there, behind him, was my employee manual, crawling across the floor, spine opening and closing, gripping the mats, as it gummed its way past the locker rooms, beelining toward that big gate.

Uh oh. Not good.

I had to grab that book before Kevin saw it. I scrambled, hopping, ducking, and diving my way through the maze of beefy creatures and hulking metal machines, eyes glued to my employee manual. It flopped and snarled, moving like it was on a mission.

I cleared the machines and landed in the aisle. The book took one look at me—I mean, I think. It doesn't have eyes, per se—and ran. "You get back here!"

I immediately stumbled and nearly fell over a very confused gremlin. He stood by my rumpled gym bag—open, contents strewn everywhere—holding my tighty whities in his hands. Just out there, for the whole world to see, stains and all.

"Sorry, dude. That book is crazy."

The gremlin slipped me a judgmental squint, then huffed as it scooped my stray socks and clean work clothes back into the bag. Well, kind of clean. Hot sauce stains, you know.

"Errf. Errrrrrr. Errrrrf." My employee manual snarfled.

I zeroed in on the sound. It stood up and opened, shaking and growling. Then it scuttled off behind the control box attached to that big gate. Great. Let's all pray it doesn't chew on wires like it chews on my shoes.

I ducked down so it wouldn't see me coming. My thighs burned like molten lava. OMG. I am out of shape. But I managed to waddle behind the gate, behind the control box, following the grunts and growls of my employee manual. My book lay open, snapping open and shut. "Errf. Errrrrrr. Errrrrf."

I grabbed it. "Ha. I got you!"

It bit me and hopped out of my hand. "Ow! Bad book. Bad! I told you to stay in the bag!"

The book whimpered. Its spine bent, and its cover turned. It opened to a page with an illustration of a hand, scrawly and ornate, with an eye in the palm. A green eye. A real eye. It glowed green, then blinked and looked around.

"Thanks for the nightmares. Now get back in the bag!"

"Grrrrrrrrrrr." It snapped at me then started to climb the back of the control panel to get away.

This was way too much work for a book. I yanked and yanked and finally peeled it off the console. It wriggled out of my hand, catapulting its weird leathery body up up up, flying through the air toward the controls. I jumped after it. That's when I realized the book wasn't growling at me.

Well, maybe. Probably not. I'm still not really sure.

All I know is when I stood up, the controls on the panel moved all by themselves. Buttons pressed in, boop boop booping, and the numbers on the LED display changed. A red switch flipped on. Then a big metal lever on the side chink chink chinked from down to up, all by itself. The lever said, "Emergency override" in big yellow letters. It clicked into top position, and a red light flashed on the console.

That's not good.

My employee manual jumped right at whatever invisible force had pushed those buttons. It hit something—or some *thing* hit it—

because it somersaulting through the air, smack into the rim of that giant gate, so hard even I was seeing stars.

Oof. That had to hurt.

I reached down to grab that emergency lever. I'm not the smartest guy, but even I know not to mess with the emergency override on a hell gate. I had one hand on it, when suddenly, my feet were in the air.

Then. *Splat.*

That was my face. Hitting the floor.

Ow.

I face planted right into the mat in front of the control box, eyeball to sole with a pair of shiny saddle shoes.

Shit.

The Cookie Scout—the one who bubbled down to nothing—looked up and around, like she was searching for something. She was still in nice little girl form.

Angel rolled into my nose. "Lloyd, is that you? I can't see. Are you all right?"

"Help meeeee!" I whispered. "Demon!"

"What demon? I don't see anything. Wow. Everything is blurry. Must be a bad connection. Hold on. I need to reset my Ethereal Net connection."

Too late. That demon scout picked him up and shook him really hard. "Ooooh! I have one of these!" She shook and shook, then stopped and waited for a reply. "Huh. This one's broken. It sucks."

Tell me about it.

She threw it. Angel hit the mat, and red liquid splurted out. "You!"

Uh oh. The demon scout grabbed a fistful of my hair, pulled my head up and looked me in the eye. Her little girl mouth split into a row of dripping fangs. "You stole my unicorn."

Her icy white cheeks split into a wide chasm filled with dripping fangs. She raised a hand that was quickly morphing into a claw. "Give it back. NOW!"

CHAPTER 6

HER CLAW CAME DOWN SO HARD I saw stars. That demon scout slapped me over and over again across the cheeks, so many times we settled into a rhythm.

"Give." *Slap.*

"Me." *Slap.*

"My." *Slap.*

"Unicorn!" *Slap.*

Rinse, repeat. And man, did it hurt. I couldn't fight back. Until my kicking feet finally managed to stick on something long enough to push me right side up. I pushed and *rrrrrrrip.* "Ow!"

As I stumbled away, my hands shot to my head and came back wet with blood. I turned around. The angry scout held a fistful of my hair.

She looked at it. I looked at her.

"Wow, that had to hurt. Sorry, fat guy. Know what? You deserve it. Thief!" She threw that fistful of hair on the floor and came at me. She knocked me flat on my back and was on top of me, claws out, scratching at my pockets.

"I don't have your unicorn!"

"Liar! Unicorn! MINE!"

I pushed her up and away while I formulated a plan. Come on, brain. Think! Nope. I got nothing. So I screamed. "Help! Help meeeeeeeeee!"

I'm in a gym full of strong guys. One of them will help me.

Any second now.

Nope. No one came. No one even noticed I was in trouble. Because every single demon, vampire, monster and gremlins had their back to me. They stood in a semicircle around Zack, *clapping?* They ooh and awed as he spun a hundred-pound barbell on his boney index finger like it was a toy. While pumping it up and down. Well. Guess they're over Trog!

The demon scout, no longer content to dig in my pockets like a rabid gopher, opened wide and tried to bite me, so I stuck two fingers straight into her eyeballs like a Stooge.

That just made her angry "UNICORN!"

"Zack! HELP!" I screamed.

The scout wrapped her freezing cold claws around my neck and squeezed.

Gack! Can't breathe!

Zack's boney skull face appeared behind her. "What are you guys doing down there?"

"She...kill...meeeeee!"

Zack scratched the top of his skull like he was confused. "That's weird, right? Cookie Scouts don't usually kill people, do they?"

"You seriously have to ask?"

"I'm a reaper. I have no idea what you all do when you aren't dying."

"Help....meeeeeee."

The scout shook my neck and cracked the back of my skull against the floor.

Thump. "Ow."

Thump. "Ow."

Apparently, we had a new rhythm.

I managed to punch her in the eyeball. Again. Then, she did

something I never saw coming in a million years. She cried. "Meanie pants."

While she punched me. Ow. Ow. Ow.

"She's right. That wasn't very nice of you, Lloyd." Zack said.

"Wha—me?? I-uuuuuuuuuuh. Shit."

Okay. If that sounds like a weird response. Let me explain. All of a sudden, a low, loud hum rattled the entire gym. Even the can lights on the ceiling shook. It felt like an earthquake. Then, a dark shadow fell over everything, and the room went totally silent, apart from gasps.

Gasps.

If a bunch of demons and werewolves are gasping, this shit's bad. The demon scout let go of me and hid behind the control panel.

Zack floated over to the center of the gate. It glowed. Eerie. Black. "I don't think it should be this color. Do you?"

A long, green thing, thick as the trunk of a fat tree—except slimy, really slimy, as in absolutely dripping—emerged from the center. It rose above Zack's head, huge and looming, stretching out over the now silent gym members. It shook like a wet dog, showering everything in slime.

Shlup.

Including us. Ew.

"Shoot. This was my last clean robe," Zack said. "Good news, though. It's a meek eel. Totally harmless. Delicious, though. They make great sushi. My girlfriend's favorite. I mean. My EX girlfriend Eeeerrrrrrrrr. Hurrrrrrr. Hurrrrrrrr."

The meek eel opened its mouth, revealing row upon row of razor sharp red spikes, dripping with goop. "Sssssssseeeeeeeeeee."

The things hovered there, hissing, squinting with its glassy white eyes as if it were trying to get a look at the place, but the light was too bright.

"Oh. My bad. That's a terror eel. They'll definitely kill everyone here. Pretty fast, too. I bet the guys at dispatch are in the weeds right now! Aw, man. I'm already here. I could have saved everyone the commute! But, I can't reeeee. Eeeeee. Eeeeeep. Hurrrr. Hurrrrr. Hurrrrr."

"Don't just stand there!" I screamed. "Do something!"

But Zack? Useless. He rumpled into a useless pile of crying bones.

"Everyone hide! I will protect yooooooooooooooooo," A heroic voice rang out. It was Hunter. He bounded up off the top of an ab machine, hurling his body straight at that terror eel. His aim? Spot on. He landed right on that terror eel's slimy face. Unfortunately, the terror eel opened its mouth, and Hunter slid right in.

Well, he's lunch. Shit.

It was up to me to end this. Yeah. You heard that right. I scrambled to the control panel. And froze. It wasn't exactly straightforward. Dials and digital screens flashed weird symbols. My heart kicked my ribs. No pressure. I only needed to save everyone, and I didn't know what the fuck I was doing.

So basically, like every day of my life.

The gym was dark and getting darker. The eel thing didn't much care for light. It scraped its body against the ceiling, ripping can lights off of the scaffold. They plummeted to the ground, sparking, crashing against the weight machines as everyone screamed and took cover.

My employee manual? It had clearly regained consciousness. It knocked over a dusty cardboard box behind the panel. "Help!"

It looked at me. Dug a broken Thigh Cruncher out of the box and threw it right at my head. I ducked. Geesh. Thanks for nothing, stupid book!

I grabbed the override handle and pulled. Oof. It didn't move. That thing was really on tight. I put my foot on the box and pulled with all the force of my body.

Crunk. The lever moved a notch. Yes!

Crunk. And another. Hazzah! Fat guy for the win!

Then something wrapped around my belly and squeezed me so tight I thought my head was gonna pop off.

A voice whispered, "Let go. Don't ruin this for me!"

When I looked up and around, no one was there. I threw an elbow, and whatever it was dropped me right on the lever. Boy howdy, the weight of me falling on it crunked that thing right back into place. The gate edges clink clink clinked, recalibrating.

A loud whir shook the gym.

Shump.

The black oozing center zipped closed, chopping that terror eel off at the neck. Its fat body crashed to the floor and split, sending slime and guts flying in every direction.

Holy shit. I did it! I shut the gate! I killed the monster. I DID IT! ME!

Angel wobbled up to me.

"Did you see that?" My chest puffed, even though my butt really hurt where it hit that lever.

I wanted to cry. I felt like a helium balloon. Flying high, light. Relieved. Because oh my God. I did it. I saved the day. ME. My head buzzed. I'd finally done it. Who's the sidekick? Not me! "Be sure to add that to my checklist."

"Lloyd? Is that you? I can hear you, but I can't see." Angel looked at me, triangle spinning.

"You saw it. You were right there!"

Angel's triangle stopped. "Why is it so smoky in there?"

The terror eel bucked. Oh, no! It's not dead! I grabbed that Thigh Cruncher and wielded it like a hammer. The eel's mouth opened, rising up up up. Then split in half. Hunter stood in side it. Alive, arms up. He held a broken piece of eel jaw in one hand, and a chunk of eyeball in the other.

Angel's triangle stopped spinning. "Wow. Did you see that? He ushered everyone to safety, jumped straight into a terror eel's mouth, then ripped it apart from the inside. Have you ever seen someone so heroic?"

"But—"

Angel just rolled away. Did he even see what I had done?

Everyone emerged from their hiding places to gather around

Hunter. They hoisted him up on their shoulders and chanted his name. I slumped down to the floor in a puddle of defeated loserdom. Seriously? Kill me now.

"Tough luck, fatso." The demon scout stuck her head out of her hidey hole behind the control box. "Now give me my UNICORN!"

Something came at me, and something snapped. Red hot rage rushed over me. I lifted up that Thigh Cruncher and punched it right through her face.

PLAP.

She erupted like a pus volcano, covering everything in a four-foot radius in bubbling black goop, including me.

Oh.

We were both surprised, judging by the look on her cold white face when it exploded. Wow. Go me. I'm two for two tonight. Not that it mattered.

Hunter was the hero of the day. Even Zack floated over to congratulate him.

Zack high fived Hunter. And Hunter immediately dropped to the floor, passed out cold.

Huh. Or.

Wait.

No, he couldn't be. I'm sure he's fine.

Gunther the demon ran to Hunter's aid. Well, he tried to. He grabbed Zack to move him out of the way and immediately fell face down on the floor. Wow. He just dropped. Fast.

The crowd closed in around them. Voices kicked up. Suddenly, white cold hands grabbed the front of my T-shirt and dragged me across the gym. It was the vampires, and they looked mad. "Here he is. This is his fault. He broke the rules. He brought death into this gym. The eel was a distraction! Drain the useless blood bag!"

"What? Noooooooo!" I flailed, but it didn't matter.

He threw me down on the mat next to Zack. A wall of angry shouts and faces pressed in tight around us.

"Explain yourself. Speak!" The vampire demanded.

"I'm sorry, guys. I don't know what happened," Zack said. "I don't think I reaped them. I mean, I'm suspended. I don't have my scythe. I didn't think I could reap, even if I wanted to. But you're right. They're dead. So maybe? Honestly, I don't know. This is new territory for me. My bad."

"Dead?" The word caught in my throat.

Hunter and Gunther? They hadn't gotten back up. They were lying, stone still, on the floor, stiff. Right where they dropped. There wasn't a single mark on them, and we all knew they'd survived the eel.

"Zack," I said. "What did you do?"

Another reaper materialized out of thin air right next to me. The monsters went tomb silent and stepped back.

He said, "Sorry I'm late. Traffic was just awful. I'm looking for..." A scroll materialized out of nowhere. He opened it and read for a few seconds. Then he looked at the two dead guys on the mat. "Holy shit, Zack. Did you do that? Unauthorized reaping? Again? Wow. Just. Wow. Anyhoo, I better motor. I'm running late as it is. Excuse me, boys. I'll see you all later. Heh heh. Get it? Later? Because you all are gonna die, eventually? It's a joke. No one? Really? Tough crowd."

Reaper two stepped over Hunter and Gunther's bodies and floated off in search of. Well, probably the demon scout I'd reduced to mush. Again. Because he sure didn't do a very good job reaping her last time.

Zack slumped. "I can't believe he still has a job, and I don't. Death is not fair."

The crowd descended on us, a flurry of hooves and claws and angry, cold hands. Seconds later, I was outside in the icy darkness, flying off Bubba's porch. I landed face first on the frozen ground. Chunks of dirt and snow lodged in my teeth. Ow.

My busted up Huffy arced through the air and landed next to me with such force the frame bent and the back wheel popped off.

Fluffy's big dog head leaned in over me, nostrils flaring, teeth bared in a growl. "You brought death into Bubba's. If I see your face ever again, I will rip you apart!"

The angry mob stomped back inside, slammed the door shut and locked it behind them. The plastic flowers and pink flamingos rattled. Angel eight ball wobbled out from between two plastic daisies. "So, um. Planet Pump it is then."

CHAPTER 7

I DRAGGED MY BUSTED—AGAIN—HUFFY down Cemetery Boulevard, past the creaking metal gate of the Eternal Spector Memory
Gardens, past the rubble of Monster Burger, into the 24/7 Demon
Mart parking lot. I was wet. Bruised. Beaten. Coatless. And my body
had frozen nearly solid in the ice cold winter night.

Zack followed me. Talking. The entire way.

Lucky me.

He went on and on about what a great time he had a Bubba's.
Yes. You heard that right: *Great* time. Apparently, he didn't realize
this was the worst night ever. Maybe he was just a glass half full kind
of skeleton, I don't know, but I gotta be honest. I wanted to kill him.
Like, really really. A lot.

When we finally stepped in on the mat, covered in frozen eel
slime and scout guts, DeeDee and the cleaning crew were pushing
the butt end of a red, heart-shaped mattress through the stockroom
door.

"Hey guys." She didn't look up. "Reaper can use the emergency
mattress Morty stores in the beer cave. Don't ask. Seriously. Just
don't. We're definitely gonna need clean sheets. And Lysol. Lots and
lots of Lysol. Trust me. Can you give me a hand?"

She looked at me and dropped the mattress. "Oh my God. Are you hurt? What is this stuff all over you?" She descended on me, patting me down for mortal injuries. "What happened?"

"We had an amazing night. Totally awesome." Zack gushed. Again. "I was nervous going to Bubba's, but wow. What a nice bunch of guys!"

"He's kidding." I could not listen to this again.

"I'm serious! Were we at the same gym? It was so great. When the eel showed up, I thought for sure it was gonna be a bloodbath, but only two people died! TWO! So many survivors. What a rush! Definitely a nice change of pace. Until today, I didn't realize how much it sucks to watch so many people die all the time. I feel like I'm floating on a cloud. You know, I think I might actually like being unemployed. It sure is easier to make friends when you aren't harvesting immortal souls. Trust me, I've tried. People spend the whole ride up or down crying. Or begging. Either way, they're not really in the mood to make friends."

I said nothing. Great? Nice? Amazing? These were not words I would use to describe my night.

DeeDee's eyes were round as silver dollars. "Two people died?"

"Make that three. And no one showed up to reap them, either. We just had to plunge Glug out of the toilet! You wouldn't think a ghost could clog, but apparently they can." Kevin stood in the door, his ghostly body covered in a light coating of dust and eel slime. Huh. Weird. I didn't know ghosts could get dirty. "Captain Dipshit and his first mate here made quite a mess. I don't know what you were thinking. Who brings a reaper to their first night at Bubba's?"

"My name is Zack. Reaper is a job. And I don't have uhh uh uhhhhhh joooooooob." He lifted his bone hands to his eye sockets and sobbed.

Oh good. He's back to normal.

"Yeah? You didn't look unemployed when Hunter and Gunther dropped dead. Wait. Your name is ZACK? You've gotta be kidding. Zack. Did you just get kicked out of a frat house?"

"It's short for Zackumzaphielhermesiappotholonian. And I wish I had a frat house. Because it means I'd have brothers who care about meeeeeeeeeeee. Uuhhhhh. Heerrrrrrr. Hurrrrrr."

"Wow, kid. I thought you were the train wreck." Kevin rubbed his forehead like he had a migraine.

"But." DeeDee looked at me. "Didn't they tell you what happened to Trog?"

"Hang on, sweets. It gets worse. Dipshit here opened the portal inside Bubba's and let in a terror eel. We're lucky we're not in a full on eelpocalypse right now. You royally screwed the pooch, kid. Royally."

"Lloyd, is this true?" DeeDee had this look in her eyes, I can't explain. Anticipation. Like her heart would fly or fall, depending on the next words that came out of my mouth.

My face flushed. "No. I...!"

"I saw you, kid. I saw you messing with that control panel. And I saw this asshole helping you." He pointed at Zack.

"I closed it. I didn't open it!"

"Then who did?"

My lips flubbed. I didn't really have a good answer for that one. The controls seemed to be moving on their own. But there was something there. Something real. Because it had grabbed me. "I'm not sure. It was invisible?"

"Invisible. Wow. That's the best you could come up with?"

I knew how it sounded, but it was true.

"I don't know what to say, kid. I didn't want to believe Fluffy and the rest of the guys, but we all saw you by the controls. Then boom, eel." He shook his head and his fat body quivered, as if the thought was too horrible to finish. "You really did open the gate and let that thing through, didn't you?"

"Lloyd, no!" DeeDee looked at me. "That can't be true."

My heart kicked up. "It's not! The Cookie Scout attacked me!"

"Oh, so now it's the Cookie Scout's fault. Classic." Kevin shook his head. "Look. I realize the gate was probably an accident, but just fess up already. We melted that scout down to goop, and we all know no demon can recover from that."

"But—" Seriously. How did he not see? She was right there!

"You know what your problem is, kid? There's always a but. Always an excuse. You skate by on luck and hope it's enough. You've worked here what, like four months now? And you still don't know what you're doing. You still haven't read your employee manual. And now this? Luck isn't enough. Luck runs out. Skills last. I'm sorry, kid."

"Kevin. What are you saying?" DeeDee reached for me. Then stopped, because eel guts.

"You know what I'm saying." Kevin looked away.

"No. He's one of us," she said.

"Sorry, sweets. I love the kid, but tonight was a shit show. It's too big a mistake to overlook. Ten bucks says your replacement's already in the lot," Kevin's ghost head poked through the glass. He looked left, then right. "You're a good kid, but you're incompetent. We can't go on like this forever."

My heart hit my shoe. He's asking me to leave, isn't he? Suddenly, my eyes went blurry. Wet. All I could do was stare at my shoes. I couldn't look DeeDee in the eyes. This can't be happening. Not like this.

Ding.

Well. That's it then. I'm fired. My replacement really did show up. I didn't look, not right away. What if he was more handsome than me? More heroic? More perfect for DeeDee? I couldn't bear it.

"Good news. It appears The Beast has not yet infiltrated Sinbad's."

Oh.

Someone stepped in the door, but it wasn't my replacement. It was Faust. He stood on the mat. Snow steamed off him like he was a hot griddle. "The doomed souls gate has not been breached. The ladies were very gracious and most agreeable in answering my inquiry."

He straightened his tailored, expensive blazer and the button of his shirt popped, revealing traces of glitter and lipstick all down his chest. Stripper lipstick. Something caught his eye. The cleaning crew. They had abandoned the mattress for snack time. They gathered around an end cap and ripped open a bag of Zapp's. They shoved those chips in like hungry walruses. "My word! What on earth are these?"

"The new cleaning crew," DeeDee said. "They've been here all week. You didn't notice?"

"I must have overlooked them. I have been rather preoccupied."

"You think?" Kevin huffed and his eyes shot to one of the thousand "Beware" posters Faust had hung.

"Steve must be angrier than I thought. Best behavior from now on then, team. Clearly, we must earn our way back into his good graces. It appears I did not send him a large enough ham for Yule this year." Faust straightened his collar. It had lipstick all over it. His hair was sticking up on the side, too, and coated in glitter, like it'd been steamrolled by a thousand body-glittered C-cups.

"What is this? Busy evening!" Faust pulled a little scroll out of his pocket. He unrolled it and began to read. "Oh dear. Oh, my."

He looked at me and raised one perfectly tweezed eyebrows. "Come, dear boy. We have much to discuss."

My feet felt glued to the mat. In terror. And dread. Well, this is it. I really am getting fired.

He put his hand on my elbow, and I floated across the floor, light as a feather. He whisked me through the stockroom door, waving Morty's disco pimp mattress out of the way with his hand. He floated me into his posh man cave. And it was posh as ever. Well, apart from the printer spitting out thousands more "Beware" posters. Other than that, Faust had clearly gotten an upgrade when Steve rebuilt the store. The hearth of the stone fireplace was even bigger, tall enough for a reaper to stand in. The room had expanded. More bookshelves, filled with even more leather-bound books and creepy relics in glass cases. Like a live, giant cockroach in a glass case that said, "Break in Case of Emergency" across the top, and the monkey paw that gave me the finger as soon as I looked at it. Gulp. Nope. La la la la. Not looking. Nothing to see here.

Faust let go of my arm, and my feet immediately touched down on Persian rug. A real one. Faust looked down at his hands and rubbed his fingers together. "Dear Dark Lord. What manner of putrid slime is this?"

"Terror eel." And it was all over me, head to toe, dripping onto his fancy rug.

"My, my. This will never do!" He waved his hand over me. The stuff didn't disappear. His magic didn't seem to work on it. "Well, that is an unusually stubborn stain. No matter. Sit. Please. We have important matters to discuss."

He glided across the room, sinking into the leather chair behind his big, elaborately carved wood desk. Which was covered in posters? Okay, then.

I took a deep breath. This will all be fine once I tell Faust the truth. "I didn't do anything wrong. This is all a misunderstanding. The Cookie—"

"Cookie?"

Yes! He gets it!

"What an excellent idea." He snapped his manicured fingers and a silver plate, topped with artfully arranged stacks of Peanut Butter Patties appeared on his desk. "I am a bit peckish. I quite love these, don't you? So sinful. Please, do try one. And, do sit down."

My heart sunk. Cookies? I didn't mean cookies! He waved his hand again. I floated across the floor, and sunk, slime and all, into the plush armchair. Oof. He was gonna have to throw it away. No amount of scrubbing would ever get the eel off the upholstery.

"I suppose you know why I've called this meeting."

My guts tied in a knot. "I can explain. Bubba—"

"Oh, yes. I am so happy you're availing yourself of your free gym membership. DeeDee has had quite the transformation at Bubba's hand. He is a master of his trade. Now, let's get to the point, shall we? My accountant, Mr. Beale, sent me a note. It appears you haven't cashed your blank check. The one I wrote to you as a reward for your role in thwarting that unfortunate incident with the living challenged last month. You do remember, don't you?"

"Huh?"

"The, how do you say? Zombies? I must insist that you give it serious consideration, and do not wait too long to use it. It is very powerful magic, and cannot lie dormant in this world too long, or else the spell will sour. So, I encourage you to reflect upon your true, pure desires and put the check to good use. Preferably by the end of this fiscal year, which is in three weeks. Remember, it must be used for something true, something sincere, never for selfish purposes, lest the spell produce bad results. As we discussed."

"Wait. The check? Seriously?"

"I applaud your self-control."

"You do?"

"Speaking the truth to your mother instead of wishing her questions away. It was an honorable choice. Jennifer is a lovely woman." He cleared his throat. "If I may be so bold, if your father ever meets an untimely end, please do let me know. I would like to add my name to her dance card."

My jaw dropped. These fools needed to step off my mom already.

"She's hot, kid. Get over it. Mmph. Mmm. Num num." Kevin sat in the middle of that silver plate of cookies, stuffing one into his mouth. Well, trying. Wait. Succeeding? Holy shit. He actually managed to lift one end of a cookie and take a bite. "Jesus, I told you all not to open the box, but no. I could smell the damn cookies all the way out by the register. My diet is totally shot now. You all know I'm a stress eater. It's been a rough night."

He chewed. Mmmphing and yumming, even though only about one in twenty bites actually bit. Still, an impressive record for a ghost.

"Kevin, my good man. This is a private meeting. Is there a reason you insist on attending?"

"You're firing him. I need to be here for that. Oh, and you forgot to summon his replacement. Snap to it. Look at me. We're already short staffed."

"Why on earth would we fire young Master Lloyd?"

Kevin recounted all the night's events to Faust. The gym. The gate. The eel. Hunter and Gunther. Everything except the part where it wasn't my fault, and I totally closed the gate and kicked demon scout ass. It's like he didn't see the Cookie Scout at all. Just me, flailing upside down by the control panel. Kevin's voice sounded strange. Flat, monotone. He practically chanted the facts, like he was in a trance. His eyes looked weird, too, staring off at nothing. If he were a cartoon, he'd have those hypnosis corkscrews twirling in his eyes.

I squinted. "You all right, man?"

"Are you certain, Kevin? I did not sense anything out of sorts, and these are serious accusations."

"Mmmph." He swallowed hard and thumped his chest to make sure the cookie lump went all the way down. "I was there. I saw it with my own two eyes."

"No. I closed the gate. I killed a demon!"

"I didn't see any demons or scouts, just you, standing by the control panel flopping around, waving your arms. You were all over that thing. Then, boom. Eel. Look. Even if it was an accident, kid, you still did it."

I couldn't believe Kevin sold me out.

"And the two souls who died?" Faust asked.

"That was Zack!" My voice shook. I could not believe I was being blamed for this. "Totally not my fault."

"The kid literally brought death to the gym as his plus one."

"He followed me!"

"You could have portalled him back to the store!"

"Boys. Please don't argue. We'll get to the bottom of this."

Faust raised an eyebrow, and I went stiff.

Uh oh. He's doing that magic thing. The one that makes me share all my deep, dark secrets? Shoot. Zip it about the masturbating,

Lloyd. PLEASE! Although, in my defense, I had significantly cut down. Not on purpose. Jobs just tend to eat up a lot of porn hours.

My lips flubbed, and I told him everything that happened at Bubba's, even the embarrassing parts. I ended with a crescendo of, "I killed the demon scout with a Thigh Cruncher!"

Faust said, "Do keep working on those squats. It sounds as though you are ripe for improvement."

Then Faust eyeballed Kevin. His ghost went stiff, and he sat there, silent, as if in a trance. "Interesting. You're both telling the truth."

He snapped his manicured fingers, and Zack materialized out of nowhere.

"Ooo. Cookies!" Zack clapped his bone hands and dug right through Kevin into those Peanut Butter Patties. It took him a minute to notice we were all staring at him. "Oh. Hey guys. DeeDee just showed me how to make microwave mac and cheese. Mind blown. How do they get those noodles to cook in that little cup? The living world. It's so amazing!"

"We're having a bit of a disagreement and would like your input. What transpired at Bubba's this evening?" Faust leaned back, stared down Zack and and waved his hand. "Tell me everything."

Ha! Vindication, here I come.

But Zack? He didn't go stiff. He didn't speak as if compelled. He said, "It was great! Only two people died. How awesome is that? Mmm. These cookies are amazing. I'm more of a Skinny Mint guy myself. You know, I once had to reap a whole Cookie Scout troop. Well, almost whole. One survivor. Anyway, a car plowed into their stand outside a WallDrugs. They let me keep the cookies. Nice girls."

"Anything else?" Faust raised an eyebrow.

"Nope. This was the best night of my life. To be honest, though, it was kind of a blur. So much excitement. People actually surviving is a new experience for me."

My heart hit my shoe. That hypno thing didn't work! And Zack was clearly not very observant.

Faust clapped his hands, and Zack dematerialized. Gone in an instant. His mouth puckered like he'd just smelled rotten eggs. "That is the most optimistic, good-natured reaper I have ever encountered. His mind is filled with love and light. Disturbing. Such strange creatures. Well, then. It seems I have little choice."

His eyes rolled back into his head, and his mouth moved, spewing chants like that taser thing in the weapons safe. His chair sparked like it was electrified. A bright white light flashed, and something fell out of a white portal in the ceiling and thunk. It hit the desk. It was Angel eight ball.

His triangle said, "Ow. Wait. Where am I? Shit!"

He tried to wobble away, but Faust put a hand on him. "Let go! I can't be seen with you, I'll lose my wings! I need this job!"

"Yes. I know this is an unusual collaboration, but these are desperate times. Can you shed light on this evening's events? The fate of your ward is on the line."

Phew! This is all good. If anyone has my back, it's my guardian angel.

His triangle turned. It said. "Evening hazy."

Fuck me. Really? Some angel.

His triangle turned again. "I couldn't see anything in there. It's like Bubba's was in a fog bank. Now get your cloven hoof off me, devil."

"Very well, then." Faust let him wobble right off the desk and crack onto the rug. "We seem to have quite a mystery on our hands. Oh. Just a moment."

Faust sunk his hand into his blazer and pulled out a file. "We may have our answer. My, my. Mr. Beale is running late today."

I never thought I'd be so happy to see one of those creepy magic envelopes. Surely, my vindication lay inside.

Faust opened it and settled in to read. "Hmm. Interesting. This is most unusual."

"You're telling me. The kid's a klutz, but I never saw this coming.

Shame. I liked him, too." Kevin shook his head. "I'm really gonna miss that MILF of his."

"We cannot be too hasty. As the senior employee, and as management, you do know we have a protocol for this. We do not pass judgment until a thorough investigation has been completed. And, for now. It's not. Beale needs more time."

"No way. That scumbag soul sucker knows everything in the snap of a finger! It shouldn't have taken him this long!"

"Yes. However," Faust took a single sheet of paper out of the folder and showed it to us. It said.

Investigation inconclusive. Evidence clouded.
Possible magical interference. Case still pending.

Well, shit.

"That's settled, then. Rules are rules." Faust looked at me. I could swear he smiled, ever so slightly. "Lloyd stays until we can complete the investigation, and until such time as his culpability can be proven beyond a shadow of doubt."

Uh, did you catch that? Awful lot of big words.

"It means you're not fired, kid. Not yet. You're on probation." Kevin snapped his little roach fingers at me. "That means mind your P's and Q's. No mistakes, got it? Not a single one. Now wash the eel spit off of you and get back to work."

CHAPTER 8

Wow. What a terrible night! But things were finally looking up. A warm, soapy, soothing, amazeballs shower awaited me in the magic healing bathroom. I was totally amped. That shower was the best thing about this place!

I stepped out of Faust's office, and my nose landed right in Zack's butt hole. Well, where his butt hole should be. He was bent over, eight feet of completely buck naked skeleton, scratching his ankle. His pelvis bone waved right in my face.

"What are you doing?" I pushed him away. Seriously. "Gah! Put some clothes on!"

"Sorry. I didn't know you were in here. I had to get these robes off. This eel slime is really gross. I can't wait to wash it off." Then he floated, right through the green door, into the shower.

Into my magic shower.

Shit. Seriously? I looked to the sky. "God? What did I do to deserve this?"

God didn't answer. The only voice was Zack, calling to me through the door. "Have you seen this shower? Deluxe! You should try it sometime."

The water kicked on.

Sigh. Rub it in, Zack. Rub. It. In.

Well, then. Guess I have a hot date with the utility sink. Yay.

Zack left a trail of dirty robes on the floor, in a line, all the way down the hallway. One of the cleaning crew started to drag a robe into their cardboard box, to use as bedding or something, but took one whiff and pushed it back out.

Good call. Eel slime? It was thick like tar, stunk like molting walrus, and was nearly impossible to wash off. Trust me, I tried. Although, antibacterial soap straight from the wall hanging industrial soap dispenser probably wasn't the best tool for the job, but it was all I had. I was halfway through my third face full of stinky faux-lemon scented suds when a tiny voice said, "Here's the deal, kid. Since we're under some sort of magic cloud and you're on probation, I gotta write down everything you do wrong in this book. Lucky me. More paperwork. Anyway, it all goes in your file, so don't mess up. It ain't easy holding a pen when you've got no body!"

I cracked my eyes. Kevin floated on the wire rack of cleaning supplies, next to a pink gel pen and matching glitter notebook.

"Wouldn't it be easier to write in a ghost book?"

"Oh, look who's the funny guy now."

I actually wasn't joking. I mean, it might be a thing? I didn't get to say that out loud, because a big blob of antiseptic soap lather slid straight into my eyes. "Aaaaaah! It burns!"

"Do us both a favor and stay in line. I don't want to write a novel in here, you feel me?"

"Yeah, yeah. I get it, okay?" I buried my face in a towel and tried to wipe the sting out of my eyes. "Leave me alone."

"Why are you so salty? I'm trying to help you."

"Are you? You weren't exactly falling over yourself to stick up for me back there. You threw me under the bus. It's like you want me to get fired!"

"You gotta be kidding. We can't lie to Faust. You know that. I told him exactly what I saw." He poked my arm with one of his tiny legs. Or tried to. It went right through. "I'm the last guy who wants you fired. I hate training new employees! Besides, I almost got you broken in. Almost."

"Whatever. You don't get it."

"Oh, I get it. You don't get it. Your problem is you, kid. Stop fumbling through your life and take control of it already. Confucius and Kevin say: wherever you go, go with all your heart. Or all your ass. Huh. Don't remember. Point is, be a full ass like I been telling you. The world doesn't need more half asses."

I looked at Kevin. Kevin looked at me.

Huh. That was actually pretty deep for a roach.

"Hey. I can be deep. I got feelings, you know. I read. Look, I'll lay it out straight. I want you to stay. But Dee and I need to be able to count on you. Especially now, given my delicate condition. We got no room for half ass. Besides, if you actually got good at your job, grave-yard shift might finally beat Junebug for employee of the month. We were so close. Twice!"

He pointed to the wall around the employee lounge door. It had thousands of employee of the month plaques, floor to ceiling, so many, so tiny, that all this time, I thought they were wallpaper. Because it was a repeating pattern, every plaque exactly the same: Junebug's big blonde hair, frosty pink lipstick smile and giant cleavage staring back at us.

"Wait. We didn't get one? But we saved the world. TWICE!"

"Kid, we'd have to stop the biblical apocalypse to beat Junebug. Don't let the big hair fool you. She's one tough cookie. See?"

He pointed at the November and December pictures. A gold star sticker in the corner read, *Honorable mention: The Graveyard Shift. Lloyd Lamb Wallace, DeeDee B. Woznowski, and Kevin Lee Roach.*

"What the hell does Junebug do on dayshift?"

"What doesn't she do on day shift? Just pull yourself together, kid. We only gotta win once to get in the raffle for a trip to Jamaica.

Look at me. I need a tan! Every damn year, Junebug comes home lubed head to toe in coconut oil, tanned so brown she looks like an espresso bean. It's my turn! I need a pina colada. *Need*."

I squinted at our tiny gold star. "DeeDee's last name is Woznowski? Eek. What's the B stand for?"

"Don't ask. Hot chicks always get the ugly names. It's how the universe keeps shit fair. Anyway, watch yourself, kid. Study up on the rules because everything you do wrong goes in your file. Everything, no matter how small. So straighten up. I hate new hires. And finish up here, because I need you out on the floor. Apparently, we gotta teach the cleaning crew how to clean. Thanks a lot, Steve." He flipped four middle fingers to the sky. "Bring a fresh mop bucket out with you. I'm paying you to scrub the floor, not your face."

I hurried, but it took a good ten minutes to get most of the eel and Cookie Scout off. No matter how much I scrubbed, I still felt dirty. Slimy. And smelled vaguely of molting walrus.

When I pushed the mop bucket past the shower, I could hear Zack in there singing to himself. Still. Taking his sweet old time. Yep. Thanks, Zack. Thanks for thinking of me while I washed my body in the same sink where we wrung out mops soaked in demon guts. It's fine. Totally fine. I'm sure it's sanitary.

I wheeled the mop through the stockroom door, and DeeDee grabbed me the second I stepped out. She pulled me behind the pyramid of Cherikee Red pop two-liters, and whispered. "Listen. You aren't getting fired on my watch. We've been through too much."

Her grey eyes met mine. Her black liner a flawless cat eye over a sparkling black shadow. Her blood red lipstick totally amazeballs. "Here's the plan. Kevin is required to track every mistake, right? So don't make any mistakes. Easy peasy."

"Great plan." Yeah. Uh huh. "I'm screwed."

"I'll help you, silly. I won't let you go. Not like this. You can't get fired. Not after all we've done. It'd break my heart. Plus, we'll never get a shot at Jamaica this year if we have to train a new guy."

She winked and smiled. It was the sweetest thing I had ever seen in my whole life. My body felt light, like I had sprouted wings and swooped, flying high. She was like a hot goth angel, arriving in my hour of need. Which was more than I can say for my real guardian angel. That jerk.

"Before I forget, keep your eye on Kevin," she said. "Let me know if you see anything strange."

"He's a dead talking cockroach. Everything about that is already strange."

"You know what I mean. Oh, and keep him away from bright lights, okay?"

"What?"

"Just a hunch. Better safe than sorry." She tensed up.

Ding.

Uh oh. The door.

I turned around. Slowly. And nearly ruined a perfectly good pair of underpants. Because a werewolf stood on the welcome mat. A giant one. Fluffy, teeth bared, growling. I tried to run, but I didn't make it one step before a giant paw landed right on my shoulder.

"YOU!"

Woah boy. Room spinning. "Are you here to kill me?"

His eyes narrowed. He dropped a charred, slime covered black thing on the floor. "You left your bag at Bubba's. I found it in the rubble. This drop off is only a courtesy, so you didn't come looking for it. Maybe now you will heed my warning: Death is a fickle friend. Beware. It always comes oooooo. Oooo. Oooh. Ack! Dammit!"

Uh, weird warning, but okay.

He dropped back on his giant haunches, lifted a paw and scratched behind his ear. Again. "Dammit. Friday can't come fast enough. You got any flea collars?"

"Aisle five." DeeDee pointed. "On the house."

Fluffy loped off on all fours over to the pet supplies. He ruffled around for a minute, and jumped back to the door, straightening something on his neck. "Thanks, Dee. I owe you one. See you in spin class next week? Gym should reopen by then. Gotta run. Still waiting for the reapers to come for Gunther and Hunter."

Then he was out the door, across the lot. And as I watched him go, I wondered what it must be like to work in the nice part of town. You know, the part where a giant werewolf running down the street might actually raise an eyebrow?

I reached for my gym bag, but hesitated. I'd just washed off all the eel goop, and my bag was absolutely drenched in it. I definitely didn't want to get more on me.

DeeDee got it. She said, "There's a box of rubber gloves by the sink."

The bag rattled. I jumped back, arms out to protect her.

"What is that?" She stared down over my shoulder.

We watched the bag writhe and wrinkle and buck. An icy blue string rose from the zipper. It poured up out of that bag like a waterfall in reverse, pooling into a glowing blue puddle. A puddle in the shape of a man. A man with rippling abs and tousled hair?

Aw, man.

A ghastly blue face turned to me and said, "Hi, Champ. Wow. That was a rough first night, huh? Don't be discouraged. If you're willing to work hard, I'm confident we can get that bod ready for swimsuit season. Nice place you've got here. If we move the pop bottles aside, there's plenty of space for push-ups, squats and curls. Everything we need."

Holy shit. It was Hunter. A ghost Hunter. He floated out of the bag, chipper as ever. He looped the 2-liter pyramid and stroked his chin, totally unruffled by the fact that he was dead and not in a physical body. There was no trace of anger or suspicion or distrust in his face. He seemed so happy, I swear, if he had a tail, it'd be wagging. Maybe I'd be happy too, if I'd brought my eight pack abs into the afterlife.

"You wish," Angel eight ball hit my foot. Yep. Always an opinion. "Now *that* is what a man should look like."

Uh. I hope Angel didn't expect me to look like this. A workout is one thing, a miracle is another.

DeeDee tugged on my sleeve. Because another ethereal blue form rose out of the bag. We watched blue gas pour up and out, much more this time, so much so that it looked like someone had turned the dial to the Niagara Falls setting.

She said, "This isn't good."

Well, that's reassuring.

The smoke formed into a wide, thick figure. It stepped out of the bag. With hooves. And horns. Yep. The blue cloud formed into Gunther. Big, buff, and from his pout and furrowed brow, none too happy to be here and dead.

Kevin ghastly blue head rose from behind the counter. "If my dickhead roommate finds out I'm dead, do not let him touch my records, you hear me? He isn't in my will. He gets nothing." Then he saw the ghosts. "Well, shit."

He floated over to that little pink book and tried really hard to pick up that pink glitter gel pen.

"Put that pen down. I didn't do anything!"

"Uh huh. You brought a reaper to the gym, and now we've got ghosts. I don't want to work with ghosts, do you? Ghosts suck! All they do is float around like they own the place, pretending they're still alive!"

I looked at Kevin. Kevin looked at me. Clearly, the irony was lost on him.

Gunther and Hunter floated around the store, whispering about treadmills and weight racks. "Okay. I see your point."

"Yeah, you do," he huffed. "Now put that bag in your locker. Jesus. It smells like a hundred cows with diarrhea had a convention in there."

"Fine." I carried it—holding it out as far away from me as possible —through the stockroom. I made it as far as the employee lounge door. I hesitated, as thousands of smiling Junebugs watched my every move.

I hadn't been in there since Chef—Well, since the zombie incident. The room was empty now. But who knew for how long? Steve took Earl back to Pennsylvania to—nope. I couldn't even think about that. You know what? I'm not gonna. The bag smelled like a cow's butt hole. I'd just throw it away. I stuffed it into the trashcan by the utility sink. My eyes watered. Eep. That smell. It's like the eel guts ripened with age.

I almost had the bag all the way in, when it bucked. Uh oh. I stepped back. Another ghost? The wonky zipper finally gave way, and something shot out.

"Aaaah!" It flew at me. Fast and landed, right on my head, like a face hugger. I peeled it away. It was my employee manual. Dirty. Eel soaked. Mad. "Holy shit!"

Aw, man. I could not let Kevin see this book. His stupid pink pen would never stop writing. I dropped it in the sink and grabbed the nozzle. It needed a bath. Wait. Can I wash it? It's paper.

Grrr. Errrrr. Errrrrrr.

Its pages kicked like feet. It kicked open, back to that drawing of a hand, scrawly and ornate, with an eye in the palm. The eye glowed green. Then it blinked, like a real eye, looking straight at me. "Aaaaaaaah! Hell NO! Why are you so creepy? I thought you were supposed to help me?"

I grabbed a dust pan off the wall and flipped the cover shut.

Nothing in there could be worth looking at that kind of creepy. I grabbed the book, and, steeled by a fear greater than memories of zombie chefs, kicked open the lounge door, walked that bucking book over to my locker, and shut it in. I spun the combination lock, then I leaned against the door with all my weight, just to make sure it latched.

The book kicked.

Thump. Thunk. Thump.

"Bad book. Stay!"

It whined like a weird dog.

"Who you talking to?" Kevin floated up to me. I swear, he came right through the wall.

"Uh. Nothing. No one. Just myself."

"Yeah, well. Get your thumb out of your ass and get on the floor to help DeeDee. We gotta have these ghosts squared away before the gate opens." Kevin shook his head. "I gotta feeling we're gonna be waiting a long time for that reaper."

CHAPTER 9

I PASSED out face down on my bed, despite the thin veneer of eel slime, head to toe, all over my body. It had been a long night. Hunter made me do squats. Lots of squats. Man, he loved squats. And burpees. And sit-ups. And lunges down the chip aisle and back, in between all my regular duties at the 24/7 Demon Mart. Hunter did exactly what he'd done when he was alive, over and over. So the good news? I had my very own personal trainer. The bad news? He never got tired or wanted to quit. Because he was dead.

It was exhausting. I barely made it up the stairs to my room, and that was the last thing I remember.

Until my nostrils burned like I'd snorted Sriracha. I opened my eyes. I didn't know how long I was out, but I knew it wasn't nearly long enough because the blinding winter sun bore through the window, lasering out my retinas. An unholy smell, like burning elephant turds, filled my room.

Zzzzz. Zzzzz.

What the..? Something landed on my face.

Smack. Ha. Got it! I pulled my hand away. A small black fly lay crumpled in my palm.

Zzzzz. Zzzzzzz.

A black cloud of flies swarmed around me. Ack! It'd brought friends.

I rolled over, swatting, trying to figure out how they all got in here, and came face to face with a skull. "AAAAAAAH!"

I plooped right out of bed, straight onto the floor. Into a pile of festering black fabric. And I mean absolutely festering. The smell was so bad my eyes watered. A swarm of flies puffed up out of it when I landed.

"Are you all right?" Zack asked.

"What are you doing here? How did you get into my house?" My heart kicked my ribs. "What is this stuff? You brought flies?"

Reaper in my house! Nope. No way. He had to go!

"Sorry, man. I didn't want to wake you up. I've been standing here for like, three hours."

"What time is it?" I grabbed the clock. Eleven a.m. "What do you want?"

"The little roach guy said we're peas in a pod. Or something? I think that means you can help me."

Gah. Kevin!

"What do you want?"

"I don't have any clean clothes. Kevin says I can't be naked anymore."

"So?" That pile of stinky black stuff I was sitting in must be his dirty laundry. Great. Just great.

That's when I noticed he was wearing only boxer shorts. On the plus side, he wasn't buck naked. But I don't know where he got his undies. They were bright yellow with little goldfish printed all over them.

"What do you want me to do about it?"

"Can you wash them? I don't know how."

"You're kidding."

"Well, no. My girlfriend did all the laundry. We were together five thousand years. Eerrrrrrrrr. Herrrrrrrrrrrr. Five thousand years and she dumps me, just like that. Hurrrrr."

"You didn't do laundry once for five thousand years? No wonder she dumped you."

He slumped and started to sniffle. "I knooooooooooooooow. I miss her soooo mu uh uh uuuuuh."

Aw, man. I better get him to stop crying, or we'll be here all day. "Sorry, man. It's okay. But, surely you did laundry before you had a girlfriend."

"No. My mom washed my clothes. I wasn't lying. I really don't know how."

"You've never done laundry? How old are you?"

"Um. I don't know. How old is life on earth? All the reapers started in the amoeba division when we were kids, so..."

He started counting on his fingers, then he saw me looking at him. Then he looked at me. Never mind. Doesn't matter.

"You can't stay here. Take your clothes back to the store and wash them in the sink. Or use the magic shower. I'm pretty sure if you wish them clean, the shower will take care of it. Okay. Problem solved. Bye!"

He slumped and sighed. "Uuuuuuuuuuuuuuuuuuuuuuuh."

"Get out." I snipped.

"I don't know how all that works. Can you show me?"

"No! I'm sleeping!"

"Okay. I'll just hang out here until you wake up. Then we can go back to the store together. And you can show me how to wash clothes in the shower."

"What? No! Leave me alone."

"Uuuuuuuuuuuuuuuh." His shoulders sunk even more. Then he sniffled and rubbed his nose hole with his bony knuckle. "I'm so looooooooooooooooneleeeeeeeee."

Oh my God. My dry, aching, exhausted eyeballs stared at the ceiling. I can't believe this. Why me?

"You're my only friend. Hurp hurp. I need help. I don't have anywhere else to go. And Kevin says I can't be outside in the daytime. Someone could see me."

"People can see you?"

"Some of them. Hurrrrrrrrr." He cried. And cried some more until he got up to blow his nose on the dirty bath towel I'd left on my desk chair. Then my Xbox suddenly caught his eye. He leaned in, poking the controller with his bony finger. "What's this? Ooooo. You've got one of these magic cartoon boxes! I've reaped a few guys who were using these."

He looked around. "Where are your crunched up, empty cans of energy drinks?"

"Hands off." I popped up off the floor and swatted his hand away. Dude. That Xbox was the best thing I owned!

Tap tap tap tap.

We both froze. That was a knock. On my door. Uh oh.

"Honey? I know it's early, but I heard voices. Are you chatting online with your little friends?"

Shit. My mom. Red alert!

"Since you're awake already, I'm coming in. I've got stuff for you."

My heart punched my tonsils. Mom. In here? With a reaper? "Uh, just a minute!"

I flew straight at Zack, pushing him into the closet. Dude. I knew my Mom. That knock was a courtesy tap. A "just in case you're masturbating" knock. She wasn't gonna wait. She wouldn't be dissuaded. "Mom, get out" had never kept her out of anywhere!

"Hey!" Zack waved his arms and tried to swat me away as I wrestled him straight into the closet and shut the door right on his foot. "What do you think you're doing? Ew! It's a mess in here! Wow. This is the most disgusting closet I've ever seen. And I reap people, dude. I've been to, like, a million crime scenes. Did someone die in here? The floor is sticky."

"Shh! Quiet. Mom can't walk in here and see the angel of death!"

"An *angel*, not *the* angel. There are like seven billion people in the world. Plus all the corporeal demons, sea creatures. And like, zillions of amoebas. One guy can't handle all that. We're not miracle workers."

"Shhh!" I jammed the door shut, but his massive bone toes were still in the way. I pushed the door more.

"Ow!" He howled, but he didn't move. I had no choice but to elbow him back into the closet bar, which collapsed, burying him under a pile of my clothes.

"Everything okay in here?" Mom stepped in.

"Fine! Just cleaning up!" I plastered on a fake smile as I stood in front of the closet and pretended everything was cool. Nothing to see here, Mom. There's definitely not a grim reaper in my closet, no sireee.

She had a basket of fresh, clean folded laundry in her arms. A pile of my mail sat on top of it. "Here you go, honey. You left your laundry on the floor again. And after we bought you that nice hamper. You really need to use it."

She pointed at it. It was covered in fast food wrappers and dirty socks. Ahem.

"What is that horrible smell?" She waved her hand in front of her nose, then locked in on the pile of dirty reaper robes on the floor. "What is this? Where did it all come from?"

Shit. She can see it.

"Uh. Well. Mmm." I got nothing.

"Did you have another sewer back up at work? Goodness. That's a smell. And the flies!" She batted through the black cloud, then knocked the wrappers off my hamper, bent over, and started stuffing the reaper robes into it. "Did you bring this home from work?"

Angel eight ball rolled out from under my bed and eyeballed me with his triangle. "Please don't sin. Lying to your mom is a two for one. Lying and dishonoring your parents. Please. I'm drowning in paperwork as it is and your audit is right around the corner."

I kicked him back under the bed.

"Um. I have been asked to wash it." What? That wasn't technically a lie. Vague isn't lying. Is it?

"Oof. This is a doozy. That nice Mr. Faust should have paid for laundry service. But, I guess it's too late now. We'll have to take care of it. We sure can't leave it like this."

Mom started to drag the hamper out of the room.

"No. Don't touch that." Like, literally don't. I didn't need my mom handling hell eel guts. It might raise some questions. "Uh. I can wash it."

"Aw, you're so sweet, but you've been up all night, honey. My hard working little boy needs to rest." She pinched my cheeks so hard my lips puckered. "Besides, from the looks of it, it's going to take two or three cycles to get this stuff out, and if you wait, it won't be done in time for work. You know how long it takes our old machines to cycle. They're on their last legs. I'll run it while you're sleeping. I'm working from home today. Van's in the shop. Besides, I'm so proud of you. Taking on extra projects at work. I like the initiative. You know, this is the longest you've ever had one job!"

"Don't be too happy, Mom," I muttered. "I'm about to get fired."

"Like hell you are." Angel shot me some stink triangle from under my comforter.

"Did you say something, honey?"

"Uh. No. Thanks, Mom. I owe you one."

She whisked that hamper of putrid eel gut-soaked stuff out of my room, and when I finally heard her thumping down the stairs, I breathed a sigh of relief. Just in time, too. Zack popped straight out of that closet with such force he knocked one of the doors off the hinges.

"Man, that closet is small. And creepy. What is *that*?" He pointed to the cave of garbage, broken toys, and lost socks my employee manual had fashioned into a cave.

"That's where my employee manual lives."

I mean. Usually. Now it was locked up. Where it should be.

"Really? I've never seen a book do this before." Zack leaned down in to get a closer look at the cave hole. Something gray shot out and fwapped him right on the face. He jumped back. "Aaaah! What the hell was that?"

Shit! How did my employee manual get here! That door was locked!

Then Gertrude rolled out. Like literally rolled, because she was so fat she was round like a beach ball, and she was missing a front leg, so she really didn't have much to stop her—right out of the cave.

Zack jumped back. "Oh shit. That cat is still alive? The Smites Department put out a bunch of conditional hits on that thing. Nine lives indeed." He rubbed Gertrude on her immense belly. She purred, then immediately passed out, dripping drool onto the carpet. "So, uh. Anyway, can we talk about the village washerwoman? Wow. Hot, right? Lucky!"

He put his hand up, waiting for a high five.

"The what?"

"The washerwoman. The blonde?" He pointed at my door. "As the guys from Gamma Pi said when I reaped them after fall hazing, 'Hubba hubba, I gotta chubba!' Man. Washerwomen look so much better now. In the middle ages, they were covered in scabs and boils. Let me tell you, there were no babes during the bubonic plague. Not a single one. Cowpox was pretty bad, too. That was a waste of hot milk maids, if you ask me."

"Oh my God." First Morty, then Kevin, then Faust, and now Zack? Kill me. "That's not a washer woman. That's my mom."

"So your mom does your laundry?" He looked at me. I mean, I think. He doesn't have eyeballs. "And you made fun of me?"

"No. It's not like that. I know how to do my own, she just does it sometimes, okay? When she wants to. What are you mad about? She's washing your clothes, isn't she?"

"Not to uh, pry, but is your dad still alive? I wouldn't ask, but Kevin said the best way to heal a broken heart is to be 'balls deep by the end of the week.'" Zack made air quotation marks with this bone fingers. "No one compares to my girlfriend, but your mom. Well, she's the first thing that's made me tingle down there in a while. Signs of life, know what I mean?"

My jaw dropped so hard and so fast, I swear I got carpet in my teeth. I glanced at his boxers, and for a hot minute I wondered how that would work. Then. Nope. Forget it. Just hell no. All these guys needed to back off my mom. Because, ew. "That's it. You have got to go."

"I can't leave. I'm naked!"

"Not for long."

CHAPTER 10

As the wise and all-knowing Anonymous once said, "you don't have to go home, but you can't stay here."

I held my phone to my ear, hands shaking, butt pressed firmly against my bedroom door, just in case Mom's spidey sense kicked in and she decided to barge in. Finally, DeeDee answered. She had barely gotten in a hello when my lips started flapping, fast. "Zack followed me home. He can't stay here. My mom is here. What do I do?"

"Gee. You picked up a stray, too?" she asked. "Bring him to my place. Junebug has enough on her plate. We can't ask her to babysit a restless reaper. Hunter made her do three hundred squats this morning, and Gunther keeps trying to look down her shirt. Like she doesn't have enough to manage on day shift."

I was about to ask her what, exactly, Junebug did on dayshift, but I heard barking in the background. "Bad, boy. Bad! Get your nose out of there! I gotta go," she said, "See you soon, okay?" and hung up.

We had to wait until Mom got in the shower to make our escape. It was the only way. The second the tap squeaked and the ssssshh-hhhh of water kicked on, we made our escape. Down the stairs and out the front door. Look at me, being responsible and doing the right thing. Home free!

Or not. Shit. We made it as far as the driveway. Where we now stood, in the freezing cold, staring at the snow piled up around my four shredded tires. Yeah. I see what Angel means about getting things fixed. Be prepared, right? I was not prepared. Ergo, our escape plan was immediately complicated by a lack of transportation.

"Wow. The Smites Department did a much better job on your car than on your cat," Zack said.

"Tell me about it. We're gonna have to take the bus."

"If you give me the address, I'll just fly there."

"Absolutely not!" I couldn't set an unattended grim reaper loose on Columbus. Plus, he was bright yellow. Someone was bound to notice that.

Yes, I said yellow. Because Zack was no longer naked. He wore an XXXL bright yellow banana hoodie. Literally, a banana. When the hood was up, it looked like the stem.

Don't judge, okay? It was a group Halloween costume. Dad was the gorilla, in a suit so big he looked like a deflated King Kong. Mom had gotten them two-for-one at a yard sale, and size doesn't matter when you're Jennifer Lamb Wallace and there's a bargain on the line. We're on a budget. You should know that by now.

Unfortunately, Zack looked like a banana space alien. I covered his face with ski goggles and a huge scratchy wool scarf my Great Aunt Edna knitted. His bottom half looked even worse. His leg bones were really long, so we had to layer long johns, with tube socks pulled all the way up, and the pink leg warmers Mom wore to the Charity Ladies' Auxiliary 80s Ladies' Night scrunched up to cover the space in between. And flip flops, because his bone feet were so huge, none of my shoes fit. His heels hung off the back.

Let's just say his outfit and size didn't exactly help us get around town incognito. It also didn't help that we had to take the bus.

"Why are all the humans staring at me?" Zack whispered the second we stepped on. Because everyone watched the two of us walk down the aisle. It wasn't just the outfit. I'm convinced a couple of them could actually *see* Zack, like *see* see. One lady squinted, like she was *looking* looking, as she unpeeled a waxy white candy wrapper and popped a thin pink wafer in her mouth. Whatever she saw, it must have been too much for her, because her jaw dropped, and that pink candy wafer fell out of her mouth and skidded across the aisle as he walked by. When I looked back, she had passed out cold.

"Why can she see you?" I whispered. Part of me was starting to think this was a bad idea.

"Old people. They're in God's waiting room." Zack shrugged. "Well, technically you all are, but old people *know* it. They're tuned in."

While we were waiting at the second bus stop, a passing pizza guy took one look at us, missed his turn, and the front grill of his Camry wrapped around a fire hydrant. The car stopped. Unfortunately, the pizza light on the top of the car did not. And neither did the pizza guy. He shot through the windshield and hit a light pole. With his head.

"Jesus." Bile tickled my tonsils. "He's dead."

"Oof. That had to hurt. And so young, too," Zack said.

"Did you do that? I thought you were fired! Cut it out!"

"It wasn't me. He must have another reaper assigned to him. You do not reap if you don't have a scroll. Trust me. It just isn't done. Major no no. You can be thrown into the pit for that!" He looked up and around. "One of my brothers must be around here somewhere. Do you see him? He's late. That's also a big no no. You don't leave souls lying around. You need to reap them before they go stale."

Zack's ski goggles surveyed the cloudy, gray winter sky. Scanning, like he was looking for something. "Wow. That reaper is super late. Maybe there's a traffic jam on the C Forty."

"The what?"

"Celestial Highway Forty. It's the main line from—"

"Come on." I tugged on his sleeve and pulled him down the sidewalk. I could not stare at that dead pizza guy any longer. Or the steaming piles of melted mozzarella cooling on the icy street. I could hear sirens in the distance, so the squad was on the way.

This was starting to feel like a terrible idea, but it's not like I had any other option. He absolutely could not stay at my house, in my room, for eleven hours with Mom working from home. She knows when something's amiss. Always. She once busted me for sneaking one cookie out of the Oreo family size pack. ONE. Who misses one cookie out of a row that long? Her instincts were so keen, she kicked open my bedroom door the second I sunk my teeth in to take a bite.

A reaper in my room was not gonna fly. She could see his robes. What if she could see him? I couldn't take any chances.

Bus two dropped us about a block from DeeDee's condo. Thank God. We rounded the corner and a really old dude with a cane looked up at Zack, screamed, and fell right on his butt. "I'm not ready. I need more time!"

"It's okay, old person," Zack said. "I'm unemployed. Hurrrrr hurrrrr hurrrrr."

"Oh. I'm sorry, son. You'll get back on your feet soon." The old dude said. He looked at me. "Is he all right? Why is he crying?"

"Long story." I helped him up. He smoothed himself out and patted Zack on the shoulder, then shuffled out of there so fast the soles of his orthotic shoes burned rubber on the sidewalk. But he must have tripped, because he fell.

Thunk.

Head first, into a mailbox. He stopped moving. His head somehow got stuck in the slot. He had a crumpled letter in his hand.

"Oh my God!"

A solitary tear rolled down Zack's cheek. "I miss my job. Herrrrrrrrrr. I feel so empty insiiiiiiiiiiiiiiiiiiide. Hurrrr herrrrrrr."

I dialed 911. "Hello? Hi. I need an ambulance."

"Uh, it's too late for that," Zack said.

"Shhhh! Yeah. There's a little old man here on the street. He hit his head."

"The paramedics can't save him. He's stone dead."

I gave them the address and hung up. "Stop bothering me when I'm on the phone!"

"What? I'm just trying to save you some trouble."

"I can't *not* call the squad. Look at the poor guy." We both looked. He was already turning blue. He dropped his letter. "It's what you do. You have to help!"

"You silly humans." Zack looked up at the sky again. "I don't know who's working this sector. But they're late again. They're definitely gonna get written up for this. He should have been here the second his head hit the box. Well. I guess they are short staffed since I was suspended. Herrrr. Hurrrrrr. I wish they'd hur hur hurrr take me baaaaaaaaaaaaaaa."

"Jesus Christ. Pull yourself together!"

Zack straightened up. "Holy cow. Is he here?"

Ugh. The second the paramedics pulled up, I pushed Zack down the block to DeeDee's.

I pressed the buzzer and fiddled.

Buzzzzzz.

What's taking her so long? Answer, please!

Buzzzzzzz.

"Do you want me to float up there and see what she's doing?" He pointed up at the windows.

"What? No floating!" We're in enough trouble as it is. "An eight foot tall levitating banana isn't gonna help us lie low."

"Here. Let me take over." Zack pushed me out of the way. "I'm really good at this."

He pressed every single button on the panel in one quick motion.

"Dude. That's just rude."

"Old work trick. No one ever once agreed to buzz in death. We had to get in to the building somehow. You do not want to see what happens when a soul doesn't get reaped. Eeesh. Speaking of." He scanned the sky. "I still don't see anyone coming for that old man."

A voice rang from the tinny speaker. "Who is it?"

Zack said, "Candygram."

The guy buzzed us in.

"That worked?"

"Always does."

We trudged up the steps to DeeDee's condo. Zack admired the brick, hip industrial hallway. "Wow. Great place. Why do you still live with your mom? Are you, like, still a kid or something? Or, what do they call it, a slacker? How old are you, anyway?"

"What? No! Shut up."

"Just asking. I honestly don't know. It's hard for me to tell human ages. Baby, middle age, old. They're really just different types of lumpy. Humans. So doughy."

I knocked on DeeDee's door as hard as I could, whisper screaming, "DeeDee. It's Lloyd. Open up. Pleeeeeeeease."

"Did you call her first? Because showing up without calling. So Rude."

I looked at him. He looked at me. Pot. Kettle. For real?

I knocked again. And again. My stomach churned. I had a sinking feeling. Where was she? Did she fall asleep? I couldn't drag him back across town looking like this!

Suddenly, a high-pitched whine came from inside. Huh. Did she get a dog? "DeeDee. It's Lloyd!"

The door swung open.

"DeeDee, thank god! Can we come in?"

"Sure thing, Champ."

My guts landed in my shoes. Hunter stood in the door, smiling ear to ear. Blue. Dead. Smiling. Impossibly handsome. What. The. Hell.

Wait. How did he open the door?

"Come on in. We made bacon! You guys like bacon? What am I saying? Everybody loves bacon."

He opened the door wide enough that I could see DeeDee standing at the kitchen island, hovering over a skillet.

"Oooh. Human food? Don't mind if I do." Zack pushed me out of the way. He took one look at her condo and stopped abruptly. "Hold on. Do you live with vampires? I can't stand vampires. So creepy. No souls, but still alive? What's up with that?"

"No vampires," she said. "Just me."

"You sure? Because this looks like a vampire's house. So plush. I have to give them credit. They do have a keen eye for decorating."

Hunter floated in happy circles up, down and around DeeDee and Zack. And me. "What a great day! All my favorite people are here. Such a great pack!"

Uh. What is happening?

Zack pulled down his scarf and dropped a fistful of bacon into his bony maw. "Oh, man. That is good. I see why you all are so fleshy now. Human food is great!"

I looked at the weird buffet laid out before me. Fried bacon and peanut butter, which Hunter was licking straight out of the jar. Well. He was really really trying to. His blue tongue went right through the jar, coming up with nothing, but that didn't dull his enthusiasm.

"What is going on?" I asked.

"What took you guys so long?" DeeDee asked. "If you had trouble with the form, you should have called me. I could have walked you through it."

"Form?" I looked at her. She looked at me. Whatever. I grabbed her hand and pulled her into the hallway. "Can we talk, in private?"

Zack turned his full attention and enthusiasm to Hunter. "Man, all you Bubba's folks. Talk about a great group of guys! So welcoming. Sorry about you and Gunther. I don't know why you're still here. We must be short staffed. We saw two people die on the way here, and I didn't see a single reaper."

"What is HE doing here?" I tried to disguise the jealousy in my tone, but you know, nailed it.

"You tell me." She blinked at me. "Does he not like living in the cooler? I disinfected Morty's mattress. It should be okay now. Unless Lysol doesn't work on hell STDs."

"Not him. HIM," I thumbed back at Hunter.

"Oh. He followed me home. He looked so sad, I couldn't turn him away. Bubba's is closed for repairs, and Junebug was done with the squats. Really. You should have seen her face. I couldn't leave him with her, and he doesn't have anywhere else to go," she said. "I had a hell of a time getting him home. It took forever. He peed on every single electric pole, and then he got sprayed by a skunk. Wow. The smell. I gave give him a bath, but I'm pretty sure the skunk stink molecules mixed with his ghost molecules. He still stinks, and do you know what's really weird?"

"Surprise me. Because all of this is really weird."

"The water actually stuck to him. He shook dry like a dog, and it took me twenty good minutes to wipe the water off the floor. I didn't know water stuck to ghosts, did you?"

My head started to spin. Hot Hunter? Here? With DeeDee? And she gave him a BATH. Great. Just great. She had a hot naked man ghost in her bathtub. My head suddenly felt very hot and I swear the room started to spin.

Angel eight ball hit my foot. "Relax. It's fine. You were playing the long game with DeeDee anyway, right? It's not like you ever told her how you feel about her. Plus. You know, you still live with your parents. That's not exactly a panty dropper. I mean, that was fine up until the renaissance, but now? It's frowned upon. You'll definitely need your own place before you think about romance. Plus, Hunter's a ghost. I mean, this relationship isn't exactly going anywhere. It can't. Well, not physically. Know what I mean?"

"Oh my God. Just shut up." I kicked Angel down the hall.

"Having some angel trouble?" DeeDee watched him wobble away.

"Yes! Zack showed up at my house. Naked! With a pile of dirty laundry. My Mom is washing his robes right now."

"Why didn't you wash them?" DeeDee asked this as a straight, obvious question, without the slightest hint of judgment in her voice.

Angel pivoted, shooting me some triangle. Of course. Always an opinion. "Good question. Your hands aren't broken. You can work the machine. Men. Giant, walking man babies. Your moms take care of you, then the second you move in with a girl, she takes care of you. Hurrrrrrrrr. Herrrrrr. Herrrrr. You sacrifice, and you compromise, and you give them your heart and what do you get? They betray you. They LIE! Hurp."

"Uh, okay?"

"What's with him lately?" DeeDee stared at angel, who was so busy crying that he didn't even play dead.

"I don't know. He's always kind of been the worst."

"As my boy Thomas Aquinas said, 'Man does not always choose what his guardian angel intends'."

"Who? Anyway, thanks for taking Zack in. But boy. Getting him here was a fiasco. The lady on the bus—"

"You took the bus? Why didn't you open a portal?"

"Portal. What?" I didn't even know what that meant. So naturally, I ignored it. "Listen. People can see him. Like *see* him. Some people. Not everyone."

"Only the sick ones. And old ones. Or the crazies. And people who are about to get reaped. And you guys." Zack hovered right over my shoulder. If he had a nose, it would have been smack in between me and DeeDee. "And psychics. Not the hippies with the crystals, though. Geesh. Those guys—Ow!"

I elbowed him in the ribs. "I hate to ask you to take him on, but you live alone. It'd be safer here than at home with my mom. He can fly back to the store when it's dark."

"We'll portal. It's faster."

Huh? I looked at her. She looked at me.

"I get to stay here? Wow. This place is deluxe." He looked down the hall. "It's definitely an upgrade. Don't get me wrong. Lloyd is my best friend and all, but have you seen his room? Man, what a slob! Have you seen his closet? There's a cave made out of dirty—gah."

I elbowed him in the ribs. Harder. My cheeks flushed hot.

"Make yourself at home, Zack. I'm about to put in a movie. But can you do me a favor? If Hunter lays down on the sofa, scratch him behind the ear. He likes that. Just watch out for his leg. It shakes."

"Ooh! A movie!" Zack floated over to the TV and started rifling through the DVDs.

"Do you want to stay?" DeeDee asked. "I was going to watch *Poltergeist*. You know, for research. But now I don't know. Hunter might get the wrong idea. *Scooby Doo* is probably a safer bet."

"How are you so relaxed about all this?"

She shrugged. "It's not so bad. I always wanted a dog, and my condo association doesn't allow them. Well, not live ones."

She whistled at Hunter and pulled a red plastic bone out of her pocket. She squeezed it, and it squeaked. Hunter's eyes lit up. "Here, boy! Fetch!"

The plastic bone arced through the air. Hunter zoned in. He ran, he jumped, and he would have caught it. If he had a real mouth, not a ghastly ghostly one, as tangible as a wisp of smoke. Still, he scuttled after it, happy. Sniffing around on the floor on all fours, until he found it in a corner.

"Ghosts aren't much trouble if you keep them happy."

CHAPTER 11

MOM'S HEADLIGHTS flashed across the front window, stopping right on Kevin, who had his fat blue face pressed through the glass, like he was waiting for me.

Uh oh. I had the deep dark sinking feeling I was in trouble. Again.

Mom patted the basket of reaper robes on my lap, now clean, fresh out of the dryer, still warm. "Honey. I don't know what was on this, but it gummed up the washer. If it happens again, tell Mr. Faust to try the dry cleaners. You have a good night at work, okay? I'm proud of you!"

She pinched my cheek and bid me goodbye. And when I stepped in the door, Zack's clean laundry in hand, Kevin stood on the mat with one foot tapping violently and four fists dug into his fat phantom carapace.

Yep. He was mad.

"Are you serious? You're on probation, and you can't keep it together for one day. One! Do you want this job? Because if you do, you sure fooled me."

I looked at Kevin. Kevin looked at me.

"What's wrong?"

Kevin rubbed his eyes like he had a headache. "Really, kid? Do I have to spell it out for you? You took a grim reaper on two city buses today in broad daylight. What were you thinking?"

"I couldn't keep him in the house with my Mom. She's like Sherlock freaking Holmes!"

"Why did you take the bus? That's what the portals are for!"

"How was I supposed to know that?"

"Two words: Employee manual."

Oh. Shit. "Well, I didn't know!"

"No shit. And you're late. We will talk about this after you get your meat hands over to the register and cash this guy out. You are not off the hook."

He pointed at a tubby dude in a wrinkled T-shirt standing by the register, Colossal Super Slurp in one hand, devil's chocolate donut with chocolate icing in the other. Woah boy. That guy did not know what he was getting himself into with that doughnut.

"Hurry up. He's been waiting for ten minutes."

"Really? Why didn't DeeDee ring him up?"

"She's late, too. She didn't call either. You kids. Geesh. No wonder I'm stuck here. How can I cross over knowing you two can't even show up on time? I can't rest knowing the store is unattended. You millennials are screwing with my afterlife. Now get moving."

"Fine. I'll be right there, man." I fake smiled and waved at the customer.

I rounded the counter and was halfway to the register when Gunther floated right up to that dude and said, "Mmm. Is that a donut? Is it Friday? It's my cheat day!"

He opened wide and sunk his demon mouth around the guy's donut. Gunther's mouth hit air, which seemed to surprise him, because he stumbled and fell. His blue ghost body cut right through that poor human, landing at his feet in a liquidy pool. The tubby guy? He didn't see or hear Gunther, but he sure felt him. His eyes went as wide and round as quarters. He shivered like a man who'd been doused in a bucket of ice water. Then, he very slowly sat the doughnut and the slushy on the counter, dropped a crumbled up bill and some change next to them, then walked straight out the door without a word. Looking straight ahead. Eyes round as dinner plates. Traumatized.

Gunther reformed. His eyes lit up when he saw the abandoned doughnut. He tried to eat it, but his head went right through the counter, down through the lottery tickets, and out the bottom of the cabinet. Again. And again. And a few more times. Dude. Gunther looked like he was bobbing for apples.

Kevin was not happy. "Jesus Christ. He's scared off two customers in the last fifteen minutes! Hey. Dumbass! You. Gunther!"

Gunther said, "Me?"

"Yeah, you. You can't eat food, okay? So cut it out. Stop walking through the customers. You're scaring them away."

"But it's cheat day!"

"Don't you get it? You don't get a cheat day anymore. You're dead. Oh, and blue is not your color. It makes your butt look fat, so hit aisle six and give me five hundred lunge presses, fatty. Now!"

"Fat? What?" Gunther cocked his head back and spun in circles, trying to get a look at his fat behind, which was not, in fact, fat. Kevin was just messing with him. Gunther spun and spun, unable to see his own butt. Still, Kevin's plan worked. Gunther eventually floated away, and I watched his head bob up and down behind the shelf as he lunged his way to a better post-life posterior.

"Is that gonna work?"

"It already worked. He's gone, isn't he? You could use some lunges, too, by the way. Mister I-want-to-be-a-hero. Pfft. I don't think all the Avengers movies you've got cued up on your Xbox are gonna help you, kid. You're gonna need more than abs to save the day."

My cheeks flushed. "How did you know about that?"

"You can't get anything past me, kid. Now, time to deal with another giant ass."

I looked at his butt, but he looked at me. Oh. He meant me. I'm the ass.

"Yes. You are. Now, let us refer to your employee manual." Kevin pulled his out of God only knew where. It was see-through. And blue. "Get yours out and you can read along."

"Uh...That book is a ghost book. See? That is a thing!"

He eyerolled me. "Where's your book?"

"It's here." I zipped up. It wasn't technically a lie.

"Here. Let me save you the trouble." He thumbed through a couple of pages, cleared his throat, and read aloud. "And I quote, in the event a supernatural creature leaves the store without prior approval and is at risk of unauthorized revelation to humans not employed by gate services, contact your local magic practitioner or designated gate level manager for assistance. If neither are available, or in case of extreme emergency, file form one three six six six for instant portal authorization. Agents are standing by to assist you."

"What does that even mean?"

"It's clear as daylight, kid. It means call me or call Doc. Or file the form. If you'd done any of that, you coulda portalled Zack's big boney ass back here instead of taking the bus."

"My butt isn't bony. I've been told I have quite the—what do you call it—babookna? No, badonka. Yeah. That's it." Zack floated in through the front door, still dressed like a big, yellow banana. He pointed a bony finger down into the laundry basket. "Wow. Are those my robes?"

He lifted the basket off the counter and sunk his face right into it. *Snuuuuuuuuuu.* "Mmmmm. It smells amazing! Hey, roach. Did you know Lloyd's mom is the village washer woman? She does a great job. She's pretty, too. Not a single scab or boil."

"Get lost, bag a bones. We're having a conversation here. Employees only."

Zack floated away, laundry in hand, sniffing it so hard the fabric nearly sucked into his nose hole.

Kevin called after him. "I told you once. Change outta that hoodie now. The yellow's so bright, it's burning my retinas. And FYI, I got dibs on Lloyd's mom. Find your own MILF."

"But—"

"Zip it, kid. We talked about this. Your mom's a babe. Accept it. How is she anyway? She looked real good just now. She still using that strawberry shampoo? Mmm." He closed his eyes and took a deep breath, like he was actually sniffing. He stopped abruptly. "Hold up. Hey. Bonehead."

Zack stopped. "Me?"

"Yeah, you. Were you just outside? I told you to stay in that cooler where no one can see you. You stay in back, got it? No more outside! Outside bad!"

"Uuuuuuuuuuuuuuuuuuuuuuuuuuuuuuh." Zack slumped, defeated, a giant forlorn banana.

Kevin turned to me. "Wait. What were we talking about? Oh yeah. I'll tell you what you were thinking. You weren't. Rule number eleven: Employees of 24/7 Demon Inc. will under no circumstances knowingly facilitate the mixing of supernatural creatures with ordinary humans outside of gate operating hours. It's in black and white, in your employee manual."

"Did you memorize that?"

"That's your question? Wow, kid."

I stared at him, blank and blinking. "But he showed up at my house. I couldn't let him stay. My mom would have caught us. I couldn't let the angel of death rattle around in my room! What was I supposed to do?"

Zack blurted out, "I'm *an* angel, not *the* angel."

He was standing in the chip aisle in his boxer shorts, loading bags of Zapp's into the laundry basket.

"Jesus Christ, where are your clothes?" Kevin snipped.

Zack pointed to a pile of yellow by the hot dog station. "You said the banana was too bright."

"Stop floating around here naked! This is a place of business!" Kevin rubbed his eyes. Again. "And he wonders why his girlfriend dumped him. You."

He pointed at me. "Next time. Call me, call Doc, or file the form.

No more boneheads on the bus. You still got that iPhone Faust gave you? Let me see it. I gotta make sure my number is in there."

"Come on, I had no idea!"

"Of course you didn't. Here. Study and learn. This is the form. It should look the same in your copy. Standard issue."

He pointed to a tiny page in his book. Which was as blue and see-through as he was. I squinted. Yep. That was a form.

"Look, kid. I don't know what it's gonna take to make this sink in. But here it is: You need to read the damn book. Reading is magic. The more you know 'n' shit, just like that blind guy on Star Trek said. Got it? It's got lots of pictures, so it shouldn't be too hard. Oh, but first, I got something else for you to read. Your little outing with Zack made the news."

Kevin pointed behind me. A newspaper—an actual paper news-paper—was spread open by the stereo. I mean, I think it's a newspa-per. It's hard to tell, because it wasn't like any newspaper I'd ever seen. It had black ink on red paper, and it seemed to be floating, ever so slightly, above the counter.

Hell Report
The latest scoop delivered to all Nine Circles
Falling Angel Alert: Former Golden Boy Embarks on Killing Spree

Golden boy Zackumzaphielhermesiappotholonian has fallen even farther from grace. Sources say the once-lauded reaper has gone on an unauthorized killing spree in retaliation for his recent suspen-sion. The Office of Efficient Eternal Soul Transference had no comment, saying they cannot discuss active, ongoing investigations, although a spokesman did issue a statement. It read, "Our workforce has an impeccable reputation, and all souls continue to be reaped in an efficient, timely manner just as they have since the beginning of life on earth." But an anonymous source inside the department confirmed rumors that Zackumzaphielhermesiappotholonian has gone rogue and has continued to reap souls illegally, without permit, since his suspension. The first incident occurred after a trans-circle gate breach at Bubba's Yoked & Choked, Kick Ass Take Names training center, Earth level, Sector 17, where the tipster said three souls were reaped. The carnage continued the next morning, when Zackumzaphielhermesiappotholonian allegedly reaped three more souls while disguised as a giant banana. The agency has denied any wrongdoing, insists there have been no unauthorized reaps, and has not sent a clean-up crew, leading some to speculate that souls still remain at the scene.

The news has sown chaos and discord in the celestial community, with many questioning how such a popular and well-known angel could fall so far so quickly. Zackumzaphielhermesiappotholonian was the OEEST's Reaper of the Month for all celestial planes for 96,320 months in a row, a record, until last week, when he was suspended without pay for allegedly reaping the wrong soul from a senior center bus headed for a racino on the outskirts of Columbus, Ohio. North America, USA. Earth level. According to The Grim Bureau of Investigations, Enforcement Division, Zack was sent to reap one Stumpy Wilson, 87, a passenger who had an aneurysm while doing Number Two in the bus' onboard latrine, and Edna Wilson, 86, who died of embarrassment at the horrific smell her husband had wrought on the unsuspecting passengers. Zack reaped the bus driver instead, leading to the death of all 37 souls on board. No reaping scrolls had been issued for those individuals. Faulty reaping is only a minor offense, in part because elderly humans tend to all look alike. However, his failure to alert the proper authorities after an erroneous reap resulted in immediate suspension due to soul spoilage. Cleaning crews are still on the scene, trapping poltergeists. Sources say clean up will likely be completed ahead of schedule, as the disembodied seniors all chose to congregate together at the closest Denny's. Spoilage seems to be minor, as wait staff at the diner have so far only reported levitating decaf coffee carafes and the mysterious appearance of carefully clipped coupons for 20 percent off Moons Over My Hammy meals.

Accusations against Zackumzaphielhermesiappotholonian have shaken the celestial order, triggering a mass audit of all activities in all departments in the Souls Management and Development Division, and shining light on inconsistencies in the checks and balance procedures and accountability standards for star employees.

Zackumzaphielhermesiappotholonian, the celebrity bad boy known as the Golden Scythe, is best known for reaping all 1,517 souls aboard the sinking Titanic in one scythe sweep, using a combination freefall, ninja roll, and Sow Chui reaping fist move. The Titanic reaping is considered one of the top ten reaps in history, behind only the Pompeii Herculaneum volcanic eruption (79 AD) and the Shaanxi earthquake (1556 AD). A clip of the Titanic reaping is the second most popular video on the All Creatures Great & Dead Network, bested only by the security tape footage of Yurialaempholalmodephianous mistakenly delivering former Fuhrer Adolph Hitler to Heaven's Pearl Gate, South Entrance, a blooper that is considered the most humiliating flub by any reaper in OEEST history. That epic mistake led to Yurialaempholalmodephianous' disgrace and immediate, permanent reassignment to janitorial services, soul residue division.

Since his fall from grace, Zackumzaphielhermesiappotholonian has sought asylum at Transmundane gate 23, sector 17, and is rumored to be sleeping in a refrigerator once used to store mops and reanimated corpses. Hell Report has not been able to reach him for comment. His former girlfriend, a low-level clerk in the Office of Mortal Destiny Management, Nobodies Division, did not return calls for comment.

"No wonder he didn't have anywhere else to go." Kevin shook his head. "They sound pretty pissed."

"I don't believe it." I looked at Zack, who must still be on a bacon kick and a little unclear about the line between human and pet food. He stood in aisle five, eyeing a bag of Beggin' Strips like he was seriously considering eating it.

"Yeah. That this guy was a massive hero? Me either. Seems like a garden variety dumbass to me."

"Not that. He just seems so..."

"So what, kid? Boney? Death like? Look at him. He was literally made to do one thing: Reap. He's been doing it for thousands of years. You think he's magically gonna stop? Look what he did to me. And to Gunther. Maybe he doesn't know he's doing it, but old habits, kid."

"But. I thought—"

"Look, kid. You are not a thinking man, so let me do the thinking for you: Do your job. Don't speculate. Don't get involved. The best thing we can do is stay out of it. We do not want to go messing around in angel business. They're scary, weird, powerful, and frankly, they're a pack of assholes. Best thing we can do is keep Zack away from people until his investigation is done. No more bus rides. Got it? Read over that form. You're gonna need it if he gets out again. Go on, then. Hang up your coat and get to work. DeeDee's late, so you're on gate duty."

CHAPTER 12

THE CLOCK STRUCK MIDNIGHT. Gunther's head bobbed up and down in aisle six, as he lunged his way to a better ghost bod. Kevin floated on the counter, trying—and failing. Again—to load the cheap cigarette racks.

Still no sign of DeeDee. I took her place by the beer cave door, but I was too nervous to sit. The stool felt like it was made of needles, so I paced. DeeDee was never late. Taking Zack to her house seemed like the perfect solution at the time—she had a lot more experience with supernatural creatures—but I regretted it more with each passing minute.

Zack stood in the pet food section, going bottoms up on another bag of Beggin' Strips. Seriously. This had to be the third one. I watched him hold the open bag over his jawbone, pouring the chunks in. He seemed so sweet, and so dumb, but I could not get that *Hell Report* article out of my head. Did he really kill all those people? On purpose? Did he kill DeeDee?

No. I shook it off. It couldn't be right. The numbers were all wrong. Only two people died today, and Zack wasn't anywhere near either of them. And only two at Bubba's, and it looked like—okay, well, it looked like Zack reaped them, but not on purpose. He seemed as surprised as they were.

It's fine. I'm sure it's fine. DeeDee's just running late. Maybe she overslept.

"Hey. Zack." My voice cracked. My throat was dry. "Was DeeDee okay when you left?"

"Mummm. Mummm. Mmmmph. Yeah. She was asleep on the sofa."

"Oh, okay."

Phew.

No. Wait. Asleep or taking a dirt nap? Oh God. I dug my phone out of my pocket. My hands shook as I called her.

Again.

Straight to voicemail.

Again.

Mailbox full. Can't leave a message.

Again.

Gah! Shit. Shit. Shit! I threw the phone. "If my employee manual weren't a rabid bitey monster, I could have portalled Zack here, and DeeDee would still be alive!"

Kevin looked at me. "What did you say?"

"Uh, nothing, I was just uh..." Deflect! I was in enough trouble as it is. "Uh...thinking about that Black Sabbath *Dehumanizer* album. It looks cool. Maybe we can play that tonight?"

"Good eye, kid," Kevin slugged over to the stereo and started flipping through records. Well, trying to. Right now, all he could do was walk through them. He was sticking halfway out of *Rainbow Rising* when he said, "Wow. Now I know what it feels like to have the music inside me. Literally. Anyway, *Dehumanizer* is an underrated album. You know they brought my boy Dio back for that one, first time in ten years."

"Did you say Dio? Was his first name Don? John. No Ron. Ronnie? Numm mmmmm." Zack's jaw crunched the last of the Beggin' Strips. He swallowed and thumped his ribcage to get the bits down. To God only knows where. I mean, I didn't see a stomach. "Little guy? Curly hair. Studded bracelets?"

"Yeah. That's him." Kevin looked at Zack with friendly interest, for the first time, and raised a single arm for a high five. "I didn't know you liked to rock. My man!"

"Oh. I don't. I reaped him."

"You WHAT?" Kevin instantly turned purple, as his blue ghost body swelled up with red rage. And I mean swelled. He puffed up so far, so fast, he looked like he was about to explode.

"I remember now. Ronnie James Dio." Zack nodded. "Real chatty. He yapped the whole way. He had a lot of questions. Dude talked a lot about wizards. I thought that was weird. I mean, come on. Wizards? What grown-up is still into wizards?"

"Oh. HELL. No!" Kevin raised a roach fist and brought it down hard on the counter.

Thunk.

Uh, that roach fist made actual contact. Weird.

Ding.

The door. Thank God. DeeDee's here! My heart soared.

Splat. Nope. Heart on the floor. It wasn't DeeDee. It was Fluffy. Growling. Angry.

"What are you doing here? It's flea dip night." Kevin snapped back to normal. Well, normal for dead. Blue. See-through. Obese.

"Hey, Gunther. Wait." Fluffy stopped cold, as he watched Gunther lunge. Then he pointed a giant paw at Zack. "Why is Gunther still here on earth? Why hasn't a reaper taken him home?"

Zack shrugged. "Beats me."

"Take care of it. He deserves better."

Zack said, "There's nothing I can do about it."

But Fluffy didn't hear him. He loped over to me and thrust an old metal coffee can into my hands. It had ice blue water in it. A squid-shaped pool toy floated near the bottom. As I peered down in, a face formed. A face with frills on each side. Gills. Its mouth blubbed.

"Aah!" I dropped the can.

Fluffy caught it and handed it right back to me. "Careful. Glug is only happy in the water. And don't even think about pouring him down the drain. We had a hell of a time getting him out of the pool filter. Thank God for that darned toy. He really loves it."

Holy shit. Glug makes three. Which means *Hell Report* got it right. I stared at Zack. At the clock. At the front door. DeeDee, where are you?

"No one came to reap him, and as much as we love him, we can't take care of him while we repair the gym." Fluffy growled. "Ghosts are nothing but trouble. You're the one who brought the reaper to Bubba's, so you take care of him until your reaper finishes the job."

Fluffy padded off to the door, adjusted the flea collar around his neck, and disappeared into the cold, black night. Zack didn't look like he was in any hurry to finish the job. He floated behind the counter and started flipping through Kevin's records.

"Careful with those! They're all I got in the world!"

Ding.

DeeDee stepped in. She took one look at me, and the ghost of Glug sploshing around in my coffee can and said, "Bummer. I guess Glug won't be helping me improve my backstroke anymore."

I had never been so happy to see her. I felt like I was flying. Until Hunter floated in behind her. On a leash?

"What's wrong with you?" Kevin asked him.

"There are leash laws, and I'm a good boy."

"Dumbass." Kevin shook his head. He pointed an angry leg at DeeDee. "You're late. And keep it kinky on your own time, sweets."

"It's not what it looks like, I swear. He wouldn't leave the house without it. Then, he made me walk him all the way here. I think he actually peed on a couple trees. I had no choice. I couldn't leave him alone for twelve hours. He chewed up my *Summa Theologica* while I was in class this afternoon. I've got a paper due next week. I didn't know ghosts had teeth!"

"Good boy." Kevin reached out and patted ghost Hunter on the head. "Keep chewing up the books. Her philosophy degree is a pain in my ass."

"Ha ha. Very funny, Kevin. It's actually very interesting. Aquinas believed angels were pure spirits, capable of illuminating the minds of humans. This is all very exciting, don't you think?"

Kevin wasn't laughing. Or interested. He was rolling his eyes. DeeDee led Hunter over to the stool. She had a giant fuzzy dog bed under one arm, and a shopping bag in the other. "I do have good news. I stopped by the store and picked up a few things that might help with our ghost problem. But first. Come on, boy. Let's get you all settled in."

She plopped the dog bed in front of the weapons safe and led him to it by his leash, which somehow magically floated around his ghost neck.

"Uh. How does that work exactly? He doesn't have a body."

"Beats me," she shrugged. "He really, really wanted it. I've been thinking. Floating tea cups. Floating leashes? Maybe that's how hauntings work. Ghosts who really want something."

"Hauntings?"

"Duh." She looked at me, then pointed at Gunther and Kevin. "What do you think this is?"

The store flashed blue.

Aaah! Ghost! Oh wait. Never mind.

The beer cave door kicked open. Morty stepped out, thumbs sunk in a giant silver belt buckle, spurs clinking the linoleum. He looked like a TV show cowboy. Plaid shirt, snakeskin boots, leather chaps. "Say, pardner. Did you move my love bed? Don't throw it away. I like to have at least one emergency stabbin' cabin ready to go at all times. Always gotta have a backup, know what I mean?"

I knew what Morty meant. And let me just say, ew.

His jaw dropped when he caught sight of DeeDee, holding Hunter's leash. "Well, smack my ass and call me Charlie. Hallelujah! Don't get started without me. I'll be right back."

He stepped back into the beer cave.

DeeDee scratched Hunter behind the ear. "Who's a good boy?"

"I'm a good boy." Hunter yawned. "We'll get those squats in after my nap, okay Champ?"

Then, he smiled and panted and walked in little circles around and around on the dog bed, before plopping down in the middle, curled up in a ball. Like a dog.

"This is so weird."

"Tell me about it." DeeDee tossed that red squeaky bone toy into ghost Hunter's lap. Well, through his lap.

Morty kicked open the beer cave door, and I immediately wished I could take my eyeballs out to wash them. Even Glug dove into the coffee can to hide. Because Morty was no longer a cowboy. Oh, he still had the boots on, but the rest of the outfit was gone, replaced by a leopard print man thong paired with some sort of leather harness thing and a studded dog collar. He held a leather whip.

"Uh. Isn't that a bit much for the Temptations Tavern crowd?" DeeDee said. "I thought Friday was country night."

"Don't play coy with me. I see what's going on here." Morty purred and boot scooted on up to DeeDee, leopard thong thrusting. "I've waited so long. Finally! I'm ready, baby. I'm all yours."

DeeDee stood wide eyed as Morty handed her a leash. The other end attached to a ring in his studded collar. He handed her the whip. Then he turned around and waved his bare-thonged hiney at her. "I've been bad. So, so bad."

"Um. Morty. What are you doing?"

"You know what I'm doing. Come on, girl. Spank it. I deserve to be punished." He looked back at her, then down at Hunter and said, "Is this not how you want me to play it? Hold on. Let me start again."

He cleared this throat and said, "Arf?"

"Oh my God." DeeDee's hands shot to her mouth. "I think I just threw up in my mouth. Yeah. Yeah. I did."

Me, too. Me. Too.

Glub glub. Glug, too.

"Don't tease me, baby. I been waiting forever. He's your dog. I wanna be your dog, too. That's what we're doing here, right? I'll lay at your feet." Morty pointed at Hunter. "You got room for one more in there. The three of us can make a pack. Three's a good number for other things, too."

Morty's eyebrows jumped up and down.

DeeDee went green, then gulped down another tonsil tickler. She handed Morty's whip back. "Sorry. That is not what is going on here."

Morty slumped. He looked as deflated as a Valentine's Day helium balloon on Easter Sunday. "You sure?"

"Oh, I'm sure. It's not too late for the cowboy. And we still have your mattress. It's in the cooler. Zack's using it right now."

Morty stood up, stick straight, wiggled his collar, and sniffed the air. His hips moved in slow circles. DeeDee tried really, really hard not to look. We both did, but I swear his thong was practically glowing, so it was hard—uh, I mean, really difficult—not to stare. "Oommm. You all feel that? There's been a disturbance in the sexy force."

Morty adjusted his package.

Okay, then. Moving on.

"Anyway." DeeDee focused instead on the shopping bag she'd lugged in. "I learned a few things from Hunter. Ghosts are happiest when they're doing the things they did when they were alive. That gave me an idea. It's worth a shot. Here. Put a couple of these in each corner. It might keep Gunther and Hunter away from the human customers. Junebug has enough to deal with on day shift."

DeeDee opened the shopping bag. It was filled with free weights. All shapes and sizes. The girl was a bonafide genius.

"Get over here and help me, kid!" Kevin screamed.

Zack dropped one of Kevin's records on the turntable as Kevin waved his blue legs. "Careful! Don't you dare scratch that. Watch your big boney mitts! Blah blah blah."

Kevin didn't actually say "blah blah blah." He said something else, but I absolutely did not hear it. I couldn't have even if I wanted to, because all the blood from my big brain packed up and headed south. To my little brain.

Because a naked woman had stepped into the store. Well, mostly naked. She wore the tiniest thong I had ever seen—tied in little bows at the hips—and spiky platform heels. Her hair was long and blonde in thick, lustrous waves. I mean, I think she was blonde. It was hard to tell for sure because she was blue, head to toe. And see-through. But hot damn, she was the hottest, curviest see-through ghost dancer I had ever seen. She could haunt me all day long.

Morty pointed like a dog, with his nose and his. Um. You know. "Who is this majestic creature? I've never seen a woman so beautiful. Well, apart from your mom. She's still my number one. But this broad is a close second."

I opened my mouth to object, but Morty clapped his hand over it. "Shhh. Don't scare her away! I told you there was a shift in the sexy force."

"Is that a thing?" I said, but it sounded more like "Im mwhat a fwing?" through Morty's hand.

"Yes it is, my man. I can't believe my luck. This is it! I've always wanted to dip my wick in a human ghost, but the reapers get 'em so quick, I've never even gotten close! She's my unicorn."

His bottom lip quivered, and a solitary tear rolled down his cheek. "Never stop dreamin', my man, because dreams do come true! They absolutely do."

DeeDee turned around, took one look at the dead naked babe, and said, "She doesn't work out at Bubba's."

The naked ghost stripper stood there, curling the end of her hair, smacking her gum, looking bored, until she spotted the crumpled up dollar bill on the welcome mat.

Huh. The fat guy must have dropped it. Didn't matter, because she was on that dollar like a cat on catnip. Except her ghost hands kept going right through it.

"Hi, Candy. Did you get off work early?" Zack waved at her. Then his shoulders slumped. "Uh oh. It happened again, didn't it?"

Kevin got a look on his face like someone was pounding his temples like bass drums. "Let me guess. When you went outside earlier, did you happen to float across the street to the titty bar?"

"The sign was so bright and twinkly. And the human world is so amazing. And I'm so loneeeeeeeleeeeeeeeeee."

"Let me guess. You got a lap dance."

"Is that what they call it? Whatever it was, it was really great. I mean. Until she stopped moving? I thought she fell asleep."

"How'd you pay for that? Angels don't use human money."

"I used the little rectangles from the machine." He pointed. At the register.

Oh shit.

"I hate my afterlife." Kevin rubbed his eyes for a long time, then said, "Which one of you is gonna call Mel and tell him he's got a dead feature dancer in the VIP room? One, two, three: Not it."

CHAPTER 13

THE STORE WENT ARCTIC COLD, and even the ghost stripper felt it, judging by her nipples. Not that I was looking, but I was totally looking. I couldn't help it. I'm a man!

Zack dropped the needle on the record.

As Dio tinkled from the speakers, Angel hit me in the foot. "Great. Another point for lust. I told you to cut it out. Your audit is coming up. You have enough sin as it is. Wait. Is she dead? Is she a strip—Oh, no. He didn't. He did, didn't he? I can't believe this. Hurrrr. Hurrrrrr. Hurrrrrrrrrrr."

The beer cave door kicked open, sending Angel eight ball skidding into the stool. I swear I heard watery sobs as he flew. Bubby, giant and fat and happy, ducked through the door.

"Good news, Bubby," DeeDee said. "Backlash 2000 came in yesterday. I hear the Rock does a Double Rock Bottom through a table in this one. It's going to be amazing!"

As soon as his head cleared the door, the smile slid off Bubby's pincers. He froze. His eight white eyes darted back and forth between ghost Gunther bobbing for doughnuts, ghost Kevin trying in vain to flip records, and the naked chick fishing for dollars on the welcome mat. Bubby swallowed hard. He swayed back and forth, sweating. Shards of ice dropped off of him like melting icicles.

"You okay, man?"

He didn't answer me.

"Step back, foul beast!" A cry echoed through the store. A blue shape arced through the air. It was Hunter. He flew, fists ready to rain punches down on the unsuspecting Bubby. "Have no fear. I'll save you alllll!"

"Hunter, no!" DeeDee screamed. "He's our friend!"

Too late. Bubby took one look at Hunter and put his claw-tipped arms out to dull the impact. *Bloop blap bluuuuuuuuu!*

Translation: "Who the hell is this guy?" Or "Not in the face." Or "Mommy!"

I wasn't a hundred percent sure, but it was definitely one of those.

Hunter didn't land a hit. He went right through Bubby's gelatinous body, which was worse. Bubby stopped moving. His eyes went wide. He got that same spaced out, horrified look that the tubby guy had when Gunther fell through him.

That's when Zack decided to float straight down the chip aisle with his bone hand out to introduce himself. "Hi. Are you Bubby?"

And that was it. Bubby passed out cold and fell splat, right on top of me and Morty and the coffee can filled with Glug.

Ow.

As I lay sandwiched between a giant, unconscious, jelly centipede from hell, the ghost of a gill guy, and an incubus pervert in a leopard print thong, I looked to the sky and asked, "Jesus, haven't I been through enough?"

"Hang tight, guys. I'll get Bubby up and moving." DeeDee waved an open bag of Smart Pop under his nose like it was smelling salts.

He sat up. I did not. I just laid there, clutching Glug, who was slowly leaking out of his now-crushed coffee can. My ribs felt like they'd been steamrolled.

Morty hopped up out of there, full blazes. Downstairs. If you know what I mean. He winked at me and said, "Not the worst sandwich I've ever been in."

Oh, God. Ew.

Zack said, "Bubby. I've been waiting—"

Bubby froze. Then, plap. He passed out, splayed across on the floor. Again.

"—to meet you." Zack slumped.

Popcorn arced through the air, raining down over Bubby's fat jelly blue body. The cleaning crew was right on that. Because they seemed to materialize out of nowhere in any situation that involved food.

"Eee. What the hell are those?" Morty pointed. With his finger this time. Thank God.

"I'm not sure I want to know at this point."

"Just keep 'em out of my way. I got a unicorn to saddle." He straightened out his dog collar and hip thrust right on over to the welcome mat, where Candy still grabbed at the dollar bill. "What's your name, beautiful?"

I couldn't look away. Because hello. Dead or alive, there's a stripper on the welcome mat. I stared at her as she jiggled, for so long I didn't even notice when the pizza guy showed up.

Wait. Pizza guy?

Uh oh. The pizza guy was also enjoying the Candy show, eyes wide, staring at her ass—ets, as she bent down for that dollar. Unfortunately, he was see-through. And blue. Because he was the pizza guy who took one look at Zack and died horrifically today.

"Shit. Another one?" Kevin said. "We didn't order a pizza. We're full up. Scram."

Pizza guy looked at his ghost receipt. "This Transmundane Gate 23, Sector 17, Cemetery Boulevard?"

Kevin rubbed his eyes. "Yes."

"That'll be thirteen fifty," pizza guy said. "And this music is terrible. You got any WeekNd?"

"I'll kick you into next weekend." Kevin said. "Are you testing me,

God?"

Zack floated up to the pizza guy. "No one came to get you yet? Huh. Wow. Head Office is really running behind."

"Uh, Lloyd." DeeDee tugged on my sleeve. "Who is this?"

"Who?" I turned around. A blue man stood by one of the reach in coolers. And no, not the kind with drums and a Vegas show. A glowing, see-through blue man. He had a cane in his hand, dressed head to toe in ethereal tweed.

Uh oh.

It was the old guy who snuffed it in the mailbox today. He looked up and around like he was lost, mumbling, "This is the strangest post office I've ever seen. Where's my letter? I need to mail it today."

He patted his pockets.

"Excuse me." A blue nose, attached to a blue face, floated out of the candy aisle. "Can you point me to the Necco Wafers? They're my favorite candy. They're so hard to find these days. I was told that you sell them here."

Oh no. It was the old lady from the bus. She didn't pass out. She died!

DeeDee said, "Where are they all coming from?"

I did not want to answer her. Because I did not want to believe it, but it was true. *Hell Report* got it right. Three at Bubba's. Three today. Plus Candy. Which can only mean one thing: Zack the reaper was still reaping. Illegally. It didn't matter that he was a nice guy. He was a stone-cold killer.

"Hey, kid. Get over here." Kevin dug his fists into his carapace and shot me a look that would have lasered a lesser man down to dust.

I walked to the counter. Slowly. Dread filled my sneakers like lead.

"Help me write this down, will you?" He pointed to his pink gel pen and matching notebook.

"Wait. I'm in trouble? How is this my fault? Zack killed them!"

"If you'd used the damn portal, we wouldn't have three more ghosts in here. When is it gonna sink in, kid? Everywhere Zack goes, people die. And you took him out. Again. Even after the stuff at Bubba's." Kevin eyeballed the growing crowd of ghosts. We now had so many the store glowed blue. "You're in charge of him from now on. And you better make damn sure that reaper doesn't leave this store ever again. Capeesh?"

"How am I supposed to do that?"

"Don't ask me. You're the expert on getting fired and dumped. I read your file. Your mom practically had to set the sofa on fire to get you off of it. You got ideas."

"Ha ha. Funny." I looked at him. He looked at me. Oh. He was dead serious. Wow. Burn. I slumped. "But I thought I was doing—" the right things.

"Think again. The easy thing is not always the right thing." That's when Kevin screamed. And not at me. For once. "What are you doing? Nooooooooooo!"

Zack had come back behind the counter, and a record slipped right out through his boney fingers, and bloop, right onto the floor. "Oops. Sorry. I was looking for something by that cat guy. Do you like the cat guy? I don't think I like Dio. Pizza guy is right. This music sucks."

"Don't   like   Dio?   Eeeeeer.   Reap.   Urrrrt. Ronnie...broke...record...SUCK....Aarggggggh." Kevin grunted and hurmphed. He puffed up, turned purple. Then white.

Crink. Crunk. Creeeeeee.

He popped and stretched, like strawberry saltwater taffy, out. Bigger, more. He looked like a mean giant beaver. Thick. White. No longer see-through. Growling. Mad. Rising from the counter with six claw-tipped legs balled into fists. His mouth split into a tangle of fangs. Kevin   raised   his   claw   legs   and   "DEEEEEEE OOOOOOOOOOOOOO!"

Zack screamed, "Not in the face!" as Kevin punched him. Zack raised the album in front of him, wielding it like a shield. It didn't work. Kevin's monstrous leg punched right through the cover, so hard Zack flew back and hit the counter.

Pfffffffft.

That wasn't Kevin, or a fart, even though it sounded like one. That was the sound of foam raining down all over Kevin. As each puff of white foam hit him, he shrank a little. Fast, immediately, quickly down to normal size.

"Kevin? NO!" I screamed. Because Kevin wasn't shrinking. He was melting. The bottom half of his body dripped into a blue black sticky puddle on the counter. I batted the white fluffy bits away, trying to shield him with my body. Kevin snarled and flailed and scratched.

DeeDee screamed behind me. "Bad, Hunter. Bad! Bad dog. Uh. Boy."

Chink.

The foam spray stopped. Something hit my ankle. A red canister.

Oh, no. Demon slay foam. I spun around. "What did you do that for? How could you?"

Hunter shrugged. "He, um, turned into a monster. And I thought he was going to hurt you guys, and you just stood there. You looked like you didn't know what to do, so I took care of it. I mean, it says right on the can 'use this spray to subdue hostile, unidentified entities.' See?"

He pointed to the label on the can.

"At least somebody around here knows how to read. Maybe dogman here can give you a few pointers." That was Kevin. Normal-sized blue Kevin. He stopped when he saw the ripped album cover in Zack's hands. "What did you break? Oh. It's just Yngwie Malmsteen. Never mind. We're good."

In his very regular Kevin voice. No fangs. The giant angry beaver Kevin had disappeared. "Geesh, we get one dead stripper in here, and it's beaver beaver beaver."

Wait. I looked him up and down. Did he not know? Maybe he didn't remember. Kevin seemed unfazed. He pointed a blue leg at Zack and said, "These records are all I got in the world, so hands off. Got it? You got lucky this time."

Kevin then pressed his four remaining blue legs into the counter and tried to push himself out of the puddle. He didn't budge. He was stuck in there, good. Well, not so much stuck as actually melted. "What did you do to me? Great. Just. Great."

The bad news: Hunter had sprayed him with demon slay foam, and he was now half roach, half very sticky puddle on the counter. The good news? Kevin was no longer an angry, giant beaver monster, and he had stopped disintegrating. Hunter must not have sprayed him with enough for a full melt.

Kevin pushed and grunted, but it was all for naught.

"Uh, Kevin. Do you know you went full *Poltergeist* just now?" DeeDee asked.

"Ha ha. Very funny. You and your stupid movies. Give it a rest, will ya? Tell you what. You can borrow my copy of *Red Dawn*. A little Swayze will do you good. And you. Dog boy. I appreciate the initiative, but you really did a number on me. Grrrr. Rrrrrr." He pushed and pushed, like he thought his body was just gonna pop out of that puddle. Nope. Not happening. His body was the puddle.

"I am serious. You were almost at hallway mom eater poltergeist level," DeeDee said.

All Kevin said was, "Whatevs. Hand me my pen. I gotta write all this down. Dumbass here is still on probation, and I gotta be honest, it isn't looking good."

As he turned to that glitter gel pen, a wave washed over me. My guts roiled with rage. And humiliation. All kinds of things. "YOU!" I jabbed a finger at Zack. "This is all *your* fault. Not mine. Yours. I am tired of being in trouble. I am tired of being blamed for your mistakes! Go to your room and stay there. Do NOT come out. I don't want to see your face ever again."

Zack went all right. He ran straight to his room, sobbing and wailing, "Hurrrrrrr. Hurrrrr. Hurrrrrrr. I didn't mean to hurt anybody. Hurr hurr hurrrrrrrrr. I can't do anything right. I feel like I'm cursed."

Yeah. Me, too, buddy. Me. Too.

CHAPTER 14

When I stepped in on the mat and shook the snow off my shoes, I felt pretty good. Optimistic. Cautiously, considering, but still. Things were on the upswing.

My employee manual was safely contained in my locker, where it couldn't hurt anyone. Zack had been successfully exiled to the zombie cooler. He hadn't shown up at my house in his underpants, and as I looked around, I didn't see any new ghosts.

Yay, me! Now that Zack and my employee manual were contained, I could finally start climbing out of the giant festering poop-filled hole that was my work life.

"I don't know. You're the expert. Sprinkle me with some of your weird salts and magic and shit."

Doc stood over Kevin, who's back half was still melted into a sticky puddle on the counter.

"It is not that simple, Bug Man. You do not understand!"

"No, you don't understand. Look at me. I'm a puddle. Get me outta here!"

"Be patient. I will do all I can to unstick you." He raised his nose and sniffed. "You must cross over soon. The whiff of rot is already in the air."

"Oh, I see. Ha ha, very funny. You calling me rotten. That's rich. You've been recycled more times than I have, and that's saying something."

"Do not joke about these things," Doc said. "Life comes with a cost!"

"Don't I know it. Now get to work, old fart. Chop chop. Hey. Where are you going? I'm still stuck!"

Doc stepped away from Kevin, muttering, "The spirits are restless. And annoying. You. New Man. Come here."

He pulled me over to the hot food station. We ducked, just as an ectoplasmic high heel whizzed past my forehead. Candy was naked on the hot food station, spinning her ectoplasmic assets around a newly installed brass pole.

Because DeeDee had doubled down on that whole, "Ghosts aren't much trouble if you keep them happy" thing, especially after Kevin's broken record incident.

Accommodations had been made, and they were working.

Gunther was good as long as he didn't see or think about doughnuts, so we covered the doughnut case with a trash bag. Problem solved. Glug was fine as long as he was in water and had that squid pool toy. We couldn't salvage his coffee can, so we moved him to a Colossal Super Slurp cup. DeeDee used an envelope and some stickers from the office supply section to make a fake letter for the little old guy.

The pizza guy accepted Monopoly money, as long as there was a little extra for a tip. Hunter? Well, let's just say DeeDee took lots of walks to the nearest tree, and I've been doing a lot of squats. A lot. My thighs were like aching lava. And Candy? She was happy with a stripper pole and some neatly folded dollar bills. The only ghost who wasn't happy was the old lady, because we did not in fact sell Necco Wafers. Because ew. Who even likes that? Nobody under a hundred, that's for sure.

The old lady paced by the two-liter pop bottle pyramid, restless. Until DeeDee sat a tube of something wrapped in wax paper by her feet. The woman saw it and instantly became calmer, more see-through.

Doc whispered, "We could not find real Necco Wafers. I crafted a decoy. The wrapper is filled with slices of pink sidewalk chalk. I believe the woman will be fooled. They taste the same to me."

"Phew. That was close," DeeDee walked over to us. "Apparently, the old lady went full *Poltergeist* today and ripped up the candy aisle. Junebug was not happy. But, we've got a dozen packages of damaged Red Vines in the break room if you want some."

"This strategy will not last. The signs are clear. We are running out of time," Doc said. "New Man, you must speak to Zack. Ask him to call the reapers. Do it now."

They both looked at me. "Me? Why me?"

"You are his closest friend," Doc said.

"Uh, no. I'm not."

"Lloyd. Junebug told me he's been crying in his room all day. You should talk to him. I think you really hurt his feelings last night."

"Sorry. I've got nothing to say to him."

For real. I was not about to sit around talking about feelings with the angel of death. I don't even talk to myself about my own feelings!

"You must. We are out of options. No living human can contact the Office of Efficient Eternal Soul Transference. We need Zack's help. He is our best chance," Doc said. "Reapers must come to claim these souls before they spoil."

"What do you mean spoil?"

"Souls are like food, New Man. Leave them too long, and they go bad. Rotten," he said. "We must contact the reapers and hope they come quickly. If they do not, we must be prepared. We must take precautions. Happy ghosts do not stay happy for long."

"Don't listen to him. I've been dead for a week now, and I'm just fine. See? Perfectly normal." Kevin said that as he grunted and tried to unstick his melted behind from the counter.

Visions of angry beaver Kevin danced in my head. Yeah. I see Doc's point. "Uh, how are we supposed to prepare, exactly?"

"I do not know."

Great. Just great.

"I will consult my books. And you must consult yours. Both of you and report back."

"Uh. Any particular book, or..." Please say one of the ones behind the counter. Pretty please.

"Begin with your employee manual. It was issued to you for a reason."

Of course. My employee manual. Yep. It had to be that book. The crazy book.

"Now go, quickly. Make peace with Zack. We need his help. There is no time to waste."

He pushed me toward the stockroom door.

Ding.

That was the front door. We all looked. Zack stepped in onto the welcome mat. *IN.* From outside.

Fuck me. "You went OUTSIDE? I told you to stay in the cooler!"

He slumped. His eye sockets were pink from crying. Don't ask me how.

"I, uh...I felt really bad about last night, and I wanted to make it up to all of you, starting with Kevin. So here you go. I got you this. You'll love it. It's even better than Dio."

"Nothing is better than Dio."

Zack held something out to him. It was an album. Four guys in makeup and giant platform boots. It said *Kiss Destroyer* on it. "This is the cat guy I was telling you about. Funny story. I almost reaped him, but the bosses gave him a second chance scroll, last-minute intervention, so I let him go. There's this really great song on here. You have to hear it. It's my favorite. It's soooo good."

"Oh God. Don't even say it," Kevin recoiled.

Zack said, "It's called *Beth*."

Kevin's jaw dropped. I couldn't tell if it was good or bad. Wait. No. Never mind. Bad. Definitely bad.

"Of course, it's fucking *Beth*. This asshole reaps Dio and leaves

Peter Criss alive, then he comes in here with *Beth* when *Detroit Rock City* is the A side. Fucking. *Beth*. Wait a second."

Kevin stopped. He looked at his hands. At Zack standing there holding out that Kiss album. "Oh. I get it now. I shoulda known. I'm in hell, aren't I? I crossed over, and you all sent me to hell. After all I done for you."

He raised four legs to the sky. I swear, if you squinted, you could just make out four glowing blue middle fingers poking out at the very tips.

And that's when a ghost floated in through the front door. And it wasn't the pizza guy. It was a new ghost. A hipster, complete with cuffed jeans, ironic sweater vest, and pompadour.

DeeDee whispered. "I know him. He works at the record store by my house."

Well, worked would be more accurate, because the dude was dead now.

Wouldn't you know it, that hipster floated right through the counter, beelining for Kevin's records. He stuck his head into the collection and said, "Meh. Not much demand for these, but I can offer you store credit."

"Yep. I'm in hell. Clever devils." Kevin shook his head. "Hipsters. The perfect torture. These assholes act like they invented vinyl."

"This situation grows more dire by the day. These spirits must pass on. Consult the books. We need a plan, quickly," Doc whispered. "Keep close watch over Kevin. He is near rotten already. The years have turned him into a salty, bitter bug."

Then he sped right out the front door, but not before backtracking to grab a box off the hot food station. I could see a glazed donut with pink frosting and sprinkles through the clear window on top. I still didn't know what the hell he did with all those doughnuts, but at this point? I didn't want to know. Ignorance really was bliss.

"No, it's not. And this dead hipster is going in your file," Kevin said. "You had one job. Keep bonehead in the cooler, and nope. He got out. AGAIN. Where's my pen?"

"This isn't my fault. I wasn't even here! How was I supposed to keep him inside?"

"I don't know. You coulda charmed the door or something. It's called reading your employee manual. And being competent in the workplace. I give you a job, you do the job. Period."

Well, so much for feeling like this was all on the right track. I was so mad I couldn't see straight. I grabbed Zack by the robes. "That's IT! Call the reapers right now. Get these ghosts out of here."

"Uh, I can't," he said. "If I could, I would have done it by now."

"You're a reaper! This is literally your only purpose in the universe. Call your old boss. I'm sure you've got the number."

"I can't. I'm suspended. They took my scythe. I can't call without my scythe."

"We've got a phone!"

"No. I don't think that'll work. What did they say again?" Zack rubbed his chin. "Oh, yeah. 'Don't call us, we'll call you.'"

"You're useless!" I dragged him across the floor. Not easy. The dude was heavy, but I was mad. I kicked open the stockroom door and pushed him into the cooler. He stumbled and landed smack in the middle of Morty's heart-shaped love nightmare. "DO NOT come out. Ever. Do you understand me? EVER!"

"Hurrr. I'm sorrreeeeeeeeeeeeeee. Sniff. Herp. Will you stay with me? I don't have anybody else. I'm so lonely. And bored. There's nothing to do here. I miss home. Herp Herp. Hurrrrrrr."

I slammed the door. I stood there for a hot minute, steaming mad. Zack cried like a busted fire hydrant. I could hear his sobs through the thick steel, and a small part of me felt really bad for the guy. He sounded so sincere. And lonely. My heart sunk. I felt the same way after Simone dumped me. Poor guy. I shouldn't be so hard on him.

Wait. No. He killed people! I couldn't let him roam free.

"Hurrrrrr. Hurrrrrr. Hurrrrr."

Shit. But I couldn't leave him like this. What the hell was I supposed to do now?

"Mr. Wallace. I need your assistance."

That wasn't Zack. That was Faust. He stepped out of his man cave, outfitted in a hard hat and coveralls. The cleaning crew toddled out behind him wearing matching outfits. As in, they matched Faust. They wore little coveralls and had little hats with flashlights strapped to the front. They were all connected together with tiny ropes and holsters.

Um. Weird?

Faust handed me a cardboard box filled with a jumble of strange things. An iron horseshoe. Rusty old scissors. Jinx removing soap. Keep Away Enemies oil. A black pointy crystal? A couple of giant, flat blue glass beads and a handful of tiny vials labeled, "Spit of a Thousand Greek Yia Yias."

"Ms. Getley delivered these wards. Will you please put them with the rest of the cleansing supplies? We cannot be too careful these days. The Beast is a wily foe and clever with her curses."

Faust knelt down to adjust the harness on one of the cleaning crew guys. He produced a bag of Cheetohs and threw a couple into the heating return vent. Those creatures scrambled in after those Cheetohs like they were prime rib. Faust called after them, "If you see something that resembles any of the items in the slide presentation, report back immediately. Remember, special snacks are a reward for a job well done!"

Then Faust looked at me and said, "Do not worry. It is just a precaution. You never can be too careful when witches are concerned. The Beast once transformed into a viper and bit the ankles of all the people who made fun of her shoes. Half the village died that night."

"She WHAT?" I hopped, looking down and all around for snakes.

Faust shook his head, went back into his office and closed the door. I peered down into the box again. Oh, man. I was in over my head. I was gonna need more than squats to hero my way out of this place.

But you better believe I marched that box over to the rack of magic crap by the utility sink. I shoved it in between the empty spot labeled Curse Breaker and the one remaining bottle of Gut Scraper.

An index card taped on the shelf said, "Please alert the manager if stock dips below two bottles."

Shit. I totally forgot. Can you blame me? It's been absolutely bonkers around here!

I raised my finger to wipe a smudge off the bottom of the card, but stopped when I realized it was handwriting. A tiny scrawl. It said, "This means you, Lloyd—Kevin."

Double shit.

"Hurrrrrr. Hurrrrrr. Hurrrrrrrr. My life is ovuuuuuuuuuuuurrrrrr. Hurrrrrr. Hurrrrr. Hurrrrrr."

Zack cried so loud, it echoed through the hall.

Man. Poor guy. But he did it to himself. And he certainly made my life harder in the process. I mean, look at the mess he left by the magic microwave box. Abandoned mac and cheese cups, half full, cheese packs sprinkled all over. Didn't he know this wasn't a microwave?

Wait.

It's not a microwave.

Boom. It hit me like a bolt of lightning.

What's even better than happy ghosts? A happy grim reaper.

The answer was right there, in the box. I stepped up to the panel and started typing. Look at me! Using the thing. I mean, I think. I'd watched Ricky and DeeDee do it once or twice, but I had never done it myself.

I pressed go. The box lit up and *ding*.

The door smoked when I opened it. But when it all cleared, there, in the middle, was the answer. A grim reaper containment system in an old Skecher's shoe box. It wasn't fancy. It wasn't divine. But it was a solution, right here in my hands.

It was a gaming console. Well, technically. In reality, it was a cheap knockoff Playstation my Mom bought at a flea market. I didn't know if she thought it was real? Or if she just thought real ones were too expensive. She's cheap. It could go either way. But it did play games. A thousand of them, preloaded. No cartridges. That would be enough to keep Zack from leaving the store.

Take that, Kevin. I did something right!

"Really? You bought a reaper a pair of light up shoes, and you're all proud of yourself? Look at that box. You've seen his feet. Those are way too small."

"Aaaah!" I jumped. Because only the top half of Kevin floated in the air next to me. His backside was a very long, thin string of ghost...guts—Mist? Whatever—hanging out of the stockroom wall. "How did you get in here?"

"Neat trick, huh? Doesn't tickle, but I don't have a lot of options until Doc decides to get off his ass to scrape my ass off the counter."

"It's not shoes. See?" I opened the box. "For Zack. To keep him inside."

"What the hell is that?" He squinted. "Is that a Playstation?"

"It wishes."

We both stared at it.

"Why didn't you give him your Xbox? That'd be better."

Kevin looked at me. I looked at him.

"I'm not giving up my Xbox! I've got a Fortnite marathon with Big Dan and Chico tomorrow."

"Yeah, kid. Sure. You might not want to say that too loud. Not sure it will impress the ladies."

Angel rolled into my foot. "Amen. So, while I have you. I've got your file here. How are we doing on those abs? We need to get some check marks."

"Really? Shut up." I kicked him between some storage bins. So much for my moment of triumph. "You guys are the worst."

"Nice effort, kid, but uh, I personally don't think 16-bit is enough to keep that dumb ass reaper out of trouble. Which reminds me. This place needs a good mopping. Get on it. Extra Curse Breaker this time. We can't be too careful."

"Um. We're out of Curse Breaker?"

"You're kidding."

"I forgot to tell you. Because, you know. You died."

"Didn't you see my note? Where's my pen? I gotta write you up."

"What? No!"

"Fine, kid. I'll let this one slip. Mostly because I can't pick up the pen. Just fill the mop bucket, and I'll call Henrietta. Oh, and hot tip: Next time, just follow directions. That should be the easiest part of the job."

He reeled himself back through the wall, like he was the lure on the end of a fishing line.

I knocked on the zombie cooler door. "It's me. I'm, uh, sorry I was so mean. I have something for you."

"What is it?" Zack sniffled and wiped his nose as he cracked open the door.

"Surprise! Your own magic cartoon box. Now you can play!"

His black eye sockets lit up. He peered down into the box. "Wow, my very own Xbox! You're the best friend a guy could have."

"Well, it's not an Xbox."

He slumped.

"It's even better. It's got hundreds of games already loaded, and it's all yours." Man. I was really selling this thing. "You can play it whenever you want. You don't have to share. Yay fun!"

He stared at it. Shit. He didn't fall for it.

But then he grabbed me and squeezed me so tight my head felt like it might pop. "Eeeeeerrrrrrrrrr. This is the nicest thing anyone has ever done for me. Literally, because I usually only see people when they die. Hurrrrrrrrrrrrrr."

"Okay. Great. We'll get you a TV and set it up tonight, okay?"

I plastered on a big fake smile. Because dude. I was row row rowing my boat, gently out of shit creek. Slowly, but hey, every paddle counts.

He took the box and plopped down on the mattress. He inspected one of the cheap plastic controllers.

I filled the mop bucket and wheeled it out front. DeeDee stood by the register, reading her employee manual, talking to the puddle of Kevin. His arms dove into his puddle butt, over and over, coming up with nothing. "Dammit. Doc better get it in gear. I can't reach my book. I sure can feel it down there though. Oof. I don't know what part of me that is, but ouch. I gotta paper cut. You got anything?"

"No luck. Not a single entry about ghosts. No reapers either." DeeDee shook her head. "I really hope Lloyd's book has something in it, because if it doesn't, we're screwed."

CHAPTER 15

DEEDEE LOOKED at me and said, "Please tell me your book has some answers."

I immediately broke into a cold sweat. "Um, let me go check."

I tugged at my collar. Fear had me in a vice grip. Well, this was it. It was time. I couldn't avoid it any longer. I had to consult my employee manual. "Heh heh."

Dude. I don't know why I laughed. Maybe because it matched the stupid fake smile on my face? Because the thought of that book terrified me?

DeeDee raised an eyebrow as she watched me casually back step to the stockroom door, arm pits gushing like Niagara Falls.

"What's wrong with you, kid? You got the runs? Just go already. No one cares!"

"Wha? Me. Noooooooo."

But Kevin called it. I totally did look like I was on the verge of a DEFCON one dump—full turtle's head poking out—because I was drenched in sweat, butt clenched tight from stress.

I had a sinking feeling my book was not gonna be happy to see me. Ergo, it wasn't gonna be cooperative. Like. At all. Hello. You've seen that thing!

I played it cazh until I stepped back into the stockroom, then I booked it to the employee lounge. I kicked open the door, and...

Shit. No. Not my pants.

We're screwed. Totally screwed.

Because my employee manual? It escaped. My locker door hung open, bent, barely clinging to the hinges. I tiptoed closer, fists at the ready, and prayed, "please be in there. Please be there. Please."

But nope. It wasn't. No book. Not anymore. Because it had somehow managed to kick right through a combination lock and punch open a steel door from the inside. Yeah. Because that's normal.

My gym bag lay in the bottom, open. It had shredded all my clothes and formed them into a nest just like the one in my bedroom closet.

Dude.

I had to find that book. I did not need to give Kevin anything else to write in that little pink book of his. Although, maybe he'd cut me some slack. I could not have predicted this. It's a book, not a bull-dozer. How was I supposed to know it could escape?

Tink tink tink.

I stood up stick straight. So did all the hairs on the back of my neck. My ears perked up. It was the sound of glass clinking in the hallway, just outside the door. Uh oh. The utility rack.

I followed the sound. I tiptoed to the door and peeked out. Faust's cardboard box of weird junk moved. Thumping. Jiggling. Bumping against the lone bottle of Gut Scraper. It flapped, and I caught a glimpse of red. A book cover.

Ha! Got you now. I slunk closer, closer, closer, and ATTACK!

I lunged. I grabbed. "Ha! I've got you!"

And I did. That book shook in my hands, looking up at me with a spine full of little glass vials.

Chomp, chomp, fwap, slurrrrrrrrrp.

Um. Yeah. It sucked those vials—plus, judging from the flash of blue, at least one of the glass beads—in through its pages and started to chew.

"Uh. Stop. Stop that."

The book did not stop.

"Cut it out! Faust needs those." I shook it. "Stop! Cough 'em up!"

The book did not cough them up. It clinched tight.

Glurrrrrulp.

Yep. That was a swallow noise. Because 24/7 Demon Mart employee manuals couldn't just be stapled photocopies with cheerful card stock covers. Nope. They had to be animate. With stomachs. Because some asshole thought that was a great idea.

"Gah! Don't do this to me. Drop it!"

I shook it. Harder. But that just made it mad. The cover bucked, kicked into my belly, and used my pudge to slingshot itself straight out of my hand and halfway down the hall. It hit the linoleum, then scuttled away from me, spine opening and closing as it dragged itself across the floor.

It stopped suddenly, turned, and beelined for one of the cleaning crew, who was dragging a damaged pack of Red Vines into his cardboard box lair. The book bit into the other end of the package, and the two of them tug-o-war ed that candy like their lives depended on it.

Wow. They both really loved Red Vines.

I kicked into stealth mode and inched closer as the cleaning crew dude, streaked with dust from his adventure in the heating vent, clung to that licorice for dear life.

Grrrrrrr. Rrrrrrrrrr errrrr.

That was my employee manual. It growled and snarfled, then suddenly let go? The cleaning crew dude fell flat on his butt. The Red Vines dropped, undefended. My book charged. It grabbed the entire pack and sucked it in, swallowing it whole, plastic wrap and all, before that little creature even managed to sit up.

Wow. Talk about a fake out.

The book harmphed and mummmmmphed, glugging the pack into its booky innards. It was distracted, so I charged. When it saw me, its spine curled back, and it spit out a piece of plastic wrap stamped "EDVIN", as it made a mad dash out into the store.

Shit! I can't let Kevin see this! "Get back here!"

I ran after it, but my foot slipped on that plastic, and I slipped.

Dude. Did I slip, like I was on ice.

Thump.

Ow. The door hit me square in the face. Because my book kicked it closed right on my head.

The stockroom door was no match for my immense girth, because I fell right through it, landing face down on the linoleum by the Cherikee Red pop pyramid.

Double ow.

I sat up. And the scars of battle were not for nothing. Victory! I had that book cornered. It cowered behind the bottles, quaking. I put my hands out, ready to pounce, but it must have seen me coming, because it scampered away. Again.

Man. This was a lot of work for one lousy book.

"OW! My foot!" Yep. My bad. It didn't scamper away. It attacked. My employee manual bit into the toe of my Puma, like it was starving to death. "Ow! Ow! Ow!"

I shook my foot, but it clamped down harder. I shook my leg, hard, so hard my pudge vibrated. But that book didn't budge. Man, it was really on there!

"Jesus Christ, kid. No wonder you didn't use the form. What the hell did you do to that thing?" Kevin's top half floated up next to me to inspect. "Employee manuals are like dogs. You can't just stick 'em in a closet and ignore them. Look at it. It's gone feral. You have to train it. Take care of it. Tame it. You better start now, or I'll have to report you to HSPCB."

"The what?" Shake shake shake. Ow ow ow.

"Hades Society for the Prevention of Cruelty to Books. What are you waiting for? Give it a treat or something. You need that book as much as it needs you, you know."

I highly doubted that. Shake. Bite. Ow. "It already ate!"

I shook one last time, and the book flew off my shoe. Because it let go. On purpose. It arced over the chip aisle and thunked down somewhere by the nacho cheese dip end cap.

Great. Now I have to chase it down. Again.

Hunter floated up next to me. "Wow. Great cardio. You're really working up a sweat. Here. Do some squats with me." He put his arms out, feet shoulder width apart. "And one. And two. And three. Champ? Uh...Champ?"

He called after me. Because dude. No. I did not stop to do squats.

I rounded the end cap. My book looked back at me. I looked at it. Then it made a break for it. I followed it down the row of reach-in beer coolers. Limping. Me, not the book. Because ow. It really did a number on my toes.

I was moving a little slow, but I managed to gain on it because the darned book stopped to stare down each aisle, like it was looking for something, before it moved onto the next. Weird. It stopped again. It looked down aisle three, then made a break for it.

I jumped into the end, cornering it. "Ha. Got you!"

Huh. Never mind. I do not got you.

Aisle three was empty. Just me and the beef jerky and candy, sparkling under the fluorescent lights. Angel eight ball rolled out from under the gummy bears. "Can you please stop kicking me? My water level is perilously low as is."

"Shut up, already!"

"Really, Lloyd. That's the thanks I get for saving you from eternal damnation? And from love handles? You should be thanking me. That look is only good on teddy bears, not grown men. Now, about that checklist."

Gah. Jerk!

Where did that book go?

Shshshsh Shsshshshsh.

There you are.

I followed the sound. To the Slim Jim display? I scanned up and down, but I didn't see a book. Giant meat sticks. Monster Meat

Sticks. Tabasco. Hot AF. Big Boss Beef and Cheese. Yes. Yes. And Yes. But no book.

Then, one of the Slim Jim Savage Meat Sticks moved ever so slightly. The plastic-wrapped meat stick sunk down, down, down and disappeared under the lip of the display box. I looked up and down and all around, but I didn't see the book anywhere.

Huh. Maybe I imagined it.

Then a second Savage meat stick dropped, like it was slowly being sucked out of the bottom of the box. And another. And another. And more. At least a dozen of them, until only one was left. That one sunk down down down, and I grabbed the end and pulled it up. Something pulled it back down.

I pulled up. It pulled down.

Then I heard whining, like a puppy, coming from behind the hanger racks of Combos underneath.

I bent down. "Uh. Are you all right?"

My book flew out and landed next to my shoe. Sure enough, it had a spine full of Slim Jim Savage Meat Sticks. And I mean full. More than a dozen of them. The whole box!

And it *mummmph heerrrrrk. Slurrrrrrrrrp murrrrrrrrrped.* Sucked them all down.

"Wow. You really are hungry."

Then charged at me.

I screamed. "Why are you doing this to me? You're supposed to help meeeeeeeeeee!"

It stopped. It looked at me. I looked at it. It whined, then it suddenly flipped open to an illustration of some sort of craft project. It looked like sticks, tied together with string, into a crooked hexagon shape with a cross in the middle. Dude. It looked like something I made at vacation Bible school. Wonky, ugly, off kilter.

Huh. Maybe Kevin was right, and this book really was like a dog. "Dude. Do you need sticks? Because there are plenty outside."

It growled.

Okay, then. Guess not.

Its pages fluttered, turning as if ruffled by air. I totally squinted and leaned in close, trying to get a peek at the mouth that had swallowed all that junk food, but I didn't see anything. It stopped on another familiar page: A drawing of a hand, scrawly and ornate, with an eye in the palm. A green eye. A real eye that glowed green, then blinked and looked around.

Nope. Eep. Seriously. I didn't see a stomach, but I sure found its eyeball. Hello. Creepy! I closed the cover. "I'm serious. I need help. These ghosts have to go!"

It huffed and turned back to the stick art page. A line of fancy cursive words at the very bottom glowed. They said, "Clafoooo Varapa nick? Nik huh. Nickel?"

"That part was so funny, right? I didn't know you liked *Army of Darkness*. I love that movie." DeeDee stopped at the end of the aisle. She looked at my employee manual. "Anything we need in there?"

I shrugged. Dude. I wasn't gonna say, "How the hell should I know?" out loud. To DeeDee. No way.

"Okay. When you're done, come help me move the TV into Zack's room." A flash of blue light spilled through the cooler doors behind her. "Never mind. Morty's here. I'll have him do it. You keep working on that book. Let me know if you find something."

"Uh, huh. Sure."

She left, and the book bit my ankle.

"OW! Let go!" I lifted my foot, ready to stomp, then I realized it wasn't trying to bite me. It was tugging on my sock, while the other edge pointed like a dog. "Huh?"

I looked up. Zack stood at the end of the aisle, robes on, hood up, brooding. Holding a big brown scythe? I wasn't sure where he got that, but I didn't care. Because he shouldn't be out here. "Please stay in your room. DeeDee's getting the TV. I'll hook up the console in a minute."

He just stared at me with lifeless black eye sockets, an emotionless skull. He pointed his scythe. At me.

"Uh. You okay?" Gulp. My mouth went dry. Zack looked unusually serious. Like a legit angel of death. I ran my hands down my clothes and glanced around my ankles for witch snakes, but I uh, was pretty sure I was still alive. Shit. He's mad at me for locking him in the zombie cooler. He's gonna kill me, isn't he?

My book hid behind my legs. Shaking.

"Uh. You okay there, Zack? You look very, uh, grim."

He said, "Who's Zack? Wait. Do you mean Zackumzaphielhermesiappotholonian? No. Sorry. I'm Yurialaempholalmodephianous. You got the wrong guy. Common mistake. We all look a lot alike."

A scroll materialized out of thin air. He unrolled it and stared at it for a long time. Then at me. Then back at the scroll, then at me. Then he pointed his boney finger at me and said, in a deep, ominous voice, "Humphrey Edward Murphy, born April 1, 1927. Today, is the day of your death. It is your time!"

He floated toward me. Scythe at the ready. "Sorry I'm late, by the way. Traffic was terrible. The big man really needs to add another lane to the Celestial Forty. It's bumper to bumper constantly. I don't know how the guardian angels handle that commute every day." He shrugged. "But at least your cat didn't eat your face before I got here, so, you know. That's good."

"What? I'm not Humphrey! You've got the wrong guy!"

"Sure, buddy. Sure. That's what they all say. Let's go, dude. I'm already running late. That commute set me way back, so we gotta make up some time. I can't muck this up. You're my job interview." He said. "I have to get out of janitorial services. You have no idea. It's literally like wiping up the shit stains on the celestial toilet bowl of souls. The amoebas are the worst. Who would have guessed such tiny things could leave such big streaks? Those amoebas. Still mad. Spiteful little creatures."

"Angel! Help meeeeeee!" If there was ever a time a guy needed a guardian angel, it was now. But he just sat in the gummy candy section, triangle blank. "Thanks for nothing!"

"Wow. You reapers don't know your asses from your elbows." Kevin's fat top half stretched all the way from the counter, looped around the doughnut case, and right on up to Yuria—Uh. Yuri-whatzit?

"He ain't lying. His name is Lloyd Lamb Wallace. You got the wrong guy."

Thank God. Ghost cockroach to the rescue!

The reaper squinted at me. "How old are you?"

"I'm twenty-one!" I screamed it as I stumbled backward.

"Huh. Really? I never can tell human ages. You're all so fleshy." He examined his scroll, then looked around. "Is this the Shady Rest Retirement Village?"

"No. That's across the river. You aren't even in the right suburb. Geesh."

"Well, shit." The reaper slumped. "Well, close enough. You'll do. Come on."

He tried to grab me by the elbow, but I flailed like one of those wacky air guys in front of a car dealership.

"Hands off the kid," Kevin said. "You need a soul? We got plenty. Go pick one. You're welcome. Tell you what. You can thank me by taking the hipster first."

"Are you serious?" Yuri said. "You really have, like, unreaped souls just lying around?"

"What are you, blind?" Kevin thumbed a leg back. "Look around."

Yuri's eye holes darted from corner to corner, taking in all the ghosts. Lunging Gunther, squatting Hunter, the hipster hovering by the stereo, the old man and the letter, and Candy, spinning above the hot dog rollers, pining for the Sinbad's main stage. He stared at Candy for a long time until the front of his robe started to stick straight out like he was smuggling a log under there.

Anyway. Moving on.

The second reaper said, "Wait. Is this? I remember now. This is where Zackumzaphielhermesiappotholonia's staying, right? Wow, dude. Just. Wow. I didn't want to believe all the rumors, but it's all true."

"Hey. Lloyd? Which one of these attaches the magic cartoon machine to the TV?" Zack floated up, with a fistful of HDMI cables in his hand. "Yurialaempholalmodephianous? What are you doing here?"

"My man! Look at this place. All these souls. That's quite the kill count. You sure are going out with a bang, huh? Stickin' it to the man. Mad respect."

Yuri stuck out his first, waiting for a bump.

Zack left him hanging.

"What's wrong, brother?" Yuri said. "Just trying to give you props. I mean, way to send a message upstairs, right?"

"I didn't do this. I don't reap without scrolls. Ever. I'm innocent!"

"Uh, huh. Sure. Sure. Tell it to the judge. But I gotta say. No one will believe you. This looks bad. Real bad," Yuri said. "You know what they say: One angel falls, another one rises. Speaking of, I applied for your old job. I'm doing my tryout right now. Fingers crossed."

He held up two bone hands and crossed his bone fingers.

"My job?" Zack's jaw dropped. "YOU?"

"Hey. Yura-Dipshit." Kevin dug his fists in his carapace. "You gonna get these souls outta here or what?"

"Me? Oh no no no. No way. No scroll, no soul. I'm not touching this dumpster fire." He put his hands up and backed away. "But I sure will tell the guys back at Head Office what I've seen. You can count on that."

"Yeah. You better. These ghosts have got to go."

"Oof, speaking of got to go," Yuri rubbed his belly. "Mind if I use your toilet? It's been a long drive, and this dump truck has a load to drop, you feel me?"

"Uh." I pointed. "Through there?"

He floated away. But the dude must have an anus like an iron vice, because he sure took his time getting to the bathroom. He stopped to examine every single ghost on the way. He even picked up the bus lady's faux Necco Wafers and popped one in his mouth.

Right in front of her. She was not happy. She looked steaming mad, especially when he spit that pink wafer out onto the floor. "Gross! That tastes like chalk. You aren't missing anything, sweetheart." He leaned right into her face. "Or are you?"

"Hurrrr. Hurrrrrr. Hurrrrrrrrrrrr. This is the worst day of my entire life!" Zack descended into tears. His fists balled up. "He can't take my job! He just can't! He's not good enough! Hurrrrrrrrrrrr."

Hurrrrf. Hurrrrrf. Hurrrrrrrf.

For once, that was not Zack crying. My employee manual crawled right up to Zack and started hacking up a furball on his foot. Well, he didn't have fur, but it sounded like a furball. And I should know. I live with Gertrude, so I'm an expert.

Hurrrrf. Hurrrrrf. Hurrrrrrrf.

It spit out a small piece of paper, like from a fortune cookie. Zack picked it up.

"What does it say, bonehead?" Kevin snipped.

"Where envy and selfish ambition exist, there is disorder and every kind of evil," Zack scratched his head. "What does that mean?"

Kevin didn't miss a beat. "It means you need to stop being jealous of Yura-Doofus or shit's really gonna go south."

"ME? Jealous of *him*? That guy brought Hitler to Heaven's Gate! He's a laughingstock."

"Hey. That wasn't my fault. The scroll was smudged! It was raining," Yuri said, right as he kicked open the stockroom door. He rubbed his belly. "Oof. I hope you all have good pipes, because I'm about to murder a brown snake. A really big one."

Yuri disappeared, and Zack said, "No. No way. I'm not jealous. Yuri's the one who's jealous."

Grrr. Grrr. Grrr. That was my book. Biting my sock and pulling. I wiggled my foot, but it didn't let up.

"Yeah, yeah. You tell yourself whatever you need to to get through the day. But think about it. If that guy gets your job, whose gonna be jealous of who? Wait. Whom?" Kevin scratched his chin. "Fuck it. I'm a dead roach. I don't need good grammar."

Zack crossed his arms, harmphed, and turned his back on us.

Kevin put a leg up and whispered to me, "He's totally jealous."

Then he said to Zack, "Well. The signs are pretty clear. If other reapers are interviewing for your job, it's time to move on. Come see me when you're done crying. I know a guy over at Taco Bell. I'll give you his number. Because you don't have to go home, but you can't stay here."

Kevin unwound his body, all the way back to the counter.

Zack melted into a puddle of bones and tears. "Hurrrrrrrrrrrrrr!"

The bus lady's ghost paced, frantically. "I can't find my candy!"

I shook the toothy employee manual off my sock and quick stepped over there to help her look for it, because dude. I did not want the bus lady to go full ghost beaver Kevin. But those Necco Wafers? Gone. Totally missing. Then it dawned on me: That stupid reaper must have pocketed them.

Great. Just great.

DeeDee stepped out of the stockroom. "Good news, Zack. Games are ready to go. Wanna play? Zack?" Then she stopped cold and waved her hands in front of her nose. "Oh my God. What is that smell? Did one of the sewer pipes back up?"

"That was me, sweet tits. I left you quite a present in the bathroom." Yuri floated out the door behind her, then over to the hot food station, where he watched Candy twirl around the pole. She stopped when she saw him. Which was weird, because she didn't stop for anyone unless they had a dollar. She stared at him, squinting. I couldn't tell if she was mad or just thinking. Hard to tell. Yuri stared back, but he wasn't looking at her eyes. He was staring at her ass—ets. Ahem.

Her blue body flickered, but Yuri didn't notice. He said, "Ooh! A dollar. Finders keepers!"

He snatched the dollar bill off the counter, then said, "see you later, losers!"

He snapped his fingers and disappeared. Into thin air. Without a trace. At least I thought he did until I saw the front door open all by itself.

Wow. What a jerk.

"He stole my TIPS!" Candy screamed. Her ghost blonde hair turned solid white and swished around her head like she was standing in the middle of a hurricane. She stomped and knocked the hot dog rolling machine right off the hot food station. With her high heels. Because her rage had turned her solid. The loss of that dollar was too much for Candy to bear.

DeeDee ninja rolled to the register and hit "No sale." The second the drawer popped open, she grabbed a fistful of dollars and made it rain on Candy.

"What are you doing? Stop it!" Kevin's legs slapped at the air, trying to grab those dollars. "We do actually need this money to keep the doors open, you know. We're a place of business."

"Kevin. I have to. Look!"

Candy. As the dollars rained down, she turned from angry and solid back to blue and calm. And once the last dollar bill fluttered past her, uh, assets, she jumped back on the pole and did a twirl, smacking her gum, looking bored. Back to normal.

Yuri popped his head back in and said, "Oh, and Zack. I'll be sure to tell your girlfriend how well you're doing next time I'm in the office. Oops. Ex girlfriend. Catch you later."

Zack exploded into tears. "Hurrrrrr. Hurrrrrr hurrrrrrrrrrr!"

That reaper was a real asshole. Zack was a saint compared to that guy. I didn't know what it was about him, but he rubbed me the wrong way. The ghosts didn't seem to care for him either.

CHAPTER 16

"GIVE ME TWENTY, CHAMP."

I put my arms out and squatted. Oof. It burned. Still. Dude. Seriously. Like OMG, when do squats stop hurting? Maybe when you stop doing three hundred of them every night. And when your personal trainer isn't a ghost. Who's haunting you. With exercise.

And down. Up.

And...down. Up.

Down. Up.

Hunter glowed brighter, bluer, happier with every squat. "Good work, Champ. That bod will be ready for summer in no time!"

Uh, huh. Yeah. Probably not. But still, I tried. Because it was all part of the plan. Keep the ghosts happy. Keep them on the routine. And maybe get fit enough to climb a shelf next time a zombie chases me. And it was all working out. The last few days had been okay. No scared customers. No new ghosts. No angry beaver Kevin incidents.

"Hey. Dumbass. Wrap up the Buns of Steel, already. It's time to do the rounds. Start with the Necco Wafers. Grandma's getting restless. Oh, and Candy needs two more dollars if you want her to keep dancing."

Up. Down. Ow. "Fine."

As I said, with ghosts, it's all about the routine. I waddled up to Kevin, thighs on fire. Doc had left a replacement pack of faux Necco Wafers on the counter.

"Doc nailed it with the sidewalk chalk. Even if she had tastebuds, she'd never be able to tell the difference. My grandma used to give me those. She acted like they were a treat. Blech." Kevin shivered at the thought.

I looked at him. Grandma?

Then he ripped into a fresh box of Peanut Butter Patties. Instead of pretending to load the cheap cigarette racks. And I mean, he actually ripped into the cookie box. "Uh, Kevin?"

"Zip it, kid. I know I'm fat. Don't judge me. I'm dead. I need to find joy wherever I can." He raised a cookie—actually raised it—to Gunther, who was loitering by the still-covered doughnut case like he sensed the sugar was nearby, but he just couldn't pinpoint it. "Cheat day, am I right?"

Then Kevin really stuffed that cookie, whole, into his mouth. And it actually stuffed. It didn't fall through his body and land on the floor. He actually swallowed it. Because Kevin was solid, and he was off his routine. That can't be good.

I slowly backed down the chip aisle, over to DeeDee, who was wrestling with Hunter's leash, readying for his hourly trip to the tree at the end of the parking lot. And I mean wrestling. Hunter pulled and growled, DeeDee dug in her heels and wrapped the leash around her elbow, to keep him from jumping up onto the chip rack. "Boy. He's really fighting me tonight. I don't know what's gotten into him."

Hunter was panting, his blue hands pawing at the linoleum, like he was trying to dig a hole. "Down, boy. Down!"

Hunter did not stop, but he did manage to knock a couple of bags of Smart Pop off the rack.

"Uh. Does Kevin seem different to you? He isn't doing the same thing on a loop. He's off his routine."

I watched Hunter paw at the floor. Huh. Hunter wasn't following his routine, either. "Maybe Kevin's spoiling. Maybe they're all starting to spoil. Doc's right!"

"Are you kidding? Kevin's on point. He's doing exactly what he did when he was alive. Being salty and giving everyone a hard time. That's his thing. If he stops doing that, then I'll be concerned. Look."

Kevin stopped chewing long enough to yell "Stupid Hipster!" at the ghost who now perpetually hovered by his record collection.

Yeah. I see DeeDee's point.

"We have to cut him some slack. This has to be pretty scary for him. He'd never admit it to us. Besides. I'd rather have him here, like this, than have no Kevin at all." She looked over at him. She bit her bottom lip like she was upset. Then Hunter yanked his leash and nearly pulled her headfirst into the rack. "Man, I swear he's getting stronger. Can you pay the pizza guy? I need to look for Hunter's bone. I don't know where that stupid thing went. He gets restless without it."

I grabbed the Monopoly money off the counter, went to the front door, and looked out. No pizza guy. I checked the clock: 12:15. Huh. He's ten minutes late.

"If Candy asks, my stage name is Zorro. Back me up, okay?" Morty stepped up next to me wearing a black wide-brimmed hat, black satin shirt open to the waist, a cape, a black eye mask, and tight tight tight satin pants. "I've got a new angle. I'm gonna tell her I'm a male stripper. It's a sure win. I don't know what it is about chicks. They don't want to drop trow unless they feel like you can relate."

Morty's cape swished and next thing you know, he was by the hot food station trying to sweet-talk Candy as he ducked under her ecto-plasmic high heel. Um, yeah. Did I mention his attempts to woo his ghostly unicorn had thus far been fruitless? You had to give the guy credit. He was persistent.

I opened the door and stuck my head out, looking around the lot. "Where the hell is that pizza guy?"

"Oh, you mean Keegan?" Zack floated up with four overflowing Colossal Super Slurp cups in his arms. He started to fill up a fifth with Hexed Huckleberry. Which was black? Ew.

"He's in my room. We just played a killer round of *Squirrel Gangster Shoot Out*. Gaming marathon. It's a great game. The little squirrel guy is so cute, and he has a girlllllllfrieeeeeeeeeeeeend. Hurrrrrrrrrr."

He cried and floated away.

Wow. He was totally despondent. He sobbed as he grabbed a fistful of Zapp's Evil Eye bags off the end cap. Then he disappeared into his zombie cooler, slamming the door shut behind him. Poor guy. But on the plus side, since we plugged in the game station, no one else had died. That's a win.

"Bad, Hunter. Bad. Down!" DeeDee yanked his leash, and it tightened around his ghostly neck. He jerked and kicked the end cap clean off. Chip bags flew. Wouldn't you know it, the cleaning crew materialized out of nowhere to lick the spilled chip bits off the floor.

"Stomachs on legs. Disgusting. Nummm. Mummm. Mmmm," Kevin said, as he stuffed two Peanut Butter Patties in his fat blueish mouth.

Ding.

Finally. The pizza guy! I whirled around, Monopoly money in hand. "Thirteen fifty, plus tip. Keep the change."

"What the heck am I supposed to do with play money?" It wasn't the pizza guy. It was Bob the Doughnut Guy.

He stood on the mat, pink rubber gloves up to his elbows, holding a fresh pink box of nightmares. He wore a bright yellow Hawaiian shirt and was tan as a buckeye nut, apart from the white spot his sunglasses left around his eyes.

"Where you been? My doughnut case is running on fumes! Mumm. Numm. Mmm." Yep. Kevin was still chowing down on those cookies, and from the looks of it, he did a pretty good job of actually swallowing them.

"Didn't you get the email? Dolly's won best bakery in the sector. We all won a free trip to Jamai...caa.aaaa.aaaaaa." Yeah. Bob the Doughnut Guy's A's trailed off. As soon as he saw Kevin. Bluish. Dead. His bottom half melted into the counter.

His eyes went round and big as silver dollars. They darted between Gunther, the dead demon stalking the doughnut case, and DeeDee wrangling ghost Hunter on a leash. And the hipster who just pulled his head out of Kevin's record collection. Again. Then Glug, happily splashing in his slushy cup by the stereo. And Candy, blue boobs bouncing as Zorro Morty begged for her love and tried to lick the spectral bottom of her spike heel shoe.

And wouldn't you know it, that's when Zack popped out to grab another bag of chips. "Hurrrrrrrr. Oh. Hi. I'm Zack. What's your name?"

Zack waved. Bob the Doughnut guy went completely white and dropped like a rock. He passed out cold on the welcome mat, pink box still in his pink-gloved hands. Thankfully, the box was sealed. Because dude. I was not touching those doughnuts.

Kevin turned to Zack and said, "Again? Really?"

"I didn't kill him!"

Kevin stared down at the unnaturally tan, unconscious, three-hundred pound, six-foot seven-inch tall donut guy on the mat. So did I.

"Is he dead?" Please don't be dead.

"Well, he ain't blue. I'll see if he's got a pulse." Kevin jump flew off the counter—well, the top half did. He caught a lot more air as vapor than he ever did as a fat roach. He leaned in close to Bob's nose. "False alarm. He's fine. Musta been the shock of Zack's ugly mug."

Kevin examined Bob's tan, muttering, "Everybody gets to go to Jamaica but me. Stupid Junebug."

"Is Bob all right?" DeeDee led ghost Hunter to the mat and peered down over the knocked-out doughnut man.

"Might as well let him sleep it off." Kevin shrugged.

Hunter yanked his leash again and DeeDee snapped. "SIT!"

He did. For once.

"Finally! Good boy. Who's a good boy." She gently ran her hand down his ghost back like she was petting him. I swear, his back leg shook from the sheer joy of it. For a split second, I wished she would pet me like that. I think I hate that guy. Yep. I hate him.

"OW!" My foot! My employee manual bit into the toe of my Puma. It looked at me. I looked at it. "Are you hungry? AGAIN? You just ate!"

The cleaning crew wasn't the only stomach on legs around here. Well, my employee manual didn't have legs, but same idea. I still couldn't read it, but it did stop biting me, as long as I slipped it the right snacks. Unfortunately, it was really picky. It only liked Red Vine SuperStrings, glass vials of yia yia tears, and Slim Jim Savage Meat Sticks.

It bit into my sock, then flipped open to that same page. The one with the drawing of a hand, scrawly and ornate, with an eye in the palm. A real green eye. I flipped that book closed with my foot and stood on it to keep it shut. It wriggled, trying to open.

"Oh, dear. Beware the green-eyed monster. It will destroy you from the inside out." It was a voice, tiny and sweet. It did not come from my book. It came from the teeny little lady in an Easter egg yellow cardigan and cotton ball of white hair who stepped in onto the mat. It was Henrietta. "As the Bible says, envy rots the bones!"

She smiled at me as she stepped right over Bob, still unconscious. Wait. Did she just do one of her, you know, psychic things she does? Shoot. I should have written that down.

"Oh, no. I did it again, didn't I?" Zack floated up to Henrietta, leaned down in to examine her kindly great grandma face. "She's definitely dead. I'm sooooorrrrrreeeeeee. Hurrrr."

"Don't cry, dear. I'm not dead. Not yet." She patted his scapula, and we all breathed a sigh of relief. "Although, I am too old to buy green bananas."

She turned to me. "There you are. This just came in for you. Special delivery. Marked urgent."

She sunk her wrinkled little hand into her giant quilted flower-print purse, and a lump formed in my throat. *Please be a new employee manual. Please!*

Grrrrr.

Ow.

Yeah. My book bit me. It must have zoned in on my brainwaves.

"Here we are." Her hand emerged from the depths. She handed me a black roll.

"Duct tape?"

"Waterproof tape, dear." She shook her head. "I thought it was an odd order, too, but it's better if we don't question the divine."

Gee. I wonder who ordered this. Where is Angel eight ball, anyway? I was about to look, but Henrietta had more nightmares in that bag of hers. She lifted out a small cardboard box. It clinked when she handed it to me. It was heavy and filled with glass bottles. "This is all I could get. Celestial supply problems. The Heavens are in disarray. Audits! Make this last, dear. Always read the label and follow the directions."

"Read? This guy? Heh heh. Good luck," Kevin threw shade at me then stuffed another cookie in his mouth. "Mmmph. Mmmmm. Mmmmm."

"Goodness. Look at the time. I'm late for cards with the ladies."

"Ooh, bridge?" Zack asked. "I like bridge."

"Tarot. Good luck, dear." She patted me on the arm. She turned to Zack and said, "I'll see you on March 13, 2041. Bye, boys."

She shuffled over to Bob the Doughnut Guy, pulled something out of her purse, and sprinkled it all over him. She said what sounded like a prayer, and he sat up so fast, so frantic, it's like Henrietta had just jolted him to life with a set of defibrillator paddles. "It's okay, dear. They're not here to kill you."

Henrietta kicked open the front door with her thick rubber

orthotic shoes and booked it across the parking lot. Man. She's fast for a granny. Bob the Doughnut Guy stood up, smoothed himself out, and picked his magic pink box up off the mat. His wide eyes locked on Gunther. "Uh..."

Bob the Doughnut Guy sped past him, around behind the counter, clutching that box tight. Probably to keep it from shaking out of his hands. "Wow. Crazy night. Heh heh."

He tried to smile, but it was really just gritted teeth. A bead of sweat had broken out around his mustache. He tugged at his collar. "So. Um....Got another seasonal flavor for you. Special edition."

Poor Bob. Trying to pretend it's all good.

"I told you no more pumpkin spice, Bob. Mmmm. Mmmmm." Kevin chewed, but he must have turned full ghost again, because the cookie stayed intact. Even the crumbs were ghostly. He looked at the cookie. At his transparent carapace. "Shit. I can't win for losing. Oh well. It was good while it lasted."

Bob leaned away from Kevin. It was subtle, but there was no disguising it. He was scared. Great. This guy works in a bakery of nightmares. If he's scared, we're totally screwed.

"Uh..no. Heh heh. No. You'll like this one. Chocolate doughnut with peanut butter filling. Ohio buckeye flavor! Heh heh heh." Bob the Doughnut Guy fake chuckled as he wiped the sweat off his forehead with a pink, elbow-high rubber glove. Then he lifted the cover off the doughnut case and loaded it so fast his pink hands were a blur.

Gunther changed the second the cover lifted off the case. He took one look at all that frosted glazed evil and couldn't wait to get at it. His giant meaty hand grabbed, but he couldn't get at them. He grabbed again, and his hands went right through. Poor Gunther. Still vapor.

"Nooooooo!" Gunther screamed. "It's CHEAT DAY!"

His fists came down on the counter, so hard he dented the formica.

Oh, snap.

Bob the Doughnut Guy froze in terror.

"Cheat," Gunther groaned. "CHEAT!"

Gunther's shoulders popped, his head rolled in circles. He creaked and cracked. His body stretched. And stretched. And stretched even more. This dude was like salt water taffy on steroids. His arms stretched until his knuckles dragged the floor, like an angry blue demon King Kong. They were thick and muscular. With claws. His body cracked and puffed, taller, stouter, wider. So thick—so solid —he cast a shadow over us.

He lifted a big fat arm and smacked the doughnut case off the counter, grunting, "CHEAT DAY!"

That demon arm? It was not vapor. It was solid. Rock solid.

"Lloyd. Poltergeist!" DeeDee backed away, pulling Hunter back with her. "Get away from him."

DeeDee ducked as Dolly's doughnuts flew up up, arcing through the air. Kevin's ghostly blue legs waved, trying to catch them, but you know how that went.

Gunther opened his mouth, ready to eat. Not good. If he swallowed just one of those chocolate frosted ones, he was gonna turn into a really big problem, really fast.

My hands shook. *Tink tink tink.*

The glass bottles. I stared down at them, white-knuckling the box, and everything became so clear. This was my moment. I was not going to run. Henrietta just dropped the answer right in my hand, and I was gonna use it. It's my turn to save the day.

I backed away from Gunther and riffled through the box. I grabbed a bottle. Green liquid. Curse Breaker? Might work. My palms were so sweaty the bottle nearly slipped out of my hands, but I held tight. I read the label through my fat, pink, shaking fingers. Kevin said to follow directions, right? The label said: Mix with Gut Scraper."

Gunther screamed, "CHEAT!"

His fists crunched down. The counter split. Bob the Doughnut Guy ducked for cover.

"Will open portal and transport entities..."

Portal? Yes, please. A second later, I had a bottle of Curse Breaker in one hand and a bottle of Gut Scraper in the other. I uncorked them and threw them like grenades, right at Gunther, whose mouth just chomped down on not one, but three fresh-baked devil's food chocolate with chocolate frosting doughnuts.

This better work.

Nope. The bottles bounced right off of him. Shit. They dropped like stones, and shattered on the linoleum by his cloven hooves. The liquid splurped up out of the bottles, green and red, until the two streams touched.

That's when DeeDee hopped out of the aisle wielding two giant metal flashlights. She waved the lights all around Gunther like laser pointers. "Ooh! Look at the light! Go into the light, Gunther. Go into the light!"

"What are you doing?" Kevin said. "He's not a cat!"

DeeDee took one look at the liquid, the broken bottles, and catapulted herself up off the ground, straight at Kevin. She shot at him as fast as a bullet. She tackled him, and the two of them disappeared behind the counter.

Because those liquids? The second they touched, they turned to gas, sizzling and sparking, and ssssssing like a leaky air mattress with a fat dude on it. (Ask me how I know.) It was not a casual fizzle, like when you open a Pepsi. Oh no. It formed a big angry cloud of swirling purple, green and blue ribbons. They shot up all around Gunther, twirling and swirling, and twisting around his bits. And that gas? It grabbed him and pulled him down, like they were solid. Down in. As in, into some sort of hole.

I couldn't move. It's like I'd been turned into a Lloydcicle and frozen on the spot.

"Uh, Guys? What's this? What's happening? Hey. Get away from me! Get off of me! Aahhhh!" Harmless ghost Gunther returned. He punched and smacked, fighting the smoke. It was all for nothing. The harder he fought, the tighter it grabbed him. Until chunk by chunk, his body sunk lower and lower, until only one of his giant outstretched meat hands was visible, reaching out for help, for anything to grab hold of. The puddle? It slurped him right in.

Oh God. What have I done?

Even Zack was shaking. He'd grabbed onto me and held tight, finger bones quaking.

Bob the Doughnut Guy popped up from behind the counter. He swallowed hard and said, "Welp, see you tomorrow night, bye!"

He ran right through the hipster ghost, planted his hands on the counter and hopped right over, taking all the cheap cigarette racks down with him. He sprinted out the front door like he was hoping to win an Olympic medal. His tires squealed on the asphalt as he peeled out of the lot.

DeeDee rose from behind the counter, a giant fat semisolid ghost Kevin squirming in her arms. "What's gotten into you? Let me go! Shit. Whose gonna clean up those cigarettes? Hint: It ain't me."

She looked at me. I looked at her. Eyes wide. Not really understanding what just happened.

"Hey. Where's Gunther?" Kevin saw the puddle, which was now closing in on itself, shrinking down to nothing. "What did you do, kid?"

"Uh. Saved us?" I think?

"I mean, what did you pour on him? Bring that over here and let me take a look."

I picked up the box. The bottles nearly shook out of my hands as I carried them to the counter. My heart buzzed. "Henrietta said read the labels, so I read the labels."

Kevin bent down to inspect. "It says 'Warning. Do not mix with Gut Scraper. It will open a portal to transport entities to the seventh circle, ring three, boiling pit division.'"

We all stared at the now inert, evaporating puddle.

"Oof. Poor Gunther. So uh, tell me, kid. What part of that label made you say, 'Oh, this is a great idea!'"

"I didn't see that part. My fingers were in the way. He was huge. I panicked!"

"Suuuuuuuuuuuuuuuuuuuugh." That was Kevin, exasperated sighing me. "Wow, kid. Wow. You seriously half ass, dumb assed this one. Where's my pen? I gotta write you up. You better slow down. The notebook's almost full!"

CHAPTER 17

"Where's the tape I ordered?" Angel eight ball wobbled on my desk, leaking. The wood veneer underneath him started to warp. His fluid level was so low the triangle could barely turn. "I'm in really bad shape here."

"Why don't you go look for it? Can't you see I'm busy?" I shooed him away. "Gah! Can you go leak somewhere else? If you get it wet, it'll be ruined!"

"Don't get snippy with me. You know I'm trying to transfer into an iPhone. Errrrrr. Errrrrrrr. Wow. It is really hard to turn this remotely. Errrrrr." Oh, but he managed. Because always an opinion. "Why don't you top me up while you're at it? And hurry up. I've almost run dry. We need to make this thing last. I'm number 9,998,383,750,000 in line at Divine Embodiments. They're only serving No. 3!"

I rolled my eyes. He was just as bad as Kevin. Nag nag nag. So I ignored him and shooed him out of the way while I rifled through my desk drawer. Again. I had to find the blank check Faust gave me. Had to. Because it was high time to use it.

This investigation had to end. It was not my fault that eel showed up at Bubba's. It was not my fault that Zack went on a killing spree.

And it sure as hell wasn't my fault my employee manual was a biting, feral nightmare. It's not my fault Gunther—well, never mind. That was kind of my fault.

Anyway, I'd show them. I'd wish it all away. Dear Faust, please reward me by removing all the ghosts and the crying reaper from the store and replacing my employee manual with a real, normal useful book. Amen. Boom. See? One blank check, and I could finally clear my name. One blank check, and I could get back to normal life. One blank check, investigation over, problem solved.

My face flushed hot. Dammit! "I know I put it in here!" I upended the drawer again. But it didn't matter. It was still just a nest of wrinkled bills and receipts, old late notices and crumpled twenty-dollar bills.

"Thank you, baby Jesus. I found it." Angel rolled into my arm. He had that roll of tape next to him. Don't ask me how he moved it. "Wow. Look at this place. We really need to start in on the cleanliness and godliness thing. Hold on. I'm gonna put a note in your file."

I grabbed him, and I shook him. Hard. Really, really hard. Jaw clinched. I grunted at him, practically chanting. "No. More. Notes. In. My File. I'm. Done. With. Stupid. Files!"

Growrrrr.

"Stupid angel. Don't growl at me! You're a jerk. A weird nosey jerk."

Shake shake shake. *Splosh splosh splosh.*

Because yeah. Every time I shook him, more water flew out.

"You're a shitty guardian angel, do you know that? Where have you been anyway? You're supposed to help me. But no. You were nowhere around. You didn't even stand up for me with Faust. Because you're shitty! I hope you get fired! Because you're not helping meeeeeeeeeeeee."

I slammed him down on the desk. He stopped. Then he rolled. Well, clinked. I pretty much shook the last of the water out of him. "Ow. Meany pants. I told the truth. Bubba's was fuzzy. In fact, that whole block is fuzzy, especially the store. Something's wrong on your end. I reset my Ethereal Net connection twice, and it didn't help at all! And you listen here, Bub. Don't get high and mighty with me. I'm trying to upgrade you from a Nobody to a Somebody and this is the thanks I get? Sniff. Herp. I told you. I'm going through a hard time right now. Work is crazy, and my home life is hurrrrrr hurrrrrrr. Sniff. Sniff. Sorry. Pfoooooooooooooooo."

"Are you blowing your nose?"

Grrrrrrrrrrrrrrrr.

"What was that? Did something follow you home? Monster!" Angel's triangle clinked. "Quick. Grab a weapon! Do you have a flaming sword? No. Wait. Get your celestial trumpet. Those are good for pretty much everything. They can even make walls crumble. One time, at Jericho—"

"I don't have a trumpet! Where would I get a trumpet?"

Grrrrrrrrrrrrrr.

"It's there. THERE!" His triangle clinked. An arrow. Pointing at my closet.

Gulp. Sure enough. Something was rattling around in there. I tugged at my collar. "It's probably just Gertrude."

"You better double check."

I wanted to ignore it. I really did. But Angel was right. You can never be too sure. Anything can follow you home from Demon Mart, including the angel of death. I grabbed the closest weapon. Which was, unfortunately, the guitar controller for my Guitar Hero game. But it'd have to do. I clutched that plastic fretboard so tight I was pretty sure it was gonna crack in half. I tiptoed to the closet.

Grrrrr. Rrrrrrrrr. Rrrrrrrrrrrr. The floor rippled and writhed as something moved underneath the pile of dirty clothes.

"Seriously, though. You need to clean." Angel hit my foot. Leaking red all over my carpet.

"Shhhhhhhhh!"

I held my breath and reached down into my closet, guitar ready to smash whatever beast lay hidden underneath.

Hisssssssssssss.

I grabbed a dirty shirt. I yanked. I jumped up and landed, feet apart, ready to bring that guitar down like a hammer. "Hi ya!"

Gertrude looked up at me.

"Oh. Sorry, Gertrude." I patted her head. And she swatted. Not at me. Something shot out and clamped down right on my hand.

"OW!" I shook, and it flew through the air. In a flash, I saw my employee manual, spine rumpling, chewing? Flying right toward the handful of Slim Jim Monster Meat Sticks I'd left on my dresser. It landed on them, open, and started sucking them all in. "No! Those are mine!"

I dropped the guitar and scrambled after it. But it was no use. That book was hungry. He horked and snarfled and sucked them all right in. Yeah. I get it. I saw it eating all those Savage Meat Sticks, and I thought, mmmm. Those don't look half bad. But I'll never know now, will I? Because it growled at me every time I tried to step closer.

Grrrrr. Grrrrrrr.

Angel rolled up. "Uh. I've never seen a book do that before."

"Yeah. Me either."

"Did Celestial Library Services accidentally issue you a Necronomicon? Because you are not qualified for that. Trust me."

I looked at Angel. Angel looked at me. The book grunted as it chewed. "Thanks for your vote of confidence. I thought you wanted me to be a big hero."

"Baby steps," he said. "Is that its stomach growling? Is it still hungry?"

"I don't know. It ate a whole pound of Slim Jim's today already. And three packs of Red Vines. Oh. Wait a minute. I've still got one Savage Meat Stick in my backpack. Yay!"

I swear the book heard me. Because it perked up and whined like a sad dog. If books had faces, it would be making sad puppy dog eyes. I swear. Ugh. "Fine. Take it."

I unearthed my backpack from the piles of dirty laundry by my bed, unzipped it, and tossed the meat stick at it. That'll keep him busy. I don't have time to entertain a rabid book. I needed to find that blank check!

"This is so weird. Has it let you read it yet?"

"Can you make yourself useful and help me look for that check? If you want me to keep my job, I need it."

Mamrfff Narmfff Narmfff.

"I already found it. Look." His triangle clinked. It had a tiny arrow on it. Pointing at the closet cave. There, at the edge of my book's creepy hobo villain lair, was a crumpled red envelope. My blank check. I must have stopped breathing or gasped or something, because my book immediately perked up.

The book looked at me. I looked at the book. Suddenly, it shot up off the dresser, flying right at that check. Spine open.

"No!" I lunged, arms out, racing to beat it, screaming, "DON'T EAT THAT! NOOOOOOOOO!"

Snap. Crunk. Thump. Ow.

That was the sound of my employee manual snapping shut. Around the blank check. And me, hitting my head smack on the closet door and sliding face down into the carpet. The room spun for a hot minute, and when I came to, that stupid book was Muppet chomping down on my check.

I grabbed the little red end of it before it sunk all the way down in. "Let go. Bad book. Bad! I need this. NEED. You don't understand! Please let go."

It stopped wiggling, looked at me, and whined. "Yeah. You get it. Good boy. Now let go. Uncle Lloyd needs to cash this so he can keep his job and his life can go back to normal."

It eased up. *Phew.* "Thanks, dude."

But then it yanked, once, really hard, and slurp, it snatched it right out of my hand and swallowed it whole. It was a fake out. Just like the cleaning crew and the pack of Red Vines. Man, this book was crafty.

"That's it. Stupid book. I'll shake it out of you." I grabbed at it. It dodged. "Give it. Give it here!"

That book looked right at me and turned to page eleven. The portal form? Huh. Was it trying to tell me something? The page moved. I squinted. All the little blank spaces on the form were filling in, as if written in by some magical hand. Suddenly, a green portal opened up, and my book shot me two middle fingers. Yeah, I know it's a book, but I also know when a book is flipping me off. Then it dove right in and disappeared.

"Wow. That's a twist. So, what's Plan B?"

"There's no Plan B! I fought off a horde of zombies so a book—a book!—could eat my reward! Is it hot in here? Because my head is about to boil. You wonder why I didn't want to read the damned thing. Now you know. This shit ain't normal." My brain reeled. "I need that blank check!"

"That book could be anywhere." Angel said. "Best not to count on ever getting it back."

"Gack!"

No. No way. I would find that book, and when I did, I would get that blank check back, one way or another. I didn't know where all that food went after it swallowed, but I was sure as hell gonna find out. If it goes in, it has to come out, right?

I suddenly went cold. Oh god. Does that mean? Yes. Yes, it does. As they say, do what must be done. I'd get my blank check. It'll be just like that time Gertrude swallowed Grandma Linda's favorite rhinestone earring, and Mom had to sort through the litter box until it came out the other end. What goes in, must come out, right?

"Okay, so when you're done freaking out. Grab the tape and get to work, will you?" Angel said. "And fill me with filtered water this time. Tap water chafes."

CHAPTER 18

THE SECOND I stepped in the door, DeeDee grabbed me. She dragged me behind the two liter pop bottle pyramid and ducked down. "Please tell me you found something we could use in your employee manual."

Uh yeah. Only the solution to everything. But all I could do was shake my head. Because I had no idea where that book had gone.

"I was afraid of that. All right, then. I've got no choice. I'm opening the gate early."

"What? Why?"

"Look at this place! The ghosts are not happy. I don't know what went wrong. It was going so well, but now they're all so...restless. See?"

I peeked around the pop bottle pyramid.

"These records are not for sale!" Kevin punched the hipster ghost. His leg went right through, because the hipster was still blue mist. But Kevin? He was solid, white and stretched out to the size of a giant angry beaver, screaming with rage. "I SAID NO STORE CREDIT!"

Hunter trotted by with his leash in his mouth. His foaming mouth. His eyes were black, he zigged and zagged erratically, like he was frantic. Or desperate. Or, you know, rabid? He suddenly jumped up, clean over the chip rack, into aisle two. Except that his back leg must have clipped the top, because the entire pretzel section toppled, sending bags flying.

The little old guy? He stood by the slushies, staring at his fake letter. Actually holding it. And the bus lady? All I saw were bits of candy wrappers flying up over aisle three.

"STUPID HIPSTERS!" Kevin knocked the credit card machine to the floor.

"This is going downhill fast. I'm declaring emergency mode," DeeDee said. "I called Doc. He's trying to summon the reapers. You flip the Go Away charm. I'm opening the gate early."

"WHAT? That won't help!"

"I'm bringing in Bubby for backup. And Morty, too, if you can believe that. Someone has to entertain Candy."

Candy gyrated on top of the hot food station. She looked at me, winked, and starting sucking on a hot dog like it was a. Well. Ahem. You know. She must be solid, because man. She was really chewing on that thing.

"Uh. Candy seems fine." Oof. Is it hot in here?

Then Candy said, "Can you ask the DJ to put on some better music? The Happy Hour crowd's dead. They don't tip very well."

The little old guy perked up. Clearly, he was with her in spirit, because he tried to slip his ghostly letter into her garter.

"CHEAPSKATES!" She growled. Literally. Her voice went deep, throaty, and her mouth split into a giant row of fangs.

Um. Yeah. DeeDee had a point. "So, what's the plan, then?"

DeeDee held up a red DVD envelope. "This should buy us two hours."

"A movie?" She couldn't be serious. "*That's* the plan?"

"Well, since the flashlights didn't work, yes. You know, *Poltergeist* wasn't very accurate. I'm starting to think Steven Spielberg didn't know anything about ghosts."

"You think?"

"Okay, Mr. Sassy. We just need to keep them all busy. Buy some time to look through every book, every spell, every artifact and hopefully find a way to contact the reapers and contain these ghosts. Got it?"

She moved, but I grabbed her and pulled her back down. "What makes you think a bunch of angry poltergeists are gonna watch a movie? Wait. Is *Poltergeist* the movie? We don't need to give these guys any ideas!"

"No, silly. I'm breaking out the big guns. I'm tapping the power of the Swayze."

"Phew. Okay. *Roadhouse.* Good plan. That will definitely work on Kevin."

"Not *Roadhouse.* Even better. *Dirty Dancing.*"

"You're kidding."

"Uh, no. Everybody loves *Dirty Dancing.* Everybody. It's go time. Ready? Be careful."

She jumped up and pulled the emergency override. The beer cave lit up bright blue.

Dirty Dancing? We're doomed.

"Flip the charm. Go!" DeeDee pushed me into action.

I crawled across the store, around and behind the counter. And through the hipster, which felt like pouring ice cold gel right into the marrow of all my bones. Brrrr. Weird.

But, on the plus side, Kevin didn't notice me. He was so enraged by the hipster that he had picked up one of the cheap cigarette racks. He held it over his head, shaking it like a weapon. Packs of Eagle 20s rained down on me as I reached up up up and flipped the Go Away charm.

I crawled back down the length of the counter, grabbing every creepy book I could find along the way. I shuffled past the neatly labeled jars of herbs and rocks and crystals. There had to be something in this store that could save us. Then I saw it. A reflection, a twinkle of light. Oh, no. Wait. Never mind. I thought it was a magic trumpet or something, but it was Angel eight ball, wobbling on the shelf, triangle spinning uncontrollably. "What's wrong with you? I just taped you up!"

"Lloyd? Is that you? I can't see you. Is everything all right?"

"No, it's not all right. Help me!"

"Lloyd? Lloyd?"

Great. Angel chats all day long, rattling off checklists of stuff for me to do, but now? Nothing. Useless angel.

"Step aside, my man. You're in desperate need of a DJ." Morty stood over me, wearing giant DJ headphones, a black velvet track suit, and a hilariously huge fake gold chain around his neck.

"Zorro couldn't seal the deal?"

Morty slumped. "No. But I got it this time. Watch and learn."

Morty stepped over me, and hip checked the angry, beaver-sized Kevin away from the stereo. He pressed the intercom button, leaned into the mic, and purred, "And now, please welcome the sweet, delicious Candy to the Sinbad's main stage! Open your wallets, gentlemen, because this Candy would love to lick your lollipop."

Ew. Gross. But you ever want to see a ghost light up? That's how you do it. Man. She giggled and really started jiggling the goods in earnest. She bent over and—wait. What was I doing? Oh yeah. Crawling, but dude. It was slow going. You try walking on your knees while carrying creepy old magic books. They had to weigh fifty pounds!

I rounded the counter. Hunter hopped out into the aisle, and I ducked behind the boner pill and phone charger end cap. He dropped his leash and stood up. "And one. And two."

Oh. He's doing squats. At least he's back to normal!

"Hurrrrr. Hurrrrr. Hurrrrrrrr."

What the? I looked behind me. Zack was splayed out across aisle five, lying on the floor wearing only his boxer shorts and one gym sock. A dirty gym sock, end slipping off his bone toes, forming a puffy pocket. He was covered in empty crunched up cans of Natty Light and spent Pupperoni wrappers. "Hurrrr. Herrrrr. Hurrrrrrrr."

I crawled up to him. Ow. Ow. Ow. "Zack. What are you doing? Get up. The ghosts are spoiling. We need to find cover."

I said it as quietly as I could, but I'm not sure he heard me over his inconsolable sobs. He sang between cries. Something about hearing a chick calling but he couldn't come to the phone? Whatever. Song kinda sucked, but he repeated it over and over. Between sobs. Yep. Zack was sing sobbing.

"Are you okay?" I leaned in over his bone face.

He tipped up a can of Natty Lite, draining the last dregs out of the bottom. He crunched the can and dropped it. "Hurrrrrrr. Hurrrrrr. Hurrrrr. I want to die."

For God's sake. Seriously? Now? "I don't, so come on. Let's go."

I tugged on his ulna, but he didn't budge. For a boney dude, he was a like a sack of jelly.

"I caaaaaaaan't." Tears streaked down his cheekbones. "Look."

He thrust a red wrapper into my hands. Oh. No. It wasn't a wrapper.

Hell Report
The latest scoop delivered to all Nine Circles
Falling Angel Alert: Reaper office robbed, Golden Scythe No. 1 Suspect

The Office of Efficient Eternal Soul Transference was robbed last week for the first time in the agency's history. The Grim Bureau of Investigations has been hush-hush about the case, refusing to release any details about what was stolen or who might be responsible. Although anonymous insider sources say only two items were taken: A Golden Scythe and a pack of blank reaping scrolls. The missing golden scythe belonged to disgraced reaper Zackumzaphiel-hermesiappotholonian, who is under investigation for unauthorized soul reaping. He was stripped of this scythe, which was stored in the agency safe pending the results of an inquiry into all of his past and present reaping activities. Investigators would not confirm or deny these rumors. An official spokesreaper said, "We are reviewing security footage and forensic evidence. We are thoroughly checking inventory so that we can account for all that is missing. Not that anything is missing. But maybe something is missing. We aren't saying. We will conduct a thorough investigation, as per standard operating procedure, but it will take time and will not be easy. As you all know, we are unlike other angels. We all look alike, and reapers don't have fingerprints. Which sucks. So yeah. There's that."

But rumors are already swirling, so much so that the celestial AngelFace app had to be temporarily shut down to stop the spread of misinformation. The rumors say Zackumzaphielhermesiappotholonian himself is responsible for the thefts. "It would't surprise me. I mean, you should see where he's living. It's a madhouse. Full of souls. Wall to wall ghosts. He's obviously been killing people left and right," said Yurialaempholalmodephianous, a former coworker who was reassigned to janitorial services in 1945 after mistakenly delivering Adolf Hitler to Heaven's Gate. He has been embroiled in a bitter legal feud with the All Creatures Great & Dead network over rights to the video clip of the incident ever since.

"At first, I didn't want to believe the rumors, but then I saw it with my own eye sockets. He's definitely guilty. It's like he's killing just for fun at this point. If I were in charge, I would throw him in the pit and be done with him. I'm devastated. He was my best friend. My brother. You think you know someone."

The agency denies Yurialaempholalmodephianous' outrageous claims. A spokesreaper laughed out loud when Hell Report inquired about the accusations, saying, "Oh, that's a good one. He's got a lot of nerve criticizing another reaper's dereliction of duty. That's rich. Really Rich. You've seen the video footage, right? Classic!"

"If Yuri gets my job, I'll die. He took Hitler to heaven! Why is this happening to meeeee? It's like I'm cursed!"

"That's it. I'm done." Yeah. Something snapped. "You listen to me, Zack. Did you do this? Did you steal this stuff?"

"Well, no."

"See? It's fine. This thing reads like a bad celebrity gossip mag. It's all rumors. None of it is fact! Ignore it. It's trash. He is not gonna get your job. Now come on. Let's go. I need you."

"You do?" He wiped his snotty nose with his phalanges and sniffled.

"Yeah. So pull yourself together. We've got ghosts to wrangle."

"Oh." He stood up and looked around. "Huh. So it's not just the pizza guy. Keegan went kind of nuts after I won the last round of *Wrestle Dude Pow*. I thought he was just a sore loser, but..."

"Yeah, yeah. Whatever. So, any tips on how to handle spoiled souls?"

"No. I've been on time for every reap I've been assigned to for more than eight thousand years. I've never had a soul spoil before. I don't care what the papers say. Huuuuuuurrrrrrrrr."

Gah! Enough with the crying. I ducked as a whole box of Sweet Tarts flew over the aisle and nearly smacked me in the head. The bus lady growled, "Neccoooooo. Waferrrrrrrrrrrrrrrr" like a crazed lunatic.

I grabbed that reaper by the humerus: "Zack. If your boss or your girlfriend walked in the door right now, would you want them to see you like this? Or do you want them to see a reaper in peak physical condition? A reaper in charge. A reaper who is ready to be back on the job?"

"Uh." Zack scratched his skull. "The last one?"

"Then show them. Show them all what you can do. Look around. You're a reaper. Now reap! Show your bosses who's boss. You're not gonna let souls spoil on your watch, are you?"

"Well, um. No?"

"You don't sound sure."

"No!"

"Good. Now put on some clothes. We've got souls to reap!"

Zack stood up, and his chest puffed out. He looked regal. Well, except for the boxer shorts and the orange Cheetoh dust all over his rib cage. But still. He floated off to the cooler.

"Wow. That was quite the pep talk." DeeDee crawled down the aisle. "Good job. I'm impressed."

I suddenly felt warm and fuzzy inside. A weird sensation. Proud? Dude. It'd been a while since anyone told me I'd done a good job. Hold on. Just let me soak it in for a minute. Because dude. All I hear outside of this aisle is growling and screaming and candy and chips bags ripping and Hunter saying, and "One, and two. And three," and Kevin yelling, "NO STORE CREDIT."

I peeked over the aisle. These ghosts? Not so blue, not so see-through. Definitely solid. Definitely off their routine. And getting worse.

The old man circled the hot food station, waving his arms. At first I thought it was like a weird Candy worship thing. Then I saw his letter—the fake one DeeDee made for him—floating in the air above him. That letter floated over to the stereo, right over to Glug, happily swimming in his Colossal Super Slurp cup, which suddenly rose up up up off the counter, floated over to the slushy machines, and *thunk*. *Sploosh*. Upended. Glug spilled right into the top of the Kelpie Kiwi machine.

Shit.

His plastic toy squid plunked to the floor.

Double shit. Not good. Not good at all. I had a bad feeling about this.

Faust kicked open the stockroom door. Thank God. He'll save us! Maybe.

Or not. He marched the cleaning crew—outfitted in mini cover-alls, hard hats and safety goggles, and dragging a jack hammer?—out through the front door. They stood around, marking the sidewalk with chalk, chittering to each other like they were trying to decide where to dig.

Faust didn't even notice the floating letter or the angry shaking undulating grind of the Kelpie Kiwi machine.

Bubby stood in the chip aisle, digging through the racks. He raised a bag of Smart Pop and waved at me. I motioned for him to run. "Get out of there!"

He just shrugged and dug around for more Smart Pop.

"What's Bubby's job again?"

"Hmm. Human shield? Well, bug shield. Something. Honestly, I don't know yet. This was a last-minute plan," DeeDee said. "But if nothing else, he's a great distraction."

As if on cue, Bubby stood up and undulated, his rows of claw-tipped legs moving to the beat of the music as the *Dirty Dancing* opening credits rolled. One row of legs pumped back and forth while the other. Wait. "Is he doing the sprinkler dance? Seriously?"

Yep. I was quickly losing faith in DeeDee's plan.

"What? It's already working. See?"

All the ghosts suddenly stopped. But no, they were not watching Bubby bust a move. They had zoned in on the TV.

"See? Told you. Everyone likes *Dirty Dancing*. Everyone. Now give me the books. Hurry. We don't have much time." She filched them out of my hands. "I've already been through these a hundred times, but maybe I missed something. I sure hope Doc is having better luck. Oh. Is this one yours?"

"What?" I turned around, fast.

My employee manual sat calmly in DeeDee's lap, pretending to be a real book. Well, you know what I mean. A real, calm, immobile book. "Grab that book. Everything we need is inside!"

Literally. I was gonna reach down into that thing so far and rip my blank check out of its pulpy paper innards. But as soon as it heard my voice, it stood up, took one look at me, and made a run for it.

"Don't let it get away!" I charged.

But that book moved at lightning speed. It split for aisle three. Again. I rounded the corner, jumped into the aisle and screamed. "Aha! I've got you."

Fwump.

"Owwwwww!" I dropped like a rock. A sharp, deep pain ricocheted through my groin. Kicked...in...nuts.

A face appeared above me. An angry, white face. With pigtails. The Cookie Scout. AGAIN?

"Where are my cookies?" She scowled. "Did you eat them all?"

"What are you doing here? I killed you. Twice!"

She kicked me again. Right in the gut. I howled.

"You stole my UNICORN!" She kicked me. Again. Right in the hands this time, because I was not dumb enough to leave nuts unshielded twice. I rolled up in a nut-crunched ball, aching hands holding my aching junk.

"I want my unicoooooooooooooooorn!" She screamed, her saddle shoes stomped, crunching holes in the linoleum, and her mouth split open, morphing into that familiar, terrible row of jagged black teeth. Her hands stretched out into claws. She descended on me, clawing at my pants.

"Aaaah! What are you doing? No! No!" I wrestled and tried to roll away.

She clawed at my pockets like she was trying to turn up my wallet? She grunted. I couldn't make out all the words, but it sounded like "Sum...badge...doll?Do...take...corn!"

"Do I take corn?"

I had to ask. Anything to make her stop, but that just made her more mad.

She reared up and attacked, powered by rage. Before she could bring a claw down on me, I grabbed that scout by the shoulders and rolled, wresting control of her with the sheer power of chub. It actually worked. It's like I had super powered love handles. Huh. Well, look at that. I rolled. That ghost personal trainer paid off!

"Ha! I got you this time! You menace!" I held her down with my pudge. "You ruined my life!"

"Oh. Boo hoo. Whiner."

She smacked me. Right across the face. Then her ice cold body cracked in my hands.

Crick. Crack. Creee.

Dude. That felt like it hurt. No wonder she was so mad.

I looked at her. She looked at me. Her fang-lined mouth snapped and howled as the rest of her body stretched out below me, longer and taller. Her spiked tail popped out and bonked me right on the head. "OW!"

It fwacked, upturning the holiday clearance tub. Christmas leftovers spilled across the floor. CDs and tons of fat candy cane sticks and twisty lollipops that looked like unicorn horns. The scout hooked her claws into me and yanked. I grabbed a weapon. Or two. Or not. Because my hands came up with a Taylor Swift CD in one hand and a big twisty lollipop in the other. *Shit.*

"UNICORN!" She screamed.

"You play with a unicorn, you get the horn!" I sunk that delicious pink sugar swirl lollipop right into her mean demon mouth. Her eyes went wide. Her body stopped moving for a second.

Crunch. Crunch. Crunch.

No. That wasn't her bones morphing into the monstrous form of the day. Or her monstrous body about to explode into goop again. Nope. Those were yummy noises.

"Mmmm. Nummm. Mmmummm. Mummmm." Yep. She was eating the lollipop. She sucked it all in and crunched it down to crumbs in a split second. Then her eyes turned to slits, and she growled. "No free cookies, fat boy! UNICORN!"

Well, so much for that. I raised that Taylor Swift CD, ready to bring it down like a knife. She threw me backward, right into the shelf, so hard my brain rattled.

Ow. My all of me hurt.

She closed in on me. Angrier. Eyes black. I threw that Taylor Swift CD right at her gaping, foaming mouth. She smacked it away and growled, "No Tay Tay. I like Katy Perry!"

And she lunged. I closed my eyes. I'm a goner. Any minute now. Yep. She's gonna get me. Huh. What's taking so long? I opened my eyes and saw nothing but white eyes. Eight of them. And Josh

Groban. Bubby held the Cookie Scout upside down by her tail, as she thrashed and kicked, claws out. He waved a Josh Groban *Noel* CD in one of his claw-tipped legs.

Bleeeeeeee. Blurrrrrrp. Blup.

"Kevin's never gonna let you play that."

Bleeep Blooooop.

"Yeah. I know. I really need to find that book."

CHAPTER 19

IT WASN'T HARD, because my employee manual ran right behind Bubby and that thrashing, upside down demon scout. I scrambled after it. But by the time I made it to the end of the aisle, it had disappeared. Again.

Seriously? Gah! I needed that blank check! I tiptoed around, ducking out of site of passing ghosts, checking every crevice, every end cap, looking for any sign of movement. Which was surprisingly easy, considering. Because there had been a definite lull in the poltergeist activity.

Hunter squatted, but every other ghost's eyes were glued to the TV, and the hypnotic hip thrusts of Patrick Swayze. Dude. I will never again doubt the power of the Swayze. I never thought I'd say this, but thank God for *Dirty Dancing*.

DeeDee was a genius. She leaned over the counter, grabbing books while the ghosts were distracted.

Until Kevin screamed, and his fat white arms—four of them—balled up into fists and waved angrily in the air. "Nooooo! Baby just got to Kellerman's. You aren't playing that shit on my stereo. That song sucks. It ain't metal, and you know it."

"Sorry, dude. I gotta score tonight. Have to. I'm starving! I've waited so long, and this is my ace into that hole." DJ Morty pressed play and a guitar riff poured from the speakers, drowning out the movie.

It was a guy singing something about cherry pies? And sweet surprises? I don't know it was, but it didn't take long to figure out he wasn't singing about actual pies.

"HATE...WARRANT!" Kevin shook with rage. But it was more like convulsions, quick. His body seized back and forth. He suddenly grew bigger. And thicker. And whiter. His leg hit the stereo, and the music zrrrrped and died out.

"Come on, man! Are you all trying to kill me?" Morty harmphed. "I'm starving! I can't wait much longer. *Cherry Pie* was my ticket into her pie! You can watch *Dirty Dancing* anytime!"

Candy flipped her hair back, took one look at the TV screen and said, "I love this movie. It's so romantic."

Morty perked up. He was over the counter in a split second. He extended a hand to his ghost unicorn, and said, "Nobody puts Candy in the corner."

She squealed. Then she leapt into his arms, giggling. He kicked open the stockroom door and carried her through like a bride across a threshold. Well, then. Somebody's about to get a happy ending, in all possible meanings of the phrase.

Zack floated out a few seconds later. "Uh. That creepy pervert guy is about to make sweet love to Candy on my bed."

Um, no. The love would not be sweet.

Zack's whole body looked like it was wilting. "I miss my girl-friend. Errrrrrrrrrrrrrrrr. All food tastes like ash since she left me. There's no joy in my life. Everything is but a darkened, burned-out shell. A joyless shadow of my former life. I have nothing to live for. Uuuuuuuuh. Huuuuuurrrrrrrrr."

Well. Here we go again. But at least he was dressed. The robes looked clean, too.

Zack stuck his mouth directly under the Kelpie Kiwi, and let the slush splurt full blast right into his mouth. "Sugar is the only thing that makes me hapeeeeeeeeeeeeee. Hurr hurrrrr. I'm so sad. Eeeeeeeeeeeeeeeeeeeeeeee. Ew. This stuff tastes fishy. Oh. Hi Glug." He suddenly stopped. And stood up. "I don't believe it. Guys! GUYS!"

He whirled around and jumped up and down, excited. I wasn't sure why. He had slush all down his rib cage. He'd even left the machine on. A snake of slush poured out behind him, piling up on the floor. Kelpie Kiwi / Glug spilled all over the linoleum, the welcome mat, down the fronts of the cabinets.

DeeDee didn't notice. She stood behind the counter with her nose buried in a book, speed reading. Her finger moved across the page, back and forth, up and down.

A very long, very sharp scythe appeared in Zack's hand, shimmering like it'd just beamed in from another dimension. "I've been reinstated! They must have reversed my suspension!" He hugged that glittering golden scythe to his chest, kissing it with mwa mwa mwa noises, as he whirled in a circle, excited. "I think I'm gonna cry iiiiiiiiii eeeeeeeeeeeeeeeeeeeeeeeee."

"Fantastic! Can you please reap all these ghosts before the movie ends?" I asked.

DeeDee had stopped reading. She saw the scythe, put the book down, and moved closer to Kevin. It was subtle. Even Kevin didn't notice. But I knew. She wasn't gonna let Kevin go without a fight.

"Can you reap this guy first?" Kevin thumbed a leg back at the hipster. "He offers me store credit again, I'm gonna punch him straight into the first circle."

"I can't reap him without a scroll. Herrrrrrrrrr. Herrrrrf." Zack sobbed. But I think it was tears of joy this time. "Hurrrr. Hurrrrrrrr. I'm so ha ha haaaaaaaa peeeeeeee. I couldn't have done it without youuuuuuuuu."

"I'm happy for you, man." I said it, and I meant it.

A weird parchment roll, wrapped in a black ribbon, appeared in mid-air. "Look. A reaping scroll! It must be my next assignment. Oh my gosh. This is the best day ever. Zack is back!"

A feeling washed over me. Relief? I felt a hundred pounds lighter. *Phew!* Seriously. Just in time, right? The reapers really came through for us. Zack was happy, and the need to locate my employee manual was a little less pressing now that someone was finally here to remove our ghost problem.

"Well, at least they're all happy. Before they go." DeeDee looked at each of them with sad eyes. She was so close to Kevin, she was almost on top of him.

"Why are you sad?" Then it hit me. Because we all knew what reaping meant. A soul left earth, and moved on to wherever that final destination may be. Forever. It was the natural order of things. But it was definitely an end.

But no one else seemed sad. Hunter lunged in place. Glug danced, happily melding with the slushy. Zack had his nose holes deep in that scroll, reading. The old guy and the bus lady? They were dancing by the 2-liter pop bottle pyramid, inspired by the power of *Dirty Dancing*. A little too inspired. Um. Yeah. She had her leg up around that old guy, grinding. She yelled, "I feel alive!"

I averted my eyes. You would, too. Trust me. It was like watching two tumbleweeds porking.

Something tugged on my sock. It was my employee manual. And it was really ripping into my sock. "Oh, gee. There you are. Thanks for the assist today. I really appreciate all your help."

I didn't know if books understood sarcasm, but I poured it on so thick it couldn't help but get the message. It sat up. Its spine bent this way and that, like it was looking around. Then it pointed. At the television. The Swayze zzzzrted off. Then something knocked the TV right off the mount. It crashed to the floor and shattered. Oh.

Oh shit. Zack better hurry. We were out of time.

"Want...my...SWAYZE...BABY...CARRIED...WATERMEL-ON!" I whirled around. It was Kevin. Rage Kevin. White. Angry ghost Kevin.

He wasn't the only one. The happiness? All gone. All the ghosts creaked and cracked and groaned and made ghastly uuuuuuuhhhhh-hhhh sounds as they stretched and grew and changed.

"Kevin. Calm down. It's okay. I'll put on Dio. It'll be all okay. I promise." DeeDee slipped down behind the counter, between an angry Kevin and a still somehow very blue hipster.

"Get out of there. Get away from them!"

"No. She said. I won't let Kevin go. Not like this." She reached for one of Kevin's Black Sabbath albums, but it rose up up up into the air, out of DeeDee's reach, then bloop. The record slipped out of the sleeve and crashed to the ground.

Chink.

Oh shit. It broke.

The ghost hipster said, "Hands off. I made a deal to buy those. Store credit."

My book tugged harder on my sock. "Give me the blank check. I need it!"

Another record floated into the air, then crashed to pieces. Then another. Kevin's mouth split into a row of black spike fangs. He picked up the register and threw it. DeeDee ducked. It chinked into the front window, then dropped, spewing coins and bills. DeeDee was trapped back there with two angry ghosts.

Kevin moved in on her. And a shadow closed in over me. I looked up. Hunter. Big. Wide. Mean. Angry. His face moved in close to mine. He growled. "Give me twenty."

Gulp. Nope. Not now. I had to get to DeeDee. My book tugged at my sock. I screamed, "Zack. What are you waiting for? Reap! Reap!"

Zack floated toward me. *Phew.* Thank goodness.

"Hold on for just another minute, DeeDee."

Hunter's red squeaky bone floated in the air, up over his head, over mine. Hunter's giant white hand stretched into a claw and reached for that bone, ready to snatch it out of the air.

Hunter's paw came down.

Zack's scythe moved.

Hurry Zack! REAP!

A sharp, searing pain cut through my neck. Suddenly, I couldn't breathe. No air. *I'm drowning.* Then the room stopped moving. It was like a still photo. The pain. It stopped. It was just...gone. But so was every other feeling. Well, every physical feeling. My brain still reeled, like a methhead hamster running in a wheel, going nowhere.

The whole room stuck, frozen in time, except for me. And Zack. He said, "I'm so sorry, man. My first assignment was you. Both of you. You're dead."

He showed me the scroll. Two names. Lloyd Lamb Wallace. DeeDee Bertha Woznowski.

"What are the chances? Talk about a bummer. But no hard feelings, right?"

CHAPTER 20

Zack's scythe came down. Right on my head.

"Nooooooooooooooooooo!"

Bonk.

"Oh."

When it hit me, it didn't hurt.

Huh. Weird. It was actually a relief, like I'd been squeezed out of a really tight toothpaste tube, and I could finally breathe again. "Thanks, man. Wait."

I looked at my hands. They were blue. And see-through. And so was the rest of me.

Holy shit. "DeeDee. Look at me. I'm blue!"

I looked up, right at some poor guy who was covered in blood, clutching a giant open gash on his neck and face. "Aaaaaaah!"

I nearly fell over. Hunter's monster claw sunk so deep, his head was nearly cut clean off. It was hanging by a spine. Literally. Jesus. If he weren't so fat, it would have broken him clean in half! Talk about a gruesome way to go. The monster paw was still in his neck, claw poking through shredded skin. Dude. He reached right through the poor guy to grab a red squeaky bone floating, suspended in air, behind him.

Wait.

Wait a minute. I stared at the curve of his face, the blood on his shirt. I could just make out the words "This T-Shirt Is Haunted" on the front of it. Fuck. That poor dead sucker was me.

"Aaaaaaaaaaaaaaaaaaaaaaaaaaaaah!" I screamed for a long time, staring at my body. "Aaaaaaaaaaaaah! FUCK! I'm dead!"

God damn it. Hunter killed me. I knew deep down in my gut. I never should have stepped foot in a gym! Wow. My mom was gonna kill me when she found out I was dead.

Time seemed to be frozen all around me. I had the sensation of rising and falling, like I was floating in the wave pool at Zoombezi Bay. It took me a while to realize it was because my feet weren't touching the floor. I was floating. All that screaming moved me up and down like a carousel horse. "Fuck fuck fuck. I'm really dead!"

No. No way. Can't be happening. I tried to jump back into my body, but it felt like swimming in jelly. Plus, I just popped right back out on the other side. I hopped through my body and through the counter. DeeDee was by the stereo. She was stone still. Her head was down. Frozen in time. "DeeDee?"

Her shirt was wet. A white spike rose from the middle of the pool. One of Kevin's legs. It went right through the hipster ghost's blue gut and hit DeeDee by mistake. Kevin was frozen in mid-air, legs reaching for his *Rainbow Rising* album. "Oh, no. Not Kevin. DeeDee. She's—"

I cried, but nothing came out of my eyes.

"Dead. Yeah. Bummer. That's what I was trying to tell you. See?" Zack stood next to me, wagging his scroll in my face. "Geesh. Bertha. Can you believe it? Such an ugly name for such a hot chick. Shame to have that carved on your headstone forever."

Dead? "No. No way. This can't be happening. Call Doc. He can save us. Doc can bring us back." My voice was a hiss, like gas. "He brought Kevin back!"

Well, almost. I mean, he tried.

"Sorry, dude."

"Call Faust!"

"Well, you can ask him, but don't get your hopes up. I mean, he's *a* devil, but he's not *the* devil. If he were *the* devil, maybe."

Zack pointed. Faust must have stepped in through the front room door at just the wrong moment. Because he too had been poked clean through the middle, by the old guy with the letter. His arm had torn right through Faust's stomach, trying to get the letter. It floated in the air behind Faust. There was a pool of blood on his coveralls. He looked down at the huge red stain, with a vague look of casual annoyance. Unlike everything else, Faust was moving.

"My. This will never do." He wiggled backward and *spllrrrrrrrrrrrrrrp*. Ew. Yeah. That was the sound of him yanking himself off the old guy ghost's stabby arm. When he'd freed himself, his midsection was nothing but a gaping hole filled with red mush.

Ew. I could not unsee that.

"My, that stings. This won't do at all." He arched his back and rolled his head side to side, groaning. Suddenly a giant—and I mean giant—pair of shiny black wings shot right out of his back, ripping his blazer and chink. One wingtip hit the side of the slushy machines, the other ran right across the front window. His skin flashed red for a moment, and I saw...horns? Big fat ones, looping up and down around the side of his head.

Hole. Eee. Crap. If I still had a throat, it'd have a lump in it. He really was a devil. I watched as the hole in his abs closed. Smooth olive human skin knitted itself over what looked like a bright red set of washboard abs.

He looked at me. And at all of us, and said, "Well, this is unfortunate. Bad night at work, I see."

"Help us. We can't die. Not like this!"

"I'm afraid you can," Faust said.

"Do something!"

"I'm afraid I can't. There are rules about such things, you see. I, as a devil, cannot touch a soul until it has officially been doomed. I can influence and interact with living beings, and lord over doomed souls, but am powerless in the space in between. Unless it is the biblical apocalypse, but as unfortunate as this is, it doesn't qualify. You're a smart young man. You will come up with a solution. A solution that is pure of heart, without selfish motivation, I'm sure."

He looked at me and winked. Winked? I mean, I think. Weird time to wink. It was subtle, like a twitch. "And if not, well. May I say you were, in fact, the best crew I have ever had. None of you are a match for Junebug, but it was an honor to work with you. Such pure hearts, except for Kevin. But, may the judges have mercy on his soul. I have heard the second time's a charm. "

Faust casually stepped back into the stockroom like this was any other night, and his employees weren't all dead.

"No. No. No. This can't be happening. We're not supposed to die. We're the good guys. We're supposed to win. This isn't fair!"

"It's okay, bro. Let it all out. Go through all the stages of grief. Here.."

He handed me a scroll that said, "Welcome, newly departed: A handy afterlife checklist."

"Just hurry up. Okay? We need to get a move on. I have to get all three of you delivered on time. Or two? I'm not sure what I'm supposed to do with that roach guy. I better call Head Office. I can't afford to mess up. It's my first day back."

"Where's DeeDee? Her soul, I mean." I broke away from Zack and float-looped around the chips and the candy, looking for another ghostly blue shape in the store. But there wasn't one. No. No no no no no. "Where is she?"

"Relax. She's not out yet. I tapped you first," Zack said.

"Out?"

"Of her body. She's still in there. But don't worry. She's not in pain or anything. I opted to suspend time. You know, give you a little extra to cope." Zack turned his scythe. A tiny button flashed on a little control panel on the side of it. "I normally pop everyone at once, but I wanted some extra time to double check the paperwork. With the roach guy and all these ghosts, this isn't exactly a standard case. And I don't want to end up like Yuri. That guy. Did I tell you about the time he took Hitler to Heaven? Woo. Man. Seriously. Hilarious! I mean, how do you even? He'll never live that down. Anyway, you're first. Let's go."

He grabbed me by the fat bit of my arm and tugged me to the front door. He looked through the glass. And looked some more. And scratched his chin. "Huh. That's weird. I don't see the white light or a fiery pit. Do you? Usually it's all ready to go. Maybe they haven't decided what to do with you. Or they're behind. There's a big audit up there, you know."

Outside looked, well, just like outside to me, except that nothing was moving. There was even a bat, hanging suspended in midair, looking like he was painted on the moon.

"I'm not going anywhere. There has to be another way. I am not leaving. I can't die like this!"

Zack shrugged. "Well, no one gets to choose."

"What?"

"No one gets to choose how they die. You get what you get, man. No use complaining when it's all done. It's not like anyone else has it any better." He looked outside again. "Well, I don't see a destination, so I'll just take you up to Head Office and see if they know where you're going."

"I'm not leaving!" If I still had a body, I'd be hyperventilating. The physical feeling wasn't there, but the emotion was. Sheer panic. "No. I'm not leaving. Nope. No way."

"There's no use fighting it. Everyone dies. I mean, look at you. There's no coming back from that. Even if you hopped back in, there's no way that body could live." He pointed at my fat corpse, skewered like a kabob. "Sorry dude, but this is how it ends. All right. Let's go."

If I had cheeks, they would be on fire, and if I still had a body—a real body—it'd be drenched in sweat, because I was full on panicking. I was not going to hell, and I was not leaving DeeDee. I looked back at her body again, and something inside me snapped. "We're not going anywhere."

I put my foot down. Okay, I tried. My foot wasn't exactly solid. It went through the linoleum, which kind of felt like sinking my foot into a bucket of nails, but it was enough to make my point.

"Fighting it isn't going to get you anywhere. We've been reaping people since before there were people. We've used the same system for millennia. It's all very by the book, and when it's your time. It's your time. Although." He scratched his chin. "You know what? Maybe this will help. You were such a great friend, I'll throw in one free Life Flashes Before Your Eyes. Ready?"

"A what?"

Zack touched my forehead with the tip of his scythe, and everything around me moved really fast. I stood still as the world swirled around and around, disintegrating into a grey whirling cloud of shapes. It was dizzying, so it took me a minute to realize everything was moving backward. In space, in time. Then I saw pictures. Well, moments. It was hard to describe.

I'm in my room. I shove my new employee welcome pack and my employee manual into my desk drawer and forget about it. The book pushes the drawer open, but I push it back in.

I'm in bed, asleep. It's daytime. Light shines through the window. My employee manual wiggles into my bed, next to Gertrude, and tries to snuggle with us. I wake up, scream, and throw it in the closet.

I'm chanting to resurrect Kevin. I see the page number, up close, behind my hairy knee. Page 39, not page 33. The book's pages flutter, trying to turn to the right page, but I wouldn't let it. I forced it back open. I chanted the wrong words.

I'm at Bubba's. My employee manual jumped out of my hands when I tried to wrestle it off the gate panel. It hit something. A dark figure, a shadow, working the controls. An invisible creature. It moved to hit me, but my book took the hit instead.

DeeDee is alive, trying to grab Kevin's *Rainbow Rising* album.

My employee manual tugs on my sock. It pointed at Hunter's red bone. It tried to warn me, but I didn't even look.

Huh. All this time, my employee manual had been trying to help me. It wanted to help me do my job. Be good at my job. But I treated it like a monster.

The world spins again, and it doesn't stop. I see myself. Yelling. I say, "Don't blame me!" I say, "It's not my fault!" over and over. The same words. I'm in different clothes, yelling at different people, at different times. Mom. DeeDee. Kevin. "Don't blame me. It's not my fault."

My heart sunk. Was this how I spent my life? Was this who I am? Never being good at anything? Never taking responsibility for the trouble my actions and inactions caused?

The room stopped, suddenly. Zack stood next to me, reading the panel on his scythe. "So, I..uh, accidentally had this thing set to Hard Truth? So you probably didn't get the happy flashback I was hoping for. Unfortunately, it's a one-shot deal, so I can't redo it. Rules are rules. I'm sorry. My bad."

"My bad?" I stare at him. If I had physical eyeballs, I'd be blinking, because it was like staring into a flashlight. My brain had been lit up. I could see all its dark corners. "My bad. That's it. That's everything."

Every step of the way, Zack had apologized. When he messed up —even if it wasn't on purpose—he said he was sorry. He tried to make it right. He owned up to his mistakes. To the consequences, even if he didn't do it on purpose. He owned up to everything. He tried his best to do right and do a good job. Always.

Then there's me. I messed up, over and over, my whole life. And never once did I admit it was my fault. Never once did I own up and take responsibility. Or try to make things right. Ever. And there were a lot of those times. When life was too hard, or too scary, or too boring, or I didn't want to be bothered. Kevin was right. I was a half-ass dumbass.

And now DeeDee's dead, and Kevin's a ghost. My book was a

snarling, neglected beast. And it was all my fault. Because I never said, "my bad." I never owned up. I never once went with all my heart, so to speak. I never even tried to get good at my job. Or at anything, really. And now I'm dead. I'd lost my one chance.

I felt the pressure of tears in ghost eyes that couldn't cry. The churn of a guilty gut that wasn't flesh. The reel of guilt which needs no body to take root. I'd let everyone down in the worst possible way. I'd let myself down. I'd wasted my life. "I deserve to go to hell."

Something tugged on my leg, and it took me a while to realize that sensation was real, because I was totally a vapor. It was my employee manual. It looked up at me and whimpered.

"I'm sorry I was so mean to you. All you did was try to help me. I should have read you. I was scared, and I was stupid, and I just thought everything would magically be okay. I didn't do my part. I'm sorry." I reached down to pat it on the head, and it leaned into me like a happy cat. We actually touched. It purred. "I hope you get a better owner next time."

"Hurrrrrrrrrrrr. That was so sweeeeeeet. Hurrrrp." Zack sniffled. "But time's up. We've got to go."

Harrrrrffffff. Harrrrrrrrrf. Harrrrrrrrrrf.

That was not Zack crying. That was my employee manual.

Zack stopped. "Uh. Is that thing gonna be all right?"

Harrrrrffffff. Harrrrrrrrrf. Harrrrrrrrrrf.

"Yeah. Just a hairball."

"But it doesn't have hair?" Zack scratched his chin.

Hair or not, something was coming up. Because the cover undulated and heaved, then *bluuuuuuuggggggh*. It barfed up blood all over the welcome mat.

"Eeeeee! Gross." Zack jumped back. "And that's saying something. You should see the crime scenes I've been to."

I reached down to see if my book was okay. It nudged my hand. Into the puddle. Yeah. Ew. For real. "Wait." It wasn't blood. It was a wet red envelope. It was my blank check. "Oh. Shit."

"Uh, I'm gonna have to insist you wash your hands before we leave," Zack said.

I unfolded the blank check. "We're not going anywhere. I want a do over."

As I said the words, red ink filled in the blank spaces.

I looked at my employee manual. It looked at me. And it all became crystal clear. That book ate my check, so I didn't waste it on something stupid. It knew me well enough to save the check, so I'd have it when I really needed it. It kept me from making the biggest mistake of my life. Literally.

Zack slumped. "You're really making this hard on me. I told you, no do overs. The man upstairs isn't exactly handing out blank checks these days."

"God isn't, but the devil sure is." Or should I say *a* devil?

"Pull the other one." Zack peered down over my shoulder. "Wow. I've never seen a real one before. Where are we gonna get it notarized at this hour?"

"Leave the details to me, young man." Faust kicked open the stockroom door, wearing a crisp new, blood-free designer suit. "I've already contacted my accountant and notary, Mr. Beale."

Sure enough, a little embossed stamp appeared in the bottom corner, with a signature that sizzled as it burned into the paper.

"Only one space left." Faust pointed.

"Ow!" Something pricked my finger. My blue ghost blood spurted on the signature line.

"Sorry, my dear man. Standard procedure. Now. The paperwork is all in order. Good luck."

"Luck? But..."

"I am not allowed to intervene. You must persevere all on your own. There are rules. Oh, yes. The rules. Silly me."

Faust pulled a red folder out of thin air. It looked like the menu in a really fancy restaurant. He handed it to Zack. Zack opened it. Inside was a list, written in scrolly script.

"Do take care to follow the guide word for word. This is a once in a lifetime opportunity. Quite literally, I'm afraid," Faust said. "If this does not work out, there will be no second chances."

He clapped his hands, summoned the cleaning crew, still moving, still outside, about to jackhammer into the sidewalk. "We'll take a break from hammering. We don't want to distract you with the noise. We will hang the wards Ms. Henrietta so generously provided. It is a much quieter endeavor," he said. "Now. It is all up to you, Lloyd. Play well."

CHAPTER 21

"PLAY WELL? WHAT DOES THAT MEAN?"

"Apparently, you have to best me at a game." Zack pointed to a line of text in the menu thingy. "We have to play a game, and you have to beat me. You have to win. Fair and square."

"No no no. This wasn't how it was supposed to go! I used the check! We all get to live again. End of story. No strings. No catches. Alive. Period."

"Please don't yell at me. I'm just reading the rules. You get to live again if you win. It says here the game rule went into effect on Day Six. Apparently, a bunch of the amoebas created on Day Five died, and they made a stink about it. They all wanted do-overs. Millions of them. Huge headache, so Head Office put policies in place to make death final. This is one of them. You know, so death means the end, finis, all of that." Zack stared off into space for a second. "I remember that. I was just a kid. Man. Those amoebas. Talk about a pack of assholes. Be thankful they suck at euchre."

This can't be happening to me. "Has anyone ever beaten you guys?"

He shrugged. "I don't know. This has only happened a couple of times. In 1991, a Bill S. Preston Esquire and Ted Theodore Logan, and then an Antonius Black, back in the middle ages. So, you aren't the first."

"Well? What does it say?"

"You have to beat me, fair and square, at the game of your choosing. No cheating, and I can't take a fall, either. It says right here I have to play to the best of my abilities. If I cheat, or you cheat, we *all* go to hell. You. DeeDee. Kevin. Even me. Wow. Harsh."

Oh, gee. No pressure. "Well, what game? What do people usually do?"

"The other guys picked chess and Battleship."

"I don't know how to play chess!" That was gaming for the smart nerdy nerds, not basement dwelling chip eaters!

"Probably for the best. That guy lost. You get to choose the game, but it says here it has to be something close and readily available, because we have a time limit. We can't drag it out for a thousand years just because you want to avoid hellfire. I would totally do that if I were you, because hell really sucks. You really don't want to go there."

"I've got it." The one thing in the world I was good at. Well, pretty good. Okay, experienced, at least. Thousands of hours of experience. My chest puffed with pride. Video games. AwesomeDemon-ButtKicker98, this is your moment. All those hours were finally going to amount to something. "Let's go to the portal box. One Xbox coming right up."

"What portal?"

"The microwave looking thing in the hallway."

"Wait. That's a portal? Huh. No wonder my microwave mac and cheese noodles were crunchy." Zack shrugged. "And there was a pack of clean underwear next to the cup when I opened the door last time. I really needed those undies. I wonder how they knew?"

"Come on. Let's go."

Zack stopped me. "No magical intervention."

"What? That doesn't count!"

"We don't know that for sure, and we are not taking any chances. Do you want to burn in hell? I sure don't, so no portals. Try again."

My mind reeled. What the hell game was close at hand? I was at a corner store. Were we supposed to play tampon Jenga? "We don't have any games here!"

"I think I saw a jump rope in the toy section. Probably too short for me, though."

Wait. I got it. "We'll play something on your game system."

Video games—even crappy knockoffs—were my best chance, even on a console that wished it was a console. I mean, look at me. The jump rope was definitely out. You saw Zack at the gym. Even my ghost was way too out of shape to beat the angel of death at any feat of endurance. That crap plug-and-play was my best option. Video games were the one thing I was good at. Which, now that I think about it, was pretty sad. But oh well. At least I had a fighting chance. My thumbs had mashed many buttons in their time.

Besides, Zack had only been playing it for, like, a week now. He couldn't have mastered it.

Zack and I floated into the zombie cooler. I sat down on the edge of Morty's round sexcapade bed.

Ew. Just. Ew.

Thankfully, Candy and Morty were not, in fact, having sex on it. They were having sex next to it. Standing up. Kind of. Candy leaned over the bed. Morty stood behind her. Both of them were frozen in the throes of ecstasy. Well, not so much ecstasy as the taming of some infernal lust beast. Candy had turned white, solid, full poltergeist, her mouth a huge gaping maw lined with fangs, hair a wild halo of angry snakes. Morty had his arm up like a rodeo cowboy, holding on to that bucking dead stripper for dear life, mouth frozen mid "Yee-haw!"

"I'm so glad I'm going home tonight." Zack shivered. "Because I never have to touch this bed again."

Yeah. I feel you, dude.

Unfortunately, the ghost of the pizza guy sat, frozen, on the edge of the mattress, right in front of the TV, controller in one hand, mid-game. "Huh. Why didn't he change?"

Zack shrugged. "Guess he was happy? He likes this one."

Zack pointed to the screen. The pizza guy was midway through a neon yellow round of. Huh. I read the small print: *Super Monkey Barrel Smash.* Wow. Look at those pink barrels. This was quite the knock off.

"You have to pick the game." Zack skimmed the rules. "It should be two player. It has to have a clear winner in the end. Oh, and here. Sorry. I forgot."

Zack pressed a couple buttons on his scythe and my ghost blue body turned solid. Blue. But solid. Fleshy. Zack fiddled with the TV connections while I really hoped I didn't get any unidentified crusts or liquids on my brand new body. Which, now that I was looking around, seemed unlikely. The floor was littered with dirty robes, empty chip bags, and piles—huge piles—of sticky spent Colossal Super Slurp cups. Ew.

I had to kick a couple of cups away to unearth the other controller. Then I had to peel it off the floor. And I mean peel. It was stuck on there good. Ew. Man. If I live through this, I am definitely cleaning my room. For real.

I powered up the controller and yep, I'll be honest, I was sweating. The butterflies in my tummy were real. I had never had so much riding on a video game before. One game over really meant game over.

Gulp. Relax, Lloyd. You can do this.

A screen popped up. Rows of game names. There had to be a thousand of them, and I didn't recognize any of them. I just had to find one that was a knockoff of something I was good at, and hope Zack didn't know any of the tricks.

I scrolled. Wow. These games. *Mushroom Car Race Man. Mean Worm Fight. Kung Fu Street Kombat. Wrestle Dude POW?* Thousands of them. Or not. The more I scrolled, the clearer it became that a lot of the "games" were really just different levels of the first twenty games. Pirates. God bless 'em. They tried.

I flipped back to screen one. And I found it. The lucky winner. The game to end all games. I would emerge victorious, the ultimate champion. Mario—Oops. Nope. My bad—of *Mushroom Car Race Man.* "Got it!"

Prepare to eat knockoff mushroom car dust, Zack.

Zack peeled the other controller out of the pizza guy's stiff, sticky hand. And I mean sticky. A string of goo stretched from the controller to his blue hand. Zack lifted it up. To his mouth.

"Oh no. Don't—"

He sunk that bone tip into his mouth.

"—eat that."

Too late.

He groaned. "Mmmm. Hexed Huckleberry. Can you believe it still tastes good?"

Ew.

"*Mushroom Car Race Man.* Yay!" Zack was amped. "Keegan said when you get good, you can unlock a character called the Snot Father."

"Never heard of him." Okay, then. Things were looking up.

Zack plopped down on the other side of Keegan, the ghost of the dead pizza guy. The screen flickered. A sky view of a cheap 16-bit race track popped up on the screen. "You pick first," Zack said. "Only fair."

Gulp. Here goes nothing. And everything. No pressure. We chose our racers. I picked a weird, buff worm guy in a green unitard. Zack didn't hesitate. He immediately chose a purple ghost with a jack-o'-lantern head.

He said, "He kinda looks like me, don't you think? Cooler robes, though. I wish they'd let us do purple. I thought maybe after we'd reaped Prince, but no."

"Wait. Prince? *Prince* Prince?"

"Now that was one stylish dude. Sang all the way to heaven. Anyway, are you ready?"

"As I'll ever be."

He pressed start. The screen went dark, and for a second, I thought the console had given up the ghost. It probably wasn't designed to endure a full week of gameplay. Then, 16-bit lightning flashed, and a cartoon race track crackled onto the screen. One weird worm and one jack-o'-lantern—I assume. The graphics were small and fuzzy—revved at the starting line.

Dude. I should have given him my Xbox.

But too late now. This was it: The moment my whole life had led up to and depended on. My hands squeezed the controller so tight the plastic should have cracked.

A countdown appeared on the top of the screen. Ninety seconds of knock off 16-bit glitchy joy to determine if DeeDee, Kevin, and I live or die. No pressure.

I steadied the controller in my hand, my thumb hovering over the buttons. Waiting. Deep breaths.

Go time.

Click. Click. Click. Click.

I mashed those buttons like my life depended on it. Literally. My worm car rumbled to life, kicking up pixel dust all over Zack's pumpkin, who hadn't rolled a virtual inch. "Ha. Take that!"

He examined his controller. "Aw. Man. Wire's loose."

I raced forward while he fiddled with the wire. Eat worm dust!

"Got it." Zack pushed the wire in and suddenly his car shot forward. And caught up. And passed me.

Shit! *Click. Click. Turn. Click. Turn! Spray!*

Zack huffed. "Come on, man! You hit me with spore dust. I can't see."

"Good." *Click. Click. Click. Click.* I mashed. I turned. My car vrrrrrrrrrrrrrrrrrred. Then my button stuck, and I spun out. I shook the controller. "Stupid thing!"

"Geesh. I thought you'd be more fun to play with," Zack said. "But you're kind of angry."

Click. Click. Click. Click. Vrrrrrrrrr.

"I'm fighting for my life here!" *Click. Click. Click. Click.* "Eat my spores!"

Ha! Pumpkin spins out. YES!

"Oh, yeah. Right. I guess that is kind of a big deal. Nothing personal, bud. Rules are rules." Zack's bony hands bopped that controller hard. He nearly rammed my worm off the track.

Shit! Shit! Shit!

Zack's bony fingers hit the buttons fast, like the pop of a machine gun. Boy, those bones sure could move. The pumpkin hit me at turn three. My car stopped. "Nooooooo!"

Click. Click. Click. Click. I tried to hit some sort of combo. My car turned to static for a second, like it was about to disappear. "No!" Then it materialized in front of Zack's. "Yes!"

Click. Click. Click. Click. I'd show you. All I needed to save the day was a 16-bit worm car and my thumbs. I'll save you, DeeDee!

Click. Click. Click. Click.

Click. Click. Click. Click. YES YES YES!

Uh oh. That pumpkin was not out yet. It sped up. *Vurrrrr. Whirrrrrrr.*

Click. Click. Click. Click. "Ooh, yeah! Got you there!" Zack shrieked.

Shit! Thirty seconds to go, cars? Tied.

Click. Click. Click. Click. We leaned into the turn. "Come on, little worm. Drive!"

I mashed. Seriously. So hard and so fast my thumbs ached. I gripped the controller tighter, my butt on the very edge of the bed. My worm car sputtered and swerved.

Zack's pumpkin? It teleported. Shit! He's ahead!

"How did you do that?"

"I'm not telling you!" Zack jumped and grunted as he clicked, nearly bouncing me off the bed.

I held tight to that controller and mashed. Circle circle left left left. Mash. Mash MASH!

It didn't work. That pumpkin could really drive. He had the lead. The screen lit up in bursts of purple.

We closed in on the finish line. I pressed every button, but couldn't tell what did what, or if the buttons did anything at all. This was bad. Really bad.

The screen flashed. The track changed colors. Countdown. Ten seconds to go.

Click. Click. Click. Go, worm. GO!

My worm sped up. The clock ticked down.

Still tied.

Click. Click. Click. Click. Vurrrrrrr.

Huge blast. Pumpkin car shoots spores. I swerve. I spin out. SHIT!

Click. Click. Click. Click.

Seven.

Drive, worm! DRIVE! Zack's ahead. Way ahead. I pull my car back onto the track. My palms sweat. My hands shook. I mashed buttons, but the controller barely responded.

Six.

Suddenly, a pair of bright red cherries floated onto the screen. YES! Power up! I watched the cherries zig and zag as I puttered down the track. But they moved randomly, like a glitch. If I chased after them, I'd be even farther behind, and DeeDee's life was on the line. Then again, if I got them? I pressed the buttons in and held, following behind Zack, barely catching up. The clock was ticking.

Five.

Fuck it. I'm going for the cherries. They're my best chance. So I followed the cherries. I pulled off the track into pit row. I pushed my stick all the way forward. My engine revved. The car jumped ahead. The cherries zagged. I pressed into that X button like my life depended on it. My car jumped, flying, I steered toward the bouncing cherries. Shit. They're bouncing away. I turned again. Get 'em, Lloyd. Get 'em!

Three.

Click. Click. Click.

YES! Got 'em! Suddenly, the screen flashed, like Pac-Man ghosts after he eats a power pellet. My car spun and lit up like a disco ball.

Click. Click. Mash. Go, worm. GO!

A rainbow shot out of my 16-bit tailpipe, and that worm took off like a rocket.

Two.

This was my last chance. I had to save DeeDee. So I punched those buttons as hard as I could. All of them. Hoping maybe, just maybe, I could super charge that rainbow. Because this was Lloyd's Last Stand. Eternal damnation hung on the line. My worm flew. Rainbows sparked and whizzed across the screen.

But Zack pressed into his controller so hard. His pumpkin sped up. We were neck and neck, still so close, it could go either way. I needed more. I swerved. My car inched ahead of him. My tailpipe showered Zack in rainbow. YES!

One.

The worm flew forward. Zack's pumpkin car was completely swallowed up by a cloud of 16-bit red, yellow, and blue. YES!

A cheesy, tinking voice said, "Game over."

The screen flashed. Oh my God. I did it! I couldn't even see Zack's car. It was still wrapped in my rainbow exhaust. I DID IT! "Eat rainbow, reaper!"

Zack sighed and patted me on the back. "Good game, bro."

My hands, my whole body, shook. I did it. I won! All those hours of video games had paid off. Then, *thunk.* The controller dropped clean out of my hands. Or fell through my hands. Because they were blue and see-through. My body was gone.

No way. Did I lose? I must have lost! I felt tears welling in my eyes. Okay, I didn't. No tears for disembodied souls. But I sure was crying on the inside. How did this happen? How could I possibly lose? Wait. Do not even tell me that the power ups don't count. I mean, that's like the No. 1 move in racing games! Then again, this was a cheap knockoff. Kevin was right. I should have given Zack my Xbox.

"Man. Sucks!" Zack tossed his controller. "I mean, I'm happy you might not go to hell, but geesh."

"What?" I looked at the screen. The rainbow fizzled away. My worm sat in a 16-bit winners' circle. "Holy shit. I did it. I won!"

I floated right up to the ceiling, riding on a cloud. Like, for real. Not even a joke. "I get to live! We all get to live!"

"Well, yeah. I mean, technically you get to live. But boy. I don't know how you're gonna get out of this one."

I looked back down at Zack, still on the bed, reading Faust's directions and fiddling with his hourglass watch. "What do you mean, I 'technically' get to live?"

CHAPTER 22

I SHOULD HAVE KNOWN. There's always a catch, isn't there? A *chance* to live again. *A chance.* That's it. No guarantee. No magic wiping away all the tragic events leading up to our deaths. No backing up to a safe point in time. A time when there was no shit rocketing straight at a fan. Nope. Only a chance.

The gravity of what that meant was sinking in, deep. My ghostly blue body floated in the store, staring down the carnage before me, trying to come up with a plan before the world unfroze, and I was thrust back into it.

Apparently, I had won the chance to be placed back in my body exactly two minutes before I died. Two measly minutes. Because that was what constituted a "Do Over" in the celestial fine print. And a do over was exactly what I asked for, in my head, when the blank check appeared.

So yeah. Stupid me. I had exactly one hundred twenty seconds to prevent two people from dying again or my blank check was wasted, and all of this was for nothing. Because rules are rules, and the rules suck.

"Okay. Times up!" Zack ushered me closer to my physical body, positioning me just so. Then, he floated back next to his, waved his bony finger, and the scene slowly reversed. In super slow motion.

Except for my employee manual, which was on the end cap, shaking a bag of Zapp's Evil Eye chips at me, very adamantly. Dude. How can it possibly be hungry at a time like this?

And except for Faust and the cleaning crew, who inexplicably moved in real time through all of this. They were sorting through that cardboard box of weird junk, deciding which of the trinkets to hang up next. Apparently, Faust took this ward thing very seriously. As was obvious from the three hundred portraits of his ex-girlfriend burning at the stake staring at me right now.

Anyway. I turned back to my body. Okay. Deep breath. You can do this, Lloyd. Probably? I think. Hopefully. Maybe. Either way, I was out of time. I didn't really have a choice. I had to do this. I had to save us. Somehow. I just had to figure it out.

I watched as Hunter's spiky claw paw reversed, rising over me. My neck knitted back together, and the blood sucked out of my shirt, back into my body where it should be. Kevin's thick sharp leg splurped out of DeeDee's chest, out of the ghost of the hipster. The pool of blood on her T-shirt sucked back inside of her, and her head lifted. Alive. I looked in her slow motion-reverse blue eyes, and the pressure increased. No matter what happened, I couldn't let her die. Not for my mistakes. No way.

The scene rewound to just before the moment it all went south. Horribly, awfully, epically, holy shit, I'm going to die, south.

"This is it. Are you ready?" Zack asked.

"Uh. Can you back it up just a little bit more?" I wasn't sure I could prevent such a massive disaster from this close to the finish line. My blue ghost body was quaking.

"Sorry, dude." Zack showed me his watch. The sand in the little hourglass glowed green, a cosmic go signal. "This is exactly two minutes. Unless you can rewrite the celestial rules that govern time and space and do overs, it's time. This is your moment. Your one chance to get the girl and save everyone's lives. Wow. Now that I'm thinking about it. That's heavy. That's a lot of pressure. Good luck. I'm rooting for you."

"Tell me about it." I stared at Hunter. At DeeDee. At Kevin. At the demonic Cookie Scout hanging upside down in Bubby's claw tipped leg. Come on, brain! I need a grand plan. Now.

"And three..."

Think. Think. Think!

"Two..."

Dear Baby Jesus, if you're listening, I'm open to any sort of divine inspiration or intervention. Literally anything. Thanks in advance. Oh, if you're out there, it'd be super amazing if you could call the Office of Efficient Eternal Soul Transference. We need reapers. Seriously. Lots of them. We've got a heap of unreaped souls here. They deserve to go to heaven. Amen.

My brain was blank.

Huh. Really? Nothing?

What if I promise to go to church on Sundays?

Still blank. So much for divine inspiration.

"One."

Well, I was just gonna have to wing it. I shook out, which wasn't super helpful, because I didn't really have a body, so I only had mental muscles to loosen. Still, a pep talk never hurt. I will do this. I don't know how, but I will. For DeeDee. For all of them.

"Go!"

Shlooooooooooooooop.

That was the sound of me being sucked back into my body. And let me tell you. It was not easy, and it was not fun. I felt like Lloyd toothpaste being sucked back into a tube with an indescribably strong suction.

"Uuuuuuuh!" I gasped. Holy shit. Real air sucked into my lungs, because I'm breathing! I ran my hand over my chest. Heart beat, no gaping hole in my neck. Pink, fleshy skin! Yay! I'm alive! I had never been so happy to feel my love handles in all my life. *Mwa! I love you, pudge!*

I felt a little disoriented as everything moved in real time. The demon scout flailed in Bubby's grasp. My employee manual tugged on my sock. A shadow closed in over me.

Hunter. Big. Wide. Mean. Angry. Clawing at the air, desperate for his red squeaky bone. Again. It floated up over his head and straight toward me. Hunter raised his giant white hand, transformed into a clawed paw, ready to snatch it out of the air, to slice my neck clean off.

Oh shit. It's happening again! It's moving too fast. Think, Lloyd. DO SOMETHING!

I jumped up and grabbed that red bone as it passed above me. Or tried to, because some invisible force tugged against the other end and wouldn't let go. My employee manual crawled up onto the counter, looked right at me, and spit out a slip of plastic. "EDVIN."

The fake out. Yes!

I let go of the bone. It snapped back, then I reached up and grabbed it again, really fast. Whatever held the other end didn't see that move coming. Just like the cleaning crew guy and the Red Vine tug of war. Ha! "Here boy, Fetch!"

I threw that bone as hard as I could and shuffled out of the way. Hunter followed it as it arced up through the air, into aisle two, and jumped up, ready to catch it in his giant toothy mouth.

Phew. That was close.

Crack. Chink.

Shit. Broken records. DeeDee!

I whirled around. One of Kevin's records crashed to the floor in pieces. Kevin's mouth split into a row of black spike fangs. Kevin reached for the register. Again.

"DeeDee! Run!"

I bent my legs, put my arms out, and squatted down, as low as I ever had. Perfect form. And push! I used the force of that perfect squat, thighs burning, to catapult myself up up up at Kevin. I flew through the air like a big fat javelin. I cleared the counter. YES!

I hit Kevin's legs as they reached for the cash register. The force of my love handles pulled that machine right out of his ghostly grip.

"Re-CORRRRRD!" Kevin growled. His white clawed monster legs flailed in my peripheral vision.

YES! *Crunk.* Ow. Unfortunately, I crashed right into the back counter. Seriously. Ow.

"Lloyd. Dude. Are you okay?"

DeeDee reached for me. No time. I jumped up and grabbed that *Rainbow Rising* album by the sleeve as it rose up, floating in mid-air. Huh. I hung in the air for a moment, as if some invisible force was holding me up. Just like the bone.

Whatever it was, it shook me off. The album slipped right out of my hands, and I fell right through that hipster ghost and landed practically on top of DeeDee.

Kevin cracked and popped and stretched and screamed, monster legs reaching out for that record, about to shoot right through DeeDee. Again. I didn't know what to do, so I pressed my body against her to shield her. She grunted. "Lloyd. You're mushing me."

Kevin's legs poked and flapped and stretched. We were trapped. That record floated down down down, then stopped, squarely between us and Kevin, as if something were marking us with a big fat bull's eye. Some *thing*. Or some one.

"ReCORRRRRRRD!" Kevin growled.

Shit! Think, Lloyd. Think! I hopped up. I grabbed an album off the stack and lured the hipster away from DeeDee. "Kevin wants to sell you his entire collection. How much will you give him for it?"

Dude. As if on cue, that hipster—who was clear, blue and still clinging to his earthly habits, not yet spoiled—followed me, scribbling something on an invisible note pad, saying, "I can give you sixty dollars in store credit. That's very generous, considering. There's almost no demand for these."

Yeah. You wanna see a dead cockroach forget about a floating Dio album and get really mad? Kevin's black eyes turned on that hipster and lasered in on him with such intensity, it's as if they were powering up to melt his pompadour down to dust. I ducked. "Go go go!"

I wrapped my arms around DeeDee, enveloping her in a safe layer of Lloyd pudge, and I did something I have never done—I tucked and rolled us both right out of there. Okay, sure. It probably looked a hippo doing a somersault while hugging a supermodel, but who cares? It worked. When we stopped rolling, we were halfway down the counter, out of reach of the enraged Kevin.

Yes! We had survived our original appointments with death. YES! YES!

All DeeDee said was, "Ow."

Unfortunately, we still had a store full of angry, violent ghosts. All around us. No plan. No escape route.

But we did have a reaper. A gainfully employed reaper. I hopped up. Oh shit. The ghosts—no longer smoke. Solid, big, angry—were ripping apart the store. "Zack! Reap them! Now!"

He stood by the Kelpie Kiwi machine, dangling that rubber squid in front of Glug, who was still inexplicably merged with the slush and spilling out of the nozzle.

Zack looked at me and said. "Sorry. I can't. I don't have scrolls!"

"SERIOUSLY?" Yeah. I screamed. "Help Meeeeeeeeee!"

"I'll see what I can do." He plinked something into that control panel on the side of his golden scythe. "Huh. Weird. I'm locked out. The code says. Unauthorized use. Stolen property. What?" He shook it, as if that would help.

Glug said, "Have you tried turning it off and on again?"

I ducked back down. "Jesus. These angels are train wrecks. This can't be happening. What do we do?"

DeeDee didn't answer, because I was talking to her behind. Her glorious, curvy. Uh. Shoot. Focus, Lloyd. Death, hello!

Okay. Where were we? Oh yes. She was waist deep in the shelf behind the counter, throwing glass jars and rocks and gourds and all manner of weird things out as she went. "No. No. No. No. Shit. All of this stuff is designed for hell creatures. We aren't equipped for ghosts!"

My heart raced. No way out of the store. No way out from behind the counter. And that hipster wasn't gonna keep Kevin busy for long. What were we supposed to do now? I looked up at the ceiling—toward heaven—looking for any sort of divine intervention. My employee manual stared back at me, leaning over the edge of the counter, and *harrrrrffffff. Harrrrrrrrf. Harrrrrrrrrrf.*

Uh oh. I think it's gonna hurl.

Harrrrrffffff. Harrrrrrrrf. Hurrrrrrrrplip.

Plop. Tink tink tink tink tink.

Yep. It hurled. All over me. Red Vine SuperStrings and Slim Jim Savage Meat Sticks, still in the packages. Judging from the size of the pile, probably every single one it had ever eaten. Undigested. Whole.

A meat stick bounced off DeeDee's angelic behind, and when she poked her head out from under the counter to see what hit her, she said, "Well, that's weird."

My book dry heaved one last Slim Jim, then jumped off the counter into my lap.

"Dude. You feeling okay? That was a big barf."

It flopped on its back, pages fluttering, and fell open to that Bible school stick art page. Then, it pointed to the Slim Jims, to the Red Vines. "Wait. Do you want me to make one?" It shook in a way that I suspected was a yes. But it was hard to tell. Because it's a book. "Out of this stuff?"

Another shake. "Uh, okay."

Not sure how that was gonna help, but after the blank check thing? Better to listen.

At my book's direction, I gathered a handful of Savage Slim Jim Meat Sticks and shucked them out of their plastic sleeves. I laid them out on the floor, mimicking the shape on the page. A cross. Inside a hexagon. Of Slim Jims. Well, crazier things have worked.

Then I ripped into a pack of Red Vines. I stared at them. I guess these were the strings? I fumbled with the raspberry sugar goodness, but I couldn't make a knot. "They're too fat. I can't tie it!"

Then the book grabbed the end of a Red Vine and unraveled it into a handful of skinny, stretchy strings. "Oh. Super strings. I get it." The big Red Vines peeled into delicious little elastic ropes, which were super easy to tie. So I did. A candy knot in every spot where meat touched meat.

You know what I mean. Get your mind out of the gutter.

My book jumped up and down with excitement.

"Okay. Done. Now what?"

DeeDee finally came out from under the counter. With a huge, and I mean absolutely huge, flashlight. More like a floodlight.

"What are you gonna do with that? They're not moths!"

She sighed. "I know. It's all I could come up with. Everything in *Poltergeist* is all 'oh go into the light!' It didn't really work for Gunther, but it's worth one more try. We don't have anything else."

She pointed at my meat and candy creation. "What are you gonna do with that?"

"Hell if I know!"

Great. Just great. We were trapped back here, and our only weapons were a big lightbulb, the plot of a 1980s ghost movie, and a meat craft. We're screwed.

My book was clearly more optimistic, because it turned to the next page. Instructions? Hard to tell. Every word in here was in some dead language, and all the illustrations looked like the medieval equivalent of the Ikea catalog.

DeeDee ran her hand down the page. "Huh. Interesting. It's a soul trap." She tapped her black fingernail on the little Ikea guy. "You need to lure the ghosts into the middle, and voila. Well, it's a plan. I'll distract them. You suck them in. Okay?"

She moved up, and I pulled her back down.

"HOW?"

"Beats me." She shrugged. "You'll figure it out."

Before I could object, she turned that floodlight on full blast and aimed it up. A giant blue face appeared in the light.

"Aaaaaaaaaaah! Poltergeist!" I screamed.

Blooooooooooo. Burrrrrrrr. Bup.

Never mind. It was just Bubby, scratching his fat blue head with one of his pincers. He held a very angry demon scout upside down in one claw, and a very angry bitey bus lady in another. She had her poltergeist teeth sunk in one of Bubby's jelly fat rolls, and it did not look like it tickled.

"Great. Now's your chance to test your trap." DeeDee pushed me toward the flailing, angry creatures. "Go on then."

I held my Savage Meat Stick soul trap up by a thin string of Red Vine. With confidence. Or something close to it. The demon scout and the bus lady stared at it, as if mesmerized. Yes. It's working. It's working. "Oooooh. Lookie here. Don't you want to see what's in here?"

I wiggled it.

The Cookie Scout's fang lined mouth said, "I hate Red Vines. I like Twizzlers." Then she swatted, bringing her claw down right across my arm. "Ow!"

Bubby shook her really hard, then he chucked her clear across aisle five. She hit a reach in cooler door. Really hard.

Something tugged on my sock. My employee manual fell open. To the page with the scrolly script. "Again?"

It growled and bit my ankle.

"Okay! Okay!" I cleared my throat and held onto those Slim Jims white knuckled. "Clafoooo Varapa nick? Nik huh. Nickel?"

"Neek two. It's neek two!" DeeDee said. She waved her floodlight all over the store. Not a single ghost paid any attention. "Shit. Go into the light, my butt."

I said it again. "Clafoooo varapa neek two!"

And nothing happened. I was just a fat guy with a fistful of Red Vines and Savage Slim Jims that he'd made into a weird, shitty camp craft, screaming magic words like it was gonna help his noob warlock level up. Not the proudest moment of my life.

"Spielberg's full of it. Tangina did me wrong." DeeDee dropped the floodlight and raised a small white tube in front of the bus lady. "Mmmm. Look. Necco Wafers!"

The bus lady zoned in. Like laser focus. That's it. DeeDee's a genius. I held the trap out in front of the faux roll of candy as the bus lady reached for it. She screamed. "MY NECCO WAFERS," wrested free from Bubby's grip and shot at me, full force, pinning me against the counter.

Shit! She really wanted that candy.

I held tight. And something happened. Her angry white claw arm slipped through the meat hexagon. It went in, but it didn't come out the other side. It was as if it sunk into an invisible pool or another dimension. Or something.

And her arm? It was stuck. In the trap. And dude. This thing was like the quicksand in all those hokey TV shows. The more she fought, the faster it pulled her in, until *slurp slurp slurrrrrrrrrrrp*, that meaty ghost trap sucked her down, stockings and all.

DeeDee looked down in. "Dude. I hope she's all right in there."

"Oh. I'm fine, dear." Her head popped out. She was blue, transparent. Smoke. No longer big and white and mad or fangy. Unharmed. "But it's a bit of a tight fit."

DeeDee said, "Holy shit. It works."

I looked at my book. "Good thinking."

And it bowed, like, "Thanks, dude. I know. You should have been listening to me this whole time."

Okay. That last part was me projecting. Because dude. I should have been listening to him this whole time.

"Are you ready, Lloyd?" DeeDee looked at me. Alive. Beautiful, and said, "We have souls to trap."

CHAPTER 23

"I'M READY." I gripped that Savage Slim Jim Red Vine miracle and steeled myself for round two.

"Let's see what we're up against." She popped up and peeked around Bubby's midsection.

I rose just high enough for my eyeballs to clear the counter. Dude. We chickens do not transform into He-Man overnight. We just don't.

The angry demon scout stood in front of the reach in coolers, body cricking and cracking and stretching and morphing. Growing. Big. Tall as the ceiling. And extra mad. Her mouth split into row upon row of fangs. Her hair whipped, buffeted by invisible wind. She stomped so hard the entire store shook. She screamed, "Where's my UNICORN?"

Hunter? Even worse. His red squeaky bone floated up over the end cap, just out of his reach, as if taunting him. His head kicked back in rage. He howled, desperate, at the ceiling, then fell down on all fours. He stretched and cracked, bones breaking and reforming, the meaty bulk of him expanding into a huge white snarling beast. A giant...dog?

"Interesting." DeeDee glanced out the front window, up into the sky, and whispered. "Full moon. Poltergeist werewolf. Who knew that was a thing?"

The old guy? He circled the hot food station, pounding his cane so hard it chinked holes in the linoleum, screaming. "Mail. My. LETTER!"

Zack scratched his chin and shook his golden scythe, like he still couldn't get it to work. And Faust? He climbed a little stepladder in front of the door and hammered a nail in the drywall above it, whistling like this was all totally normal.

Dude. I glanced at my Savage Slim Jims and Red Vines. The ghost lady's head bobbed out of the center. The meat was already getting sticky in my sweaty hands. I prayed it would hold together. "Who should we trap first?"

Thunk. "Deeeeee ooooooo."

Uh oh. I knew that snarl anywhere. I turned. Kevin's giant angry top half landed behind the counter. He stared, fangs dripping, eyes black, at the broken bits of vinyl scattered on the floor. DeeDee stood behind him, rifling through records.

"How did you get over there so fast?" My heart jumped into my throat. "What are you doing? Run!"

She waved Kevin's Black Sabbath *Dehumanizer* album at me and said, "Duh."

Seriously? I did not save her so she could run right back into the lion's den. I mean danger. Not the adult superstore.

She slunk past Kevin, stepping over him as he cradled pieces of black broken vinyl. She made it about two more steps before the hipster floated after her, yelling, "Hey. I made a deal to buy that for store credit! Give it back. It's all or nothing. I'm not redoing my offer."

Kevin heard the words, "Store Credit" and growled. He looked up at the hipster and bared his fangs.

"Don't growl at me. I gave you the highest price I'm allowed. Your collection isn't special, you know. It's not my fault no one wants to buy these. Low demand."

Well, that hipster just dug his own grave.

Kevin jumped up—claw legs out, ghost roach monster wings flapping, right at that hipster, screaming. Unfortunately, the hipster had not spoiled, so once again, Kevin flew right through him directly at DeeDee. And me.

"Now, Lloyd. Now!" DeeDee held the album out.

Kevin snarled, "DEEEE OOOOO!"

I dangled the ghost trap in front of the cover and held on tight. That poor bus lady screamed as Kevin's sharp white legs shot out, ready to cut me in half. He landed headfirst in the meat hexagon.

Slurrrrrrrrrrrp. Shluurrrrrrrp.

His antennae went in, followed by his fat head, his legs, then his very fat carapace. The vortex was so strong, it even sucked the Kevin puddle right off the counter. I looked down. Kevin went in, but the space between the Slim Jims and me? Nothing. Just air.

"That is a really neat trick," DeeDee said.

A moment later Kevin's head popped out. The real Kevin. Well, the real dead Kevin. But still. He was himself, not a monster. Blue and see-through and smoky. "You better put that record back in a protective sleeve, or we're gonna have words, sweetheart. Wait." He looked down at the trap. "What is this thing? Get me outta here."

"You have to stay in there for a little while longer," DeeDee said. "For safekeeping. Trust me."

"Ooh. Something tickles. Oof. What the? Watch your hands, lady. That's private."

Kevin wiggled, and the bus lady winked at him.

"I'm gonna make another trap. Bubby. Cover us." DeeDee scooped up the remaining Savage Meat Sticks and Red Vines. and by the time Bubby stretched out, cracked his knuckles, and squared his shoulders, DeeDee popped up—trap in hand, saying, "Clafoooo Varapa Neek Two!"

"How did you do that so fast?"

"I love crafts. Plus, your employee manual is super helpful. Who's a good boy?" She leaned down to scratch its cover. Then she popped up, rolled right up to the hipster, grabbed that Kiss *Destroyer* album and said, "Hey. You interested?"

She wagged that album behind her fistful of Savage Meat Sticks, and that hipster perked right up. "GTFO. Does that have *Beth* on it? I love that song! Squeeeee!" He jumped right in after it, yelling "store crediiiiiiiiiiiiiiit!" and down down down he went.

"Fucking *Beth*." Kevin huffed. "I told you that hipster didn't know shit about music."

Bleeeeeeeeeeeep!

Uh. That was Bubby. Sounding the alarm. Because Hunter had just pushed off his haunches, and was now flying, claws out, straight at us. Bubby veered left and belly bounced Hunter right over the boner pill end cap into the pet supplies.

DeeDee didn't miss a beat. She slid over the counter and ran straight at the old guy, waving a piece of paper, yelling, "Do you need to mail this letter? I'm the postmaster!"

The old guy slid his hand right into her trap and said, "How much is a Forever stamp these days?" And boom. That was it. Sucked right in, tweed and all.

She looped back to the register, hit "no sale," and filched a twenty out of the till. "I'll handle the pizza guy."

"Hey. Put that back!" Kevin said. "I'm taking that outta your paycheck!"

DeeDee eyerolled him, then kicked open the stockroom door. "Hey. I got a twenty-dollar tip for the first guy who brings me a large pizza, extra cheese!"

Wow. That girl was good.

"Yeah. She's got three already, kid. You better get moving. She's making you look bad. Uh oh. Incoming!"

Hunter attacked. Again. Bubby karate chopped, but Hunter sunk his claws into Bubby and held tight. Bubby spun and bucked, but Hunter didn't let go. Oh, man. I had to trap Hunter. Boy, he was big. And scary. My knees felt like jelly, but I somehow managed to run out from behind the counter. I scanned the aisle looking for that red squeaky bone, but I didn't see it anywhere. Shit.

Bleeeeeeeeep!

Translation: "Look out." Or "holy shit. You're screwed."

Either way, I ducked, just as Hunter flew through the air and hit the end cap, sending unicorn phone chargers and boner pills skittering across the floor. Hunter righted himself, yanked that end cap clean off the shelving unit, snarled, "Give ME TWENTY!," then threw it.

Right at me. I held tight to my ghost trap and rolled as that metal rack cut through the air.

Kevin moaned. "Woah. Woo oooh. Cool it, kid. I'm gonna barf" as we rolled and rolled. Fast, until my body came to an abrupt and unpleasant stop at the tail end of the grocery aisle. I hit the shelf hard as a bowling ball, sending jars of peanut butter plunk plunking and rolling all around.

Hunter was on me in a flash. He pressed down on my chest, pinning me to the floor. "Your bod will be ready for swimsuit season, Champ." His fangy mouth spewed cold, rotten breath inches from my face. "When I eat half of you. Give me my BONE!"

He raised a paw, and my life flashed before my eyes. Again. So I whistled, like I was calling a dog. I'm not sure why. It was instinct.

Hunter stopped. My hand came up with a jar of peanut butter. "Are you a good boy? Because good boys get treats. Who likes peanut butter? Who's a good boy?"

His ghastly tail began to wiggle. I slowly unscrewed the cap and waved the delicious smoothness in front of his nose. Then I dangled the trap in front of it.

"That's right. Come on, boy. Mmm. Delicious."

His nostrils sniffled a thousand miles a minute around that jar. Hunter leaned back.

Shit. He's not buying it.

Then he catapulted forward. Giant paws, claws and all, outstretched.

Fuck. I'm dead. Still, I clung to those Slim Jims like my lift depended on it.

Kevin screamed. "Hole eeeeeeeeeee sheeeeeeeeeeeeeeeeeet!"

That snarling giant wolfman sunk his muzzle through Kevin, through the trap, trying to get at that peanut butter. And *shlur-rrrrrrrrrrrrrrrrrrp.*

Hunter sunk in in in in. Don't ask me how. Dude. It defied all natural known laws of earthly physics. But that trap opened wide, and swallowed hunter like a boa constrictor swallowing a wildebeest. Hunter sunk in until nothing but the tip of his tail hung out. It bonked Kevin right on the nose.

"Great. Now it smells like old lady and wet dog in here. Can you hurry this up? Grandma's getting a little handsy. Ow. Hey. Watch it. "

Hunter's human face squeezed out next to Kevin and the bus lady. "Hey, there, Champ. I gotta say, your form has really improved. Great squat back there. I'm really proud of you. Oof. Oh. Oh no." His head shook. "Can one of you give me a scratch? I think I've got a flea!"

"You ain't got fleas," Kevin snipped. "You don't even have a body!"

"Shhhhh." I needed to concentrate. Because the demon cookie scout was on the move. Her spiked monster tail kicked up like an antenna in the next aisle.

"Get your hand off my behind, lady," Kevin said. "I told you once already. My body, my choice."

"Shhh! I can't think!"

"What's there to think about? Hit her with the demon foam and get it over with already," Kevin said.

But it wasn't that simple. We'd foamed her once, and she'd come back. I peeked up over the shelf. Huh. She was face down, butt up, desperately rooting through the upturned piles of boner pills and phone chargers. Grunting. "Get. My...Corn...Earned...Camp!"

Something didn't compute. She was a demon. Some kind of

monster. Not a ghost. Right? She'd always been solid. White. Ice cold. Never blue, never smoke. And Zack didn't kill her.

Bleeep Bloop.

That was Bubby telling me to stand back. His jelly brow furrowed. He bounced back and forth between the counter and the wall, building up momentum, just like The Rock bounces on the ropes when he's gearing up for a big move.

"Bubby. No!"

Too late. Bubby careened forward, propelling the full weight of his jelly body forward, directly at that demon cookie scout. He flew at her. He snatched her and lifted her up up up, ready to—no way. Bubby spun her over his head, then readied to throw her straight down into the linoleum. It was his moment of glory, the Bubby version of The Rock Bottom. The Bubby Bottom.

"NOOOOOOO!" I screamed.

He stopped. He looked at me, holding a flailing demon scout over his head.

She snarled. "I want my unicorn." And then she...cried? "Hurrrrrrrrrrrrr."

Uh. What's going on?

Kevin stared with interest. "I gotta be honest, kid. I don't know either."

Was this a fake out?

She sniffled. "I just want my unicorn. I earned it."

Bubby looked at me. I looked at Bubby.

Dude. Given her past record, who's to say this wasn't a ruse? She wasn't exactly a nice girl. Well. She wasn't a girl at all. Unless.

Oh no.

She wasn't a girl...any...more? It hit me like a brick. Right on the head.

I stared at her. Her white body. The claws. The creaking, rage-fueled transformation from little girl to monster. Like Kevin. Like Hunter. Clinging to pieces of their human—and roach—lives.

"Oh my God. She really is a little girl." A dead little girl. I suddenly felt heavy, like my heart couldn't take it.

Bubby looked up at her with eight white eyes, all misty with tears. He sat her gently down on the floor and patted the top of her ghastly, invisible wind-whipped hair.

"Good work, crew. That is the very last one. That should do it!" Faust clapped. He stood atop the ladder, hanging a blue glass bead above the door. "We are now safe from the clutches of The Beast."

Suddenly, a body materialized out of nowhere.

"Aaaaaaaaah! NOT IN THE FACE!" That was not me. That was Faust. Who immediately calmed down when he realized that it was not, in fact, his ex girlfriend who had materialized in the store.

It was a reaper. I felt a rush of relief. Finally! Someone came to reap these spirits. God answered my prayers. Thank you, man!

The reaper held a box of Skinny Mints over his mouth, pouring them in and munching them down to bits. He had his scythe pressed, like a phone, to where his ear should be. He yapped away like we weren't even there. "I'm serious, guys. You need to get down here. This place is a mess. Zack totally stole that stuff. And, he murdered everyone who worked in the store. Even this weird little roach guy. No, I said murdered. No scrolls. Unauthorized. I'm telling you, the guy is a menace. Just get down here. You'll have all the proof you need. It's time to throw Zack into the pit once and for all."

The reaper hung up his scythe. Phone? And stared at all of us, all staring at him. "Oops."

"Yuri?" Zack floated up to him. "What are you doing here?"

"Uh...hey man. How's it going? Just thought I'd check in on my old buddy. Heh heh."

The reaper tugged on his collar and said something, but I didn't hear. Because DeeDee rolled up. "Thank God. They finally sent a reaper! That was a close one. FYI, I left Candy in the cooler. She and Morty aren't, uh, finished."

My employee manual hit me in the leg with a bag of Zapp's. "Not now. I'm not hungry!"

Then it fell opened to the page with the hand. Again. Only this time, the eyeball stared at Yuri.

"Huh. That's a ward against the evil eye." DeeDee said.

"The what?"

"It's like a curse you put on someone because you're jealous. They sell little glass beads and stickers that look like eyeballs all over Greece and Turkey. They're supposed to protect you. Oh. There's one. Above the door." DeeDee pointed to Faust's latest addition to the décor, then she went for the chips. "Have you tried the Zapp's? They're really good. They remind me of ketchup chips, but zesty. Yummy."

Harrrrrrrrrf. Harrrrrrrrrrrf. Harrrrrrrrrrf.

My employee manual heaved, then hacked a dozen glass vials onto the floor. Spit of a hundred yia yias. Greek yia yias.

I picked one up. The label said, "Open vial, shake spit three times over victim to break the curse. The spit of Greek grandmothers is the only cure for the evil eye."

Oh, well then. I feel a little better about forgetting to order more Curse Breaker.

There was a Bible quote underneath. "Where envy and selfish ambition exist, there is disorder and every kind of evil."

I looked at Yuri. At Zack. At DeeDee's bag of creepy eyeball themed potato chips.

"It's...it's you." I pointed at Yuri. "You did this. You killed these people and brought their ghosts here. You're trying to make Zack look bad. You're trying to get him fired."

It was all so clear. The pizza guy. The bus lady. The old man? Hunter and Gunther and Glug. Stupid me. A reaper had already come. To reap them illegally. And pin it on Zack. He even let an eel into Bubba's, probably an excuse to up the body count, but we'd foiled that plan.

"You must be crazy," he said. "Why would I do that?"

"You're jealous. Zack's a hero. The Golden Scythe. Employee of the month eight thousand years in a row," I said. "And you...you're not. You're a laughingstock. A fuck up. It was all in the *Hell Report*. I think he's trying to frame you for all of this, Zack."

"Is that true?" Zack turned to Yuri.

"Ha ha. Very funny." Yuri put his boney hands up. "Can you believe this guy? That's rich. I mean, look at him. He's the poster child for loser. Have you seen his file? He wishes he was a hero."

"Yeah. I do. And yeah, I get it. It's hard to be around people who have it together when you don't. People who are good at everything you're not good at. And yeah, I'm a fuckup. Because it's scary to try, because when you try, you might fail. Then everyone is disappointed in you. Or, people might make fun of you. Or show your clip over and over again on All Creatures Great & Dead." I said. "But none of that is an excuse to do terrible things. Or hurt people. Or drag everyone else down."

My head felt hot. I was really mad now. Some jerk killed me and DeeDee out of jealousy and spite. Not cool. "He fed all that information to the *Hell Report*, Zack. He followed you around killing people. He's probably the one who stole your scythe, too. You weren't reinstated. He brought it back here, to you, to make it look like you stole it."

"Yuri?" Zack said.

"You can't possibly believe a fleshy breather over a fellow reaper."

"Lloyd." DeeDee tugged on my shirt. "Uh, Lloyd?"

I stared down Yuri. As Zack argued with him, the cleaning crew toddled into the aisle, fresh off ward duty, obviously searching for snacks. A shadow rose over them. And over us.

"Um. Lloyd?" DeeDee squeezed my arm and moved close to me. She whispered, "get the trap ready."

A voice growled behind me. "I want my UNICORN!"

Uh oh.

I turned around, slowly. The very large, very angry poltergeist of a very dead, very sassy Cookie Scout stood behind me. She raised a claw and brought it down. Hard. And next thing I knew, I was flying straight at a shelf.

Thunk. Ow.

Direct hit. I landed upside down in a pile of Top Ramen, with an angry scout standing over me screaming, ripping through the shelves like she was looking for something.

The cleaning crew didn't notice the impending danger. They made a chain all the way up Yuri's robe, clinging tight to the black fabric. The top one sunk its head into his pocket. Yuri yanked him off, but he had quite a grip, because he took a big chunk of robe with him. The whole fleshy tower of them collapsed. But that top guy? As he fell, he clung, desperately, to half a roll of Necco Wafers. Real Necco Wafers.

That candy wasn't the only interesting thing dropping out of Yuri's pocket. A crumpled up letter. A red squeaky bone. A stripper's garter, crumpled dollars still clinging to it. And something metal. It skittered across the slick linoleum and hit me right in the arm. I scooped it up. It was a unicorn pin. Sparkly. A merit badge? It said, "No. 1 Cookie."

Kevin poked his ghost head out of the trap, which hung around a can of Pork & Beans, and said, "Oh yeah. That asshole is totally guilty. Clever bastard. He used that stuff to control us. Keep us hanging around here. Frisk him, kid. He ain't leaving here with any of my records."

The scout closed in on me, fangs bared. Breathing heavy. Her eyes, wide, desperate.

"Look. Unicorn!" I raised it up so she could see.

She snatched it right out of my hand. She looked down at me. With a little girl's face with pigtails. No claws. No fangs. Just a crying little girl. "Thanks, fat guy. I had to sell a lot of cookies to earn this. I think that mean bone man stole it. He's a liar. He told me you took it."

"Told you," Kevin said.

This poor Cookie Scout wasn't out to get me. She was just following Yuri around trying to recover the last piece of her earthly life. Yuri had lied to her, manipulated her.

Zack floated over. He leaned in to get a closer look at the little ghost girl, still clutching that little unicorn pin. "Wait a minute. I know you. You were part of the troop I reaped. But I didn't reap you. You were the survivor. You're supposed to be alive."

While he stared at her, I slipped one of those little glass vials out of my pocket and flick flick flick, three times on Zack. And flick flick flick, three times on myself. You can't be too careful, right?

"You wouldn't kill her, would you?" Zack looked back at Yuri—who was desperately scooping all this stuff off the floor. "She's just a little kid. You wouldn't do that."

"I totally would. You caught me. I'm done with the charade. Your little meat pal is right. I totally did this. I killed the kid. I killed the stripper. I killed the demon and whatever the hell that is in the slushy machine. It was totally me. I killed them all. And no, I didn't have scrolls. And yes, I forged the scrolls for this dickhead and his sweet tits coworker over there." Yuri pointed at me. "And yes, I held all of them back from their final destinations. Because it'll be worth it to knock Mr. Perfect down a peg."

"But we aren't supposed to do that," Zack said.

"Whatever. They're just people. No one cares."

"I care." DeeDee dusted the Zapp's dust off of her and stood up. "These are people. With people who love them. And you murdered them. You turned them into monsters. Why? For revenge? Because you're jealous? Wow. That is petty. Angels are supposed to be better than that. They're supposed to be better than us."

"Ha. Typical. You humans. You think you know everything. So self righteous. You wander around like the universe revolves around you. Like it owes you. You all don't appreciate life until you're about to lose it. Then you beg for it. Then you want more. Then you promise to appreciate it and make it matter. Blah. Blah. Blah. Every time. You live for what, sixty, seventy years? Pfft. Nothing." He closed in on DeeDee and my pulse kicked up. "You don't understand what it's like to live forever. It's a long time. And when you're shamed and mocked and humiliated? It feels even longer. You can't even imagine an eternity with everyone laughing at you. I messed up one time, and it's on TV, replayed. Forever."

"Well, you messed up other times. That one was just the funniest," Zack said.

"And there it is. Mr. Perfect rubs it in again," Yuri said. "All of this will be worth it if I can get rid of you."

Zack slumped. "But. Why? What did I ever do to you?"

"You win. All the time. You're perfect, a hero! Everyone loves you, and everyone wants to be you." Yuri started counting on his phalanges. "You have a perfect bod. You can't think your way out of a paper bag, yet you get all the good reaps and all the good press. You have a hot girlfriend. Everywhere you go, people fawn over you, singing your praises. You can reap now wrong. It's like good things just fall in your lap, over and over. You don't even have to work for it."

"I work for it," Zack said. "I work really hard. And I train. And I—"

"Yeah yeah. I know. Employee of the month, 96,320 times in a row," Yuri said. "I hope you enjoyed it, because it ends now. It's my turn to shine."

"Uh no. Because I'll tell everyone," I said.

"You aren't gonna tell them anything. And if you do, they'll never believe you, anyway. Don't you get it? I cursed you. This whole place is in a celestial fog. No one—and I mean no one—can see through it. Not even a guardian angel."

Yuri picked up Angel eight ball off the counter, shook him, and threw him at the floor like a fastball. "Who are they going to believe? Me or you?"

I scrambled to grab him.

Crack.

Too late. Angel hit the floor so hard he bounced. He wobbled into my leg. The triangle went flat, and water—filtered, not tap—spilled onto the floor.

"Wait. Is this?" Zack floated over to angel. He picked it up and looked down in the ball. Then looked at me and said. "Oh, no. It's you?"

"Shut up, already. I'm tired of this conversation. It's over. The reapers are on the way to throw you into the pit." Yuri grabbed DeeDee. He raised his scythe and said, "Sorry, sweet tits. I have a reaper to frame, and you two should be dead already."

"NO!" I moved. Fast.

The scythe came down.

Crack.

Right on the neck. The head came clean off. DeeDee dropped to the floor.

But it wasn't Yuri's scythe. It was Zack's. And I swung it. I cut Yuri's skull clean off. It landed right between DeeDee's legs. DeeDee, who had ducked just in time. She looked up at me, still very much alive. She smiled and winked.

"Oh, snap. Take that, Junebug. Who's employee of the month now!" Kevin fist pumped a ghostly little leg in and out of the trap. "Jamaica. Here we come!"

Yuri's body? It wobbled, like it was stunned. His scythe clinked to the floor. Then his skull turned up to us and said, "You guys are in big trouble now."

CHAPTER 24

"Oh, man. He's right. This is not good!" Zack put his boney hands on my shoulders and pulled me close to him. He was shaking. I could feel it. And I could hear it, too, because all of his tiny bones clinked together.

"Thank you, my man! You just signed Zack's death warrant *for* him. Woo. Classic. Couldn't have done it better myself." Yuri laughed. And laughed. And laughed.

"Why is he still talking?" I snipped. "Die already!"

"The only way to kill a reaper is to throw him in The Pit of Eternal Darkness and Oblivion," Zack said. "And I think he's right. I might be going there. Hurrrrrrrr."

Yuri laughed. Again.

"Shut up, already!" DeeDee snapped. Her leg reeled back, ready to kick Yuri into next week.

Zack stopped her. "They're here. Hurrrrrrrrr."

DeeDee immediately turned tail and snatched Kevin's Slim Jim trap off the pile of upturned Top Ramen. She held it tight. Her eyes were wide. Scared. She looked at me and the reflection of red light flickered in her gray eyes. "Lloyd. Come quick. We have to go."

But it was too late. Dozens of pillars of red smoke appeared inside the store, swirling, whirling, redder and thicker, like concentrated tornadoes. Each pillar turned into a red robe, worn by a tall, looming reaper. Dozens of them. Each holding a silver scythe, sharp like a Ginsu knife. Cold, eyeless sockets stared at us. They had us surrounded.

Zack sunk down behind me like he was hiding. "Oh, no. These are the bigwigs. The Grim Bureau of Investigations!"

"You're screwed, buddy! Have fun in eternal oblivion," Yuri said. He swiveled toward the reapers. "Wow. Are you guys a sight for sore sockets? What took you so long? Look what they did to me. I'm in pieces!"

One of the red reapers stepped forward. He pointed at Zack. Zack knelt down before him, held out his golden scythe and wept softly.

WTF? This isn't fair!

Then, the boss reaper said, "Lloyd Lamb Wallace."

"Uh." Maybe he wasn't pointing at Zack. "Yes. Sir?"

DeeDee grabbed my arm, but I stepped forward anyway. What choice did I have? We couldn't fight death. Not this much of it.

He snapped his phalanges, and a scroll appeared in mid-air. "Says here we got a tip about unreaped, spoiled souls from a recently deceased named Lloyd Lamb Wallace, Cemetery and Crossroads. Transmundane Gate 23, sector 17. Is that you?"

"Um. Yes?"

He looked me up and down. "You don't look deceased."

"I...came...back?"

"Near death experience, then. Forged scroll, too." He scribbled on the scroll with a feather pen that materialized out of nowhere. "Well, thanks for the tip. I think we're all pretty clear about what happened here. Take him away, boys."

The red reapers surrounded Zack. The big boss floated up to him, and said, "Give me your scythe."

Zack handed it over, and the big boss typed something into the control panel. It glowed slightly, like it was powering up. "You're good to go. Okay, boys. Bag him and tag him. We don't have forever. Wait. Yeah, we do."

All the reapers chuckled.

"No!" I squeaked.

But handcuffs came out.

Clink.

They landed on Yuri's boney wrists. Then, a red reaper grabbed Yuri's skeleton by the shoulders, which moved like a brainless automaton, and moved it toward the front door. Another one picked up Yuri's still yapping skull. "Hey. Uh. What are you doing? Zack's the bad guy! Not me!"

The boss reaper stepped up to Yuri. "Give your jaw a rest. We reviewed the security tapes for this sector. Funny thing. They were all cloudy until about ten minutes ago. And when the fog lifted, there you were confessing everything, plain as day. Villains. The monologue always does you in. You all never learn."

DeeDee and I locked eyes. She flashed a vial of yia yia spit and a thumbs up. Huh. That label didn't lie. It really did break the curse.

"Not the smartest criminal, are you? But, it sure makes my job easier. Once we had your confession, we double checked the footage of the racino crash. And surprise. It'd been doctored. We know you reaped the driver. We also scraped some of your bone fragments off the gate controls at Bubba's. Terror eels are a serious offense. You deserve the pit for this, but maybe the judge will go easy on you."

"No! You don't understand!" Yuri's skull wiggled.

"Oh. I understand. All Creatures Great & Dead is gonna have a field day with this. I heard about your job try out, too. Hilarious."

All the red reapers? They chuckled. And I swear I saw Yuri's white cheekbones flush pink. "Noooooooooooo!"

"Load him up, boys." The boss reaper motioned, and Yuri's skull dropped into that bag.

It moved as he spoke. "Guys? Guys? Let me outta here. You got it all wrong."

The boss reaper clapped me on the shoulder. "Smart move. Most people don't think to call us when they're disembodied. Usually, the last thing the recently deceased want to see is a reaper. Thanks to your quick thinking, these poor souls will be ushered off to their eternal rest. Good job."

DeeDee looked at me, and her eyebrows wrinkled together, like she was confused. "How did you call—?"

Gulp. I didn't want to answer that question. I didn't want to think about her dead ever again. She'd be better off not knowing.

Thankfully I didn't have to say anything, because the big boss picked us both up by one arm and ferried us to the welcome mat. "Stay out of the way. This is a crime scene, so we do have to close it to gather the evidence. You understand."

As if on cue, the red reapers spread out across the store with measuring tapes and tweezers, scribbling things on scrolls, dropping bits in tiny plastic bags, drawing chalk outlines. Some of them crowded around Bubby with clipboards, trying to take his statement. But Bubby took one look at them and passed out cold.

That's when I noticed Faust was still up on the ladder, holding a few of those blue glass eye wards in his hands. He looked at the ward, then looked all around, then looked at me, and said, "My. I had no idea jealousy was such a strong magic. Now I understand why envy is one of the seven deadly sins."

The boss reaper said, "Where's my list? I need an official soul tally." He put out a boney hand, and another reaper slapped a black clipboard into it. His eyeless sockets examined the page.

DeeDee pulled me close. "We have to get Kevin—"

The boss reaper floated right up to her. "DeeDee Bertha Woznowski. Deceased. No. Survivor. I see you've had quite a night."

DeeDee looked confused.

The boss reaper eyeballed her, up and down. "Oof. You don't look like a Bertha. Tough luck. That's quite the name. Now, where is Kevin Lee Roach, deceased. Hold on. There must be an error here. It says he's a cockroach? Which one of you jokers is playing with my form? And which one you yahoos is gonna get that gill man out of the Kelpie Kiwi?"

The boss reaper floated off.

Glug froze. Literally. Which is easy to do when you've merged spiritually with slushy. He hung out of the nozzle, clinging to his red squid toy.

"We have to hide Kevin," DeeDee whispered. "I won't let him go."

"Oh, I'm going." His blue antennae and fat head rose right up out of her T-shirt.

"What are you doing in there?"

Apparently, I was the only one who was shocked.

DeeDee slid her hand under her shirt and pulled out my Slim Jim ghost trap, compete with trapped ghosts. Hunter looked over the moon. He wiped his forehead and said, "Wow. I'll never forget that."

The bus lady harmphed and pursed her lips.

"But, Kevin," DeeDee said. A tear rolled down her cheeks.

"But nothing. I'm done. I've been a roach for way too long. I've been stepped on and chewed up and spit out and sprayed with Kill Em Dead. And my roommates are dicks. I'm over it. The kid is finally ready. He can do the job. You two will be just fine without me. I can move on in peace."

DeeDee descended into tears. Seriously. She parachuted immediately into ugly cry territory.

"Don't worry about me. Where I'm going, it'll be Jamaica every day," he said. "So quit the crying. We'll see each other again on the other side. When you get there, first pina colada is on me."

She nodded.

She held out the trap, and a red reaper floated up to take it from her. And that's how it went. The big boss red reaper checked his list twice, like a death Santa Claus, accounting for every soul. One by one, the reapers shuttled the souls out the front door, off to their final destination, which clearly lie somewhere at the end of the handicapped parking spots, because that is where each soul vanished.

The cookie scout went first. She gave me a hug. "I'm sorry, fat guy." Her cold little ghost arms squeezed me tight. I felt a stabbing in my heart over the pain I'd caused her. Sure, she tried to kill me, but dude. I didn't know she was a little kid! Just when I was feeling sentimental, she dug her saddle shoe right into my Puma.

"OW!" I hopped around, holding my throbbing toes. "What was that for?"

"You ate all my cookies, and you didn't pay. If I'd sold those, I coulda gotten a pegasus patch! Now we're even."

That kid. She turned to her reaper, and said, "They have ice cream where I'm going, right?" And boom. That was it. She skipped across the parking lot, pigtails bouncing, right into her afterlife and didn't look back.

DeeDee scratched Hunter behind his ghostly ear and made sure the reaper packed his red squeaky bone. And so it went. We sent those spirits to their hereafter as best we could.

Kevin was the last to go, mostly because his designated reaper seemed confused. "Man. A roach with a soul. The guys at Head Office are never gonna believe this."

"Hey, kid. A word?" Kevin whispered in my ear as soon as DeeDee sunk her face into another tissue to wipe away the tears. "Take care of our girl, okay? Dying and coming back? It changes you. Trust me. And she doesn't even know she did it. Keep an eye on her, okay?"

I looked at DeeDee, eyeliner streaking down her face.

"Hurry up, Bonehead. I've got a friend to meet on the other side. Here I come, Ronnie. We got a lot to talk about." Kevin waved at us, as the reaper carried him outside. "So long, suckers!"

Doc stood outside by the ice machine in silence, watching Kevin's procession in a solemn salute.

DeeDee didn't blink once, didn't look away, until Kevin got to the end of the parking spot. He waved at us one last time, and I swear, shot us four middle fingers as he disappeared into the great beyond.

Wait. He wasn't shooting those birds at us. He shot them at a white construction van that sped into the lot and squealed to a hard stop under the sign. That van? It was Steve. His face poked out of the driver's side, squinting at Kevin.

"Well, he said he was gonna give Steve a piece of his mind if it was the last thing he did. And he did." DeeDee said. "I'm gonna miss that little asshole."

Then she laid her head on my shoulder and cried. Doc left without a word. I swear he just disappeared the second he stepped into the frayed edge where the Demon Mart neon fizzled into complete darkness.

"That bug did naht just flip me four birds." Steve stepped in. You should have seen the look on his face when he saw all those red reapers. And upturned racks. And holes in the fresh new linoleum he'd just repaired. His eyes were as big and round as softballs, and the veins on his neck and forehead popped and locked up and down, nearly as hard as the zombie Earl dancing into the store behind him.

Woah boy. Earl. He was back. Juiced up, collar on, ready to become our new on-site zombie chef.

All Steve said—well, screamed—was "What? Yinz? IDJITS! DO?"

Faust stepped out of the stockroom. "Ah. Stephen. Just the man I want to see. I have a confession. Initially, I questioned your judgment. The choice of species on the new cleaning crew was unconventional. But, as always, I should trust in your wisdom. Wonderful, useful creatures. Excellent work."

Wouldn't you know it? The cleaning crew toddled out of the chip aisle, stuffing their mouths with spicy red powdery bits, dragging an open bag of Zapp's Evil Eye behind them.

Evil eye chips. The irony. I should have known.

"What the hell are those?" Steve jumped. "I didn't assign you a new cleaning crew!"

We all looked at them. Faust said, "Goodness. Then where did these fine fellows come from?"

"They're mine." A voice growled hot breath all over the top of my head.

I turned around. Gulp. Bubba stood behind me. Well, I think it's Bubba. Because full moon? But it was probably Bubba, because what other werewolf would be caught dead in a very large, very stretchy set of American flag pants.

"Those are my baby gremlins. Must have been delivered to your place by mistake. Easy to do. Addresses are almost the same. I'll send someone to get them in the morning. Right now. I'm here for this one."

He put a paw on my shoulder, and a rock formed in my gut. "We got a memo from upstairs about what really happened, son. The boys and I want to officially apologize and welcome you back to the gym. Stop by anytime. Oh, and here's a coupon for free flea dips for life, to thank you for taking good care of Hunter. Okay, then. I gotta go. I saw a stray cat around the corner. I need to chase it."

Bubba loped out the front door and across the lot. Yep. Remind me again to get a job where a werewolf running across the street actually raises eyebrows.

Steve shook with rage, grumbled "Idjits!" along with a stream of indistinguishable expletives. Then he led zombie Earl through the stockroom door, stomping all the way to the employee lounge, so hard I was sure he was leaving dents in the floor.

Zack floated up. "Well, we're almost done here. I can't thank you guys enough for every theeeeeeeeeeeeeeee ng." Cue tears. Dude. He roped me and DeeDee and Faust into a group hug so strong there was no escape. "I'll miss you guys so mu uhh uh uh uh."

"Can you guys take a break from the love fest and give me me a hand here?"

We all looked and immediately regretted it. Morty stepped out of the stockroom. He was naked.

And I mean naked, not just of human clothes. His human facade had been cut and split down the middle. Shredded. His human skin hung halfway off, dangling like a banana peel around his red horned face. But thankfully we were all spared a direct view of his junk because he had a very angry, very spoiled poltergeist Candy still stuck on it. And poltergeist Candy was like a claw-tipped harpy hopped up on super crack. Flailing, bitey, itching to get her claws in something.

The reapers descended on Morty.

"Watch out, boys. She's a wild one. Best night of my life! UNICORN, am I right?" He held his hand up for a high five. But no one took it. Because, ew. "Hurry, y'all. She's really on there, and it's starting to hurt."

"So...I guess it's safe to go pack up my stuff," Zack said. "Although, I don't know where I'm gonna go. My girlfriend duu uuuh uuuuh mped meeeeeeee. I guess I can stay at the RMCA."

DeeDee whispered, "It's like the Y for reapers. Poor guy."

Zack floated off, crying softly to himself. And I thought of the perfect thing to cheer him up. I walked to the magic microwave portal.

Huh. Angel eight ball sat on top. Window shattered, no water, triangle dead. Death by Yuri. I didn't know how he got there. Maybe a reaper left him here? Because he sure wasn't moving on his own. I picked him up. The triangle rattled, dead, against the plastic. And I kind of missed him. For once. "Thanks for trying to help me. I hope your audit goes okay."

I had a strange feeling inside. Sadness? Like maybe I missed him? Well, he'll probably pop up again. I mean, he is my guardian angel. We still have checklists to check and sin points to burn off, so he'll be back. Right?

Right?

I fired up the magic microwave, and in a flash, it was there. Steam rolled off my Xbox when I opened the door. Surprised? Don't be. Dude. If there's a moral to this story, it's friends don't buy friends shitty game systems. Besides, it was the least I could do.

When I stepped out, Xbox in hand, Zack was already on the

welcome mat with his bags packed. I handed him the Xbox. "This is for you."

"Really?" He held it in his boney hands, and as he wiped away a tear he said, "Does this one have Squirrel Gangster Shoot Out?"

"No. But you can keep the other console, too."

He hugged me and squeezed. Too tight. "You're the best!"

Suddenly, blinding white light poured through the windows, so intense I thought either the sun or a van were about to crash into us. The front doors blew off the hinges, like they'd been sucked out by a big vacuum. The ball of white light floated—and I mean floated—inside the store. And there in it, I saw a shadow. It looked like a giant bird. Wings?

All the reapers stepped back and whispered to each other. Only Zack turned to face the light, which fizzled down, as if it was on a celestial dimmer switch. When it flipped off, a figure stood in the entry. Huge white wings outstretched. White robes with a sparkling gold chest plate of armor, holding aloft a flaming sword.

Holy. Shit.

It was an angel. A real fucking angel. And it was a she, and she was *hot*. Long black hair and holy cow, the curves. "Stand down, Yurialaempholalmodephianous! Foul reaper, this man's soul is in *my* care!"

Her voice echoed so loud, it shook the ground. Then she looked at me. "Oh. Lloyd. You're alive. Where's Yuri? I owe that asshole a swift kick in the nuts." She looked around. "Huh. I missed it. Well, that was a waste of an intervention voucher. Typical. It was feather to feather on the Celestial Forty. You Know Who really needs to add at least three more lanes. I hate commuting."

I stared at her perfect face and smooth skin and angelic bod. Jesus, that bod.

"Well, Lloyd. You better watch for traffic and stray lightning bolts. We've got a huge hero's journey checklist to get through, and I just burned through your one angelic intervention." She tapped my shoulder, and her touch felt like warmth and happiness.

Wait. Did she say checklist? I stared at that angel as she glanced around the store. Is she? No. Can't be.

Then, her eyes locked in on the frozen food section. "Ooh. Pizza rolls! I'm not leaving here until I try those."

Oh my God. It is. *SHE* is. My voice cracked. "Angel eight ball?"

"Well, I would be, if Yuri didn't smash me into oblivion. You know, I should thank him. That little stunt got me moved to the expedited list at the Divine Embodiments Department. Fingers crossed for an iPhone app this time!"

She crossed her glorious, perfect fingers.

DeeDee leaned in and whispered, "Lucky! Your guardian angel is gorgeous. Mine was an ugly little cupid dude. Total pervert, too."

She shivered at the thought.

Even Zack seemed to be wilting in angel's presence. Who could blame him.

Then she looked at him. Then he looked at her and waved awkwardly. "Um. Hi."

"Hey." She looked at the floor. "Look. I'm sorry about what I said. About everything. Can you ever forgive me? It's not the same without you."

Tears streamed down Zack's cheekbones. "Baby. I can't stay mad at you."

"Okay," Angel said. "But you're doing the laundry from now on."

I froze. "Wait. What's happening?"

"I think they're about to kiss and make up?" DeeDee whispered.

"WHAT?"

In a flash, Zack and Angel were on each other like mating snakes, twisting around and around each other, slurping. He rubbed his boney hands up and down her glowing angelic, hot—And I mean smoking hot, as in dad's secret-stash of 1990s Playboys level hot —body.

"Wow. They're really going at it," DeeDee tilted her head like she was trying to figure out how it all worked. You know, because one of them was a skeleton. "So his girlfriend is your guardian angel. I mean, what are the chances?"

All I could squeak out was, "But *Hell Report* said she works in the Nobodies Division!"

She took her tongue out of Zack's mouth long enough to look at me and say, "Yeah. But I'm trying really to hard turn you into a some-body. Momma needs a promotion. And a raise."

Then she licked Zack's boney face like he was the most delicious rib she had ever tasted. He picked her up. She wrapped her legs around him, and he carried her toward the stockroom.

Holy shit. My guardian angel's going to bone the grim reaper in my zombie cooler. As Zack carried her off into the sunset, all DeeDee said was, "I hope they remember to change the sheets."

CHAPTER 25

DAWN APPROACHED. The moon sunk below the Sinbad's sign, and ribbons of pink sunlight crawled up through the night sky. The reapers packed up and left, vanishing in red swirling clouds, one by one, until only the boss reaper remained. Well, him and Zack, who was still in the zombie cooler having marathon make-up sex with my unbelievably hot guardian angel, judging from the unholy sounds echoing in the hallway.

The boss reaper floated to the door. "Good job, mortals. But, uh, you're gonna need to shut down until you get that big fat bug out of aisle three. We tried to move him, but he wouldn't stay conscious. He kept passing out every time he opened his eyes."

Aw, Bubby. Brave until he's face to face with the angel of death.

Boss reaper pulled a yellow ribbon of celestial crime scene tape across the front door, said, "Catch you later, because we always do," and disappeared in a snap.

I stood behind the counter, running my fingers across the edges of Kevin's albums. I heard quiet footsteps and a sniffle. DeeDee, her eyes puffy and pink and bloodshot. Still wet with tears. She walked up to me with a checklist in her hand. Because she was the manager now. "Um. From now on, I guess you can be in charge of refilling the cigarettes. And...uh...I'll run the credit card reports." Her voice shook. "We should clean up a little before Junebug and Ricky get here."

I felt my bottom lip quiver, and before I could stop myself, I blurted out, "I loved that stupid roach!"

That was it. DeeDee burst into full on tears. I held onto her. She shook in my arms. We both cried.

"What are we going to do without Kevin?"

"I don't know," she said. "It won't be the same without him."

"Excellent work." Faust stepped through the stockroom door, cradling my employee manual.

It repaid the compliment by barfing all over Faust's clean suit.

Harrrrrrrf. Harrrrrrrf. Harrrrrrrf. Bluurch.

Thankfully, it wasn't much. Just a small slip of paper, like that fortune it had horked up on Zack. Faust smoothed it out and looked it over. "No no no. Unacceptable. This won't do at all."

Faust sat the book on the floor and pulled something out of his breast pocket. A little glass case. It said, "Break in Case of Emergency" on the top. Suddenly, Faust's body went stick straight. His spine arced. He stared up at the ceiling, clutching that box in his hands. His mouth moved so fast, smoke and sparks and electricity spilled out at the corners. The sound was unholy, like ten possessed monks having a chant off in different dead languages. Totally scary, totally creepy, but honestly, preferable to the moans of ecstasy pouring out of the zombie cooler.

A white hole opened in the ceiling, but only for a split second. It disappeared as quickly as it had come. Gone in a flash. Literally.

Thunk.

Something landed on the hot food station. Judging from the *ssss* sound of sizzling, it hit the hot dog rollers.

"Ow ow ow ow!" a tiny voice screeched.

Wisps of smoke rolled off a giant fat brown pancake as it tumbled right along next to the jumbo all-beef franks.

"Help me, kid. It burns!"

"Kevin?"

"Who else would it be? Don't just stand there. Get me outta here, dumbass! I'm grilling here! Literally! Ow! Ow ow ow ow!"

I moved and fast. I pushed up over that counter, wielded a pair of tongs, and tweezed him out in under a minute. Which wasn't easy—he was so fat—but I managed to plop him onto the bun case. He stood up and smoothed himself out. He looked down at his still-smoking body and stomped in a tiny, angry circle. "Shit. Seriously? I'm a cockroach? AGAIN? And I'm still fat? Fuck me."

He shook his tiny cockroach fist at the ceiling. "Are you kidding me? How many more years I gotta work here, huh? This place is like purgatory! Everything I've done for you. This isn't funny, jerks. Fucking Pravuil, always changing the rules! What an asshole. I swear. That guy doesn't want to let anyone into heaven."

"Aw. Good. At least we have that sorted out." Faust sat the little glass box on the counter. It was that emergency cockroach box from his office. It was empty, and the glass had cracked. Faust turned and saw the first rays of sun rising up over the strip mall across the street, and said, "Goodness. Look at the time."

He snapped his fingers and fire rose out of the linoleum. Flames licked up up up, consuming his body. Then he sunk down down down, into the flames, like he was riding down an escalator. He descended, and the fire simply disappeared.

Uh. Okay, then. A devil. Not *the* devil.

DeeDee practically flew to the hot dog station. She scooped Kevin up and squeezed him so tight I thought his head was gonna pop off. His muffled voice rose from DeeDee's cleavage. "Nice view, but you're suffocating me."

She eased up. "Sorry."

He looked up at her. "What's wrong with your face? You look like shit. Your makeup is all messed up."

She looked at him for a second, then burst out into a weird projectile cry laugh.

"Chicks. So emotional. All right. Cut it out. Stop crying and get back to work. You're getting me all wet."

DeeDee sat him on the floor, reluctantly. But a smile cracked through all her tears.

"I'm going in back. Zombie Earl is gonna make me a No. 2 Double Monster Size," Kevin said. "Fuck diets. I'm gonna eat the damn burger and be happy. That scout leave any cookies?"

"Three boxes left," DeeDee said.

Kevin did that thing where he pointed at his eyes, then at mine. "Don't let the fat guy eat them all before I get back. Speaking of. You ain't leaving here without mopping. Extra Curse Breaker, okay? We still got a witch on the loose."

He kicked open the stockroom door and said, "Walk with me, kid."

I followed him in.

"So uh. The guys upstairs filled me in on what you did tonight. I got you a little something." He led me to the employee lounge door and pointed at a small gold package topped with a bow. "Well? What are you waiting for? Open it."

"Uh. Okay?" I picked it up and rattled it. "What is it?"

"From me to you," Kevin shrugged. "Open it."

I did. Inside was a big white mug that said, "World's Okayest Employee."

"Just okay?" Typical Kevin.

"You still got room to improve. See?"

He pointed at the infinite rows of tiny employee of the month plaques. All the same. All Junebug. Except for one? I had to squint, it was so tiny. But there it was: A portrait of my employee manual. Employee of the month. A gold sticker in the corner said, "Honorable Mention: Lloyd Lamb Wallace."

"Good job, kid. We're never getting to Jamaica at this rate, but I'm still proud of you. For what you did for DeeDee. And me." Kevin cleared his throat, and I swear his beady black bug eyes welled, ever so slightly, with a solitary tear. "Don't get a big head, kid. You still got a long way to go. And you better keep at it. I'm sick of looking at Junebug's face. Now get outta my way. I'm starving."

Kevin jump flew at the employee lounge door. It creaked open, and he scuttled inside. "Earl. My man. Looking good. Well, lookin' dead. But good, considering. I see they let you keep the track suit. Don't leak on it. Doesn't look easy to clean."

Kevin ordered a number two, double monster size. I looked at the mug. World's Okayest Employee. Coming from Kevin? That was high praise. Something tugged on my sock. It was my employee manual. I showed it the plaque. "You totally deserve it."

It had definitely saved the day.

Kevin poked his head out the door. "Hey. Dumbass. You want me to order you something? Earl's on fire."

"I'm good."

He thumbed a leg back at my employee manual. "You ever gonna read that thing?"

"Right now. Cover to cover."

"That reminds me." Kevin pulled that little pink glitter notebook out of—well, somewhere—and tossed it in the trash. "Yuri's in jail. Your record is clean. Investigation complete. Case closed."

A smile spread across my face as I filled the mop bucket. And yeah, you better believe I added the Curse Breaker. Happy moans poured from both ends of the hallway. From Kevin, munching on his first non-cursed Monster Burger in at least a month.

"You still got it, Earl. Mmmm."

And from the horny angel make-up sex in the zombie cooler. Ew. I can't even. I'm gonna need some time to unpack all that.

I wheeled the bucket to the stockroom door, and the angels abruptly stopped moaning. Finally! Geesh. They were like rabbits in there. My employee manual bit right into my toes. "Ow! Can we maybe ease up on the biting?"

It pointed at the zombie cooler.

"Huh? Oh."

I stared at it for a good long time. Because the zombie cooler door? It wasn't there. The thick black metal door with the yellow hazard sticker? Gone. Replaced. With a red door. Made of ornately carved wood. It had a sparkling crystal knob with a tarnished brass backplate in the shape of a face. A man with big curly horns. The door looked old, fancy. Antique.

As I stared at it, it cracked open. A chorus of enchanting voices whispered from inside, beckoning me in. I stepped closer. Oh, man. It sounded really awesome in there. Tinkling. Fascinating. Fun.

Chomp.

"Ow!" Wow. My book clamped down hard on my toes. It growled and tugged me away from the door.

I looked at the book. I looked at the door. I grabbed the handle and shut that creepy door tight. "Good call. Nothing good could possibly come out of there."

━━━

Thank you *so so* much for reading. The adventure will continue in (Re)Possessed.

If you like horror comedy, sign up for Monsters In Your Inbox my once-a-month email filled with all things funny and horror. Books, movies, and weird news! Sign up at: eepurl.com/czsoRr

BOOK SAUSAGE

"What the hell is up with the title on this page?"

Yeah, yeah. I know you're thinking that. Well, twist my arm, and I'll tell you. You know that old adage: No one wants to know how the sausage is made? I disagree. Sometimes, you just really *really* HAVE *TO KNOW* what unholy substance was ground up to make your meat. Or in this case, your book. That's why I'm pulling the curtain back, so you can see how this author killed, chopped, molded, and stuffed all of her life tidbits into the book you hold in your hands right now.

Welcome to the end of yet another 24/7 Demon Mart! I am so happy you're here. Seriously. You guys are the best. When I wrote *The Graveyard Shift*, I never dreamed we'd end up here. In part, because I had received a terminal cancer diagnosis, and it did not look like I would still be alive to write more than one. But I'm alive. I made it to remission, and I'm STILL in remission, one year later. (You want to see an oncologist tap dance into your exam room? That's how you do it, people.) Because of your enthusiasm—and the miracle of immunotherapy—there are now five books in this series, and audiobooks have been and will be made.

But alas. Let us not speak of sad things. Let us speak of happy things.

I am super thrilled that you guys have joined me on this journey. I love getting your letters and emails and DMs and Facebook and Twitter comments. (And surprise gifts. I'm looking at you, MaryAnn McD and Mike C.) Y'all always make me smile. It warms my black glitter heart to know there are other weirdos just like me out there!

Now, onto the book.

First, let me just say I know, I know. Poor Kevin, right? Dude. That little roach has really been through the ringer. You're probably thinking, "Didn't that roach suffer enough in *Monster Burger?*" Nope. No, he did not. And this is certainly not the end of his troubles. He has many highs and lows to come. But don't worry. Kevin is one tough cookie. Well, roach. And what doesn't kill you makes you stronger, right? Okay. More like what *does* kill you doesn't really kill you. At least not for long.

You're probably also thinking, "This broad is crazy. Savage Slim Jims and Red Vines? WTF!"

Yes. I am crazy. I spend way too much time wandering the aisles of local convenience stores looking at all the stuff for sale. (And thinking, "Hmmm. Could you fight a monster with that?") They're amazing repositories of capitalism's more extreme products. The flashiest packaging, displays stuffed to the brim, all designed to get us to impulse buy. Everything screams at you from the shelf, "YOU NEED ME. GRAB ME AND GO, MONKEY, NOW!"

Still, I try to use regional brands and products as much as possible, not for any big reason other than that's the stuff I am personally drawn to. If I'm on a road trip and have the choice between the big national brand and the rinky dink local stuff? I buy the local stuff. Like the Cherikee Red pop. (Their spelling, not mine.) And Zapp's. Oh, how I love Zapp's. I'm so amped that they've made the jump from New Orleans to nationwide.

But no, I do not love Necco Wafers. My grandparents loved Necco Wafers, but I stand firmly in "blech. No. Just. No" territory, and apparently so does almost everyone else. The New England Confectionery Company went out of business in 2018, and Necco Wafers were nearly lost. Until the Spangler Candy Company (based in OHIO!) bought them out and started making them again. Still, as our ghost bus lady knows, that candy is really hard to come by. They don't sell it on every corner.

You won't find the evil eye curse, or wards against it, for sale at your local corner store in the U.S. either. But the evil eye really is a thing in a big chunk of the world. When I was 23, I saved all my pennies so I could spend the summer in Greece with my best friend. As soon as I stepped off the plane, I noticed giant blue glass eyeball beads dangling everywhere. Like, everywhere. And for sale on every corner. Those beads were wards against the evil eye.

In the Mediterranean and other parts of the world, the evil eye is considered a real and very present danger. The idea is that you can bring misfortune to someone simply by being jealous or envious. And by looking at them. With squinty eyes. Or side eyes, or "I'm gonna get you," eyes. You know the look. If you have blue eyes, oof. I feel bad for whoever you're stink eyeing, because blue eyes are better at cursing. And yes, you can give the curse unintentionally.

The blue glass beads (also eye-shaped jewelry and stickers) are supposed to break the curse or ward it off. I bought tons of these things when I was in Greece and Turkey. I have a glass ward hanging on my front door right now. I have an evil eye doormat, too. Better safe than sorry!

Alas, as I learned in the Greek Isles, the ward is just the start. The best defense is a Greek grandma, or yia yia, spitting right in your face. Literally spitting, while saying something like, "I spit in your face to protect you!" Which happened to me and my bestie a couple of times, between singing, "Opa!" and drinking retsina and dancing with the oldsters in tavernas. For real. You haven't lived until an old Greek lady has spit in your face to free you from a curse. For the record: I have heard the spit of Turkish and Persian grandmas are equally effective. And if you're interested, the hand/

eye ward design in Lloyd's employee manual is called a hamsa, and it looks like this.

Now for some frank talk about Zorro, namely Morty's Zorro-themed stripper outfit. It's a small thing, but it makes me laugh, and I've been dying to use it somewhere. When I lived in New Orleans, I knew a male stripper whose stage name was Zorro. (Many of the young folks in New Orleans make their living working in the strip clubs on Bourbon Street, but that is a story for another book.) Zorro was swarthy, coiffed, and handsome, a stereotype of the Latin lover. And boy oh boy, he was all in on the theme. Like, all in. While wooing the tourists on the main stage and while walking around town in his real life. I once ran into him at the laundromat. He was still in full Zorro mode. He had his silk shirt unbuttoned all the way down to his belly button. His tight satin pants jiggling. On laundry day. Me? Not so much. I was in my least filthy jammy pants with a bar smoke-infused messy bun and the raccoon-eye remnants of last night's black eyeliner streaking down my cheeks. He rolls up, "Hello, Deniza," because, hello, Latin lover = accent. "You look lovely today." Cue hand kiss. Uh huh. Yeah. Pull the other one. But always a charmer, that one. I have no idea what happened to Zorro. He just kind of disappeared one day. I like to believe he was scooped right off the main stage—dollar bills clinging to his leopard print thong—and whisked away to a beachfront estate by a very wealthy, eccentric heiress. Maybe, just maybe, the two of them are still out there, somewhere, living their best lives.

And as for that Kevin resurrection chant. It's Latin, but dude. Don't even start with me. I know it's a bad translation. I totally ran that shit through Google Translate, because I am the only girl who ever managed to make it all the way through Catholic K-12, plus TWO Catholic colleges, without taking a single Latin class. Which I now regret. Hear that, kids? I WISH I HAD TAKEN ALL THE LATIN. Then I could lord over the less educated, a la John Cleese in *Life of Brian*. "How many Romans?"

(It's fine. I'll wait while you type that into YouTube and rewatch that scene, because it's fucking comic genius.)

Oh, good. You're back. Here is what the Latin chant words are supposed to mean. (Dear Google, please improve the translation algo for dead languages. Horror writers are counting on you.)

Ortum Exsurge tenebris domain=Rise up from the dark domain.

Kevin veni ad nos in domum suam=Kevin come home to us.

Receperint tui sumus exspiravi=We welcome your ghost.

That's where Lloyd screwed up and cursed Kevin to ghosthood. Oops!

You may have also caught the inside jokes. Angel eight ball is No. 9,998,383,750,000 in line at the Divine Embodiments Department, and they're now serving No. 3? I totally stole that from the last scene of *Beetlejuice*, which IMHO is the best ghost movie of all time. And those folks who played games with the Grim Reaper? Lifted directly from *Bill & Ted's Bogus Adventure* and Ingmar Bergman's 1957 classic *The Seventh Seal*, wherein doomed medieval knight Antonius Black plays chess with death. And I don't even have to tell you where "Clafoooo varapa nick? Nik huh. Nickel?" came from, do I? Now, that movie was totally groovy. (And *they* lifted it from *The Day the Earth Stood Still*. So see? We're all just recycling here.)

And that's it for this Book Sausage. Almost. If you really want to know what my favorite ghost movie is besides *Beetlejuice*, it's 1963's *The Haunting*, based on the Shirley Jackson novel, *The Haunting of*

Hill House. Watch the original 1963 version, NOT the remake, okay? And my favorite on-screen grim reaper depictions are in *Dead Like Me, Monty Python's Meaning of Life,* and *All that Jazz.*

Now that we've reached the end, you're probably still asking yourself, "What the hell does Junebug do on day shift?"

You'll find out. In fact, you'll be finding out a lot more about Junebug, Ricky, Kevin, Doc and the rest of the gang. Because I'm about to get crazy up in here and write my first short stories since I was in college.

You're probably also asking "Why does Kevin hate *Beth*?" Y'all. I know, okay? Some of you L-O-V-E that song, but I'm with Kevin on this one. Fucking *Beth.* And yes, I know it won a Grammy. But so did Lionel Richie's *Can't Slow Down,* which BEAT *Purple Rain.* Yeah. Read that again. LIONEL RICHIE BEAT *PURPLE RAIN.* So to the Grammy argument I say: Which one of those two albums are you still listening to? Hint: It starts with "purple."

I can't even with *Beth.* I don't know why. I just can't. Maybe it's because I'm not a rock bands doing ballads kind of girl, or maybe it's because even Gene and the rest of the band look like, "OMG, we seriously have to do this? This sucks," in the official *Beth* video. Doesn't matter. Just know that I can't help the way I feel, and this opinion is coming from a girl who A. Used to make Gene drinks when he'd visit Rick's Cabaret in New Orleans, and B. Has attended concerts on more than one Kiss farewell tour, including the 2000 farewell tour with Peter and Ace. *Beth* was the pre-planned bathroom break song. Because we knew we weren't gonna miss anything epic. You are allowed to disagree with me, of course. But let me add that Kevin is not the type of roach who could ever possibly like *Beth.* Or *I Was Made for Loving You.* You know, the Kiss disco song? Dude. He hates that song so much, he almost returned his Kiss Army badge. *Almost.*

See you next time!

WHO THE HECK IS D.M. GUAY?

DM Guay is a big geek, huge horror fan, and loves stand-up comedy. She mish-mashes her love of all that's scary/gory/geeky/funny into stories about creeps and critters, ghouls and ghosts, and all of the unseemly things that go bump in the night.

She runs "Monsters In Your Inbox" a monthly round-up of B-horror movies, horror comedy books, and weird news. Sign up here: http://eepurl.com/czsoRr

Stay in touch!
Visit her at http://www.dmguay.com.
Twitter: https://twitter.com/DMGuay
Facebook: https://www.facebook.com/DMGuay
Follow her on Bookbub.

BOOKS BY D.M. GUAY

24/7 Demon Mart

The Graveyard Shift

Monster Burger

Angel Trouble

(Re) Possessed (coming soon!)

24/7 Demon Mart Stories

(Read anytime after *The Graveyard Shift*)

Hell for the Holidays

Critters from the Poo Lagoon

Audiobook Editions

Demon Mart books 1-2 (plus Hell for the Holidays)

Printed in Great Britain
by Amazon